Whitey & the Wild Horse
Whitey Ropes & Rides
Whitey Takes a Trip
The Blind Colt
Stolen Pony
Hunted Horses
Rodeo: Bulls, Broncs &
  Buckaroos
Ol' Paul, the Mighty Logger
Buffalo Harvest
Lone Muskrat

Whitey's First Roundup

GLEN ROUNDS

WHITEY'S
First Roundup

Holiday House, New York

Contents

Getting Ready

"WE'D BETTER fix up the old chuck wagon tomorrow," Uncle Torwal remarked as he and Whitey sat outside after supper. "Roundup time is only a few days off."

"Yessir!" Whitey agreed. "And if we don't have it ready when Mr. Waccapominy Smith is ready to load up his cooking things there'll be trouble for sure!"

Whitey wasn't really much for size, but he did have a hand-me-down Stetson hat with a rattlesnake skin hatband. It was a little big, so that it often blew off—or slipped down over his eyes. But with a couple of lamp wicks stuffed inside the sweat band it did pretty well. His fancy-stitched, high-heeled boots had been bench made by a Fort Worth bootmaker for a cowboy who had given them to Whitey while they still had a good bit of wear left in them.

And whenever Whitey got a new pair of denim pants he climbed into the horse trough with them on to soak them thoroughly before going out to ride. As they dried on him they sort of took the shape of the saddle, so that with a little practice he could walk as bowlegged as any cowboy in the country! For several years he had been living on Rattlesnake Ranch with Uncle Torwal.

"Reckon you'll be wanting me to go along when you start out on the roundup tomorrow, won't you, Uncle Torwal?" he said.

"What makes you reckon such a thing as that?" asked Uncle Torwal.

"Well," said Whitey, "I'm just about a top hand, I figure."

"You'd better figure again, then." Uncle Torwal grinned. "Handling cattle out on the range is a little different from what you've been used to. Chances are the first day out you'd get us into some kind of a jackpot that'd take a week to untangle."

"Naw, I wouldn't, Uncle Torwal! Honest, I'd be mighty careful, and there isn't anything much to do here at the ranch now."

Uncle Torwal thought it over for a while.

Then he said doubtfully, "Well, I reckon you've got to start sometime. Fix yourself a bedroll tomorrow. But mind, the first bobble you make I'm a-going to send you back!"

"I won't make any bobble," promised Whitey, and no more was said about the business.

Listening to the gentle clank of the windmill, and the occasional squeal and thud of hoofs against ribs from the horse pasture, Whitey thought about what a fine thing this roundup would be. Not like the ones of other years when everybody slept in a bunkhouse nights, and simply rode out each morning to bring cattle from near-by ranges so that the branding could be done in the home corrals. For this year, early spring blizzards had caused stock from a dozen ranches to break through the drift fences to find shelter far back in the broken country. It would take several days' hard work to comb the cattle out of the brush-filled gullies and pockets, sort out those belonging to each rancher, and brand the calves.

So the roundup this year would be done in the style of the old days. A chuck wagon and a cook would go along, and the riders from the various ranches would live out on the range until the work was over. The calves would be roped and branded in the open. There would probably be night guards set on the herds being held for sorting. And who could tell—there might even be a stampede before it was all over!

The next few days were busy ones around
the ranch. The big chuck-box was opened
and the bins inside cleaned and scrubbed.
Then it was set upright at the back of the
wagon bed. The wheels on the wagon were
taken partly off so the axles could be coated
with thick axle grease. Water barrels were
cleaned and set to soak by the windmill. Tar-
paulins were got ready to cover the wagon
and to use as flies in case of rain.

Whitey had the dusty job of untangling
the bundle of rope and stakes that would be
set up for a horse corral. This was no small
job, since the apparatus hadn't been used in
years. After it was strung out it had to be
carefully coiled and tied again, ready for use.
But Whitey had no thought of complaining.

When he'd finished that, and without waiting to be told, he went to help Mr. Waccapominy Smith get his cooking things and the groceries ready. The big Dutch ovens had to be scraped and scrubbed with sand to get off the thick accumulation of grease and dust. Sacks of beans and of flour and a case of canned milk went into the wagon. Dried apricots, prunes, sugar, lard, vanilla and lemon extract, and dozens of other items were put in the bins and drawers of the chuckbox. Tin plates, cups, and eating utensils were piled in galvanized washtubs and loaded into the wagon itself, along with some kindling wood and an ax and shovel. There was no end of excitement.

A good many of the riders who were go-

ing along on the roundup drifted into the ranch the night before the start. The others, from ranches nearer the first camping place, would come along the next morning. Each man brought one or two extra saddle horses. Even though they'd only be gone a few days, there would be much hard riding and they'd need to change mounts. These horses were turned into the big pasture. After idling about for a while, the men rolled out their beds in the ranch yard and went to sleep.

Long before sunup next morning everyone was stirring. While the wrangler was driving in the horses, the cowboys rolled their beds and threw them on the wagon. Then, after they'd eaten they drifted to the corral to catch and saddle their horses. While

Mr. Waccapominy was clearing up and washing the dishes at the windmill Whitey hurried through his and Uncle Torwal's dishes in the kitchen. As soon as he'd finished he shouldered his own bedroll and had just started to the wagon to load it with the others when Uncle Torwal stopped him.

"What in the world are you carrying?" he asked.

"Just my hot-roll," Whitey told him.

"Looks more like you had a horse in there than a bed," Uncle Torwal grunted. "Maybe you better let me see it."

Whitey untied the rope and unrolled the bundle on the ground. The canvas was a regular bed tarp six feet wide and about sixteen feet long, such as most cowboys use. But on it was an untidy pile of quilts, shirts, a denim jacket, a pillow, a sheepskin coat and a fancy hackamore Whitey used only on special occasions. There were probably some other things deeper down in the bundle, but Uncle Torwal didn't bother to look.

"Were you planning on heading for Texas or some such far-off place to look for work?" he asked.

"No, sir," Whitey told him. "These are just things I thought I might need."

"Well, if you were going to be gone all summer, you might," Uncle Torwal agreed. "But we are only going to be gone a couple days, at most. Roll the jacket inside the slicker and tie them behind your saddle where you can get to them if you need them. Throw out everything but four quilts, and maybe an extra shirt and some socks. If everybody brought a bedroll that size we'd have to have another wagon to haul them all."

"Yessir, I guess you're right," Whitey agreed, and began sorting out his things.

"And instead of mussing your bedding up any old way, fold your soogans lengthwise and stack them up neat. Then when you roll your bed, roll it tight and smooth. A loose, bunchy bedroll is usually the mark of a sloppy cowboy!"

"Yessir!" Whitey said, and did as he was told. It took him some time, but when he finally threw his bedroll on the wagon it was as neat and tight as any there.

The Start

BY THAT time, the sun was coming up behind Eagle Butte. Mr. Waccapominy was already putting up the hinged front of the chuck-box that served as a work table when he was cooking. Ordinarily Whitey would have listened for a little while to the dreadful things the old roundup cook muttered to himself as he worked. But now there was no time to waste. Snatching up his hackamore, Whitey hurried to the calf pasture to catch Old Spot.

Any other morning the old horse would have been waiting at the gate, ready for the bridle, but this morning he had other ideas. He skittered around and snorted and refused to be caught. It seemed to Whitey that Old Spot was deliberately trying to spoil his day. If he didn't catch the horse soon, everybody would be gone ahead of him.

Finally, he went back to the stable where the riders were saddling up.

"Please, Uncle Torwal," he said, "will you help me catch Ol' Spot? He's spooky as all get out this morning, and won't let me within a rod of him."

"You don't say so!" Uncle Torwal said. "It sure is too bad, but I never have yet kept a cowpuncher around that couldn't catch up his own horse. Never seemed worth while, somehow."

"Yessir, I guess that's right," said Whitey, wondering if he was going to have to stay behind, after all.

Uncle Torwal went on saddling up his horse. Then he turned to Whitey again. "Get a pan of oats, and toll him up with that. If the others are gone when you're ready, come on over to the old stage crossing on Hay Creek. That's where the first camp will be. It's less than ten miles across country but there is no great hurry; so I'd go round by the old road, if I were you."

"Yessir," Whitey answered. "I'll find my way all right."

Back in the pasture he held the hackamore

behind him and shook the oat pan coaxingly. Hearing the rattle of the grain, the old horse pricked his ears and trotted close.

However, Old Spot knew a thing or two, himself. Standing just out of reach, he'd stretch his neck towards the pan, then before Whitey could lay a hand on him, he'd scoop up some of the grain with his long upper lip and whirl away. After he'd chewed and swallowed his prize, he'd let himself be coaxed back and repeat the performance.

Meanwhile Uncle Torwal and the other riders climbed on their horses and rode away.

Later, Mr. Waccapominy climbed up onto the high spring seat of the chuck wagon, hollered at his four-horse team, and drove off. The horse wrangler, with the bunch of extra

saddle horses that cowboys call the remuda, followed along behind.

It wasn't until everybody else was long gone that Spot finally let himself be caught. By that time Whitey was out of sorts, and when the horse tried his other game of pretending to bite while the cinch was being tightened he got a rap on the nose.

Once Whitey was actually on the way to the roundup, however, he felt better. It was a mighty fine morning. The sun felt comfortable on his back, while he watched the horse leave a dark trail through the damp grass.

Old Spot, in spite of the trouble he'd caused in the beginning, seemed pleased to be going somewhere. He jogged contentedly along, first pointing his ears forward as far as they'd go, then twitching them back. Now and again he'd drop his head and sneeze in carefree fashion.

Listening to the soft thudding of the horse's hoofs on the buffalo grass sod, and to the creak of the saddle, Whitey felt there was probably nothing in the world better than being a horseman.

Coming out of the big pasture, he followed the old road for a mile or two, as Uncle Torwal had told him to. Here the dust was deep and little puffs squirted out from under Spot's hoofs as he plopped them down.

But after crossing Flyspeck Johnnie Creek, the old road swung to make a big circle around some rough country. So Whitey started thinking that there was no reason why he should go the long way around when by cutting straight over the hills he'd see more interesting country. Besides, he was practically a cowboy, and cowboys didn't go around by roads. So Whitey started across country.

There was a wire gate which let him into a fenced school section. From there on there was no trail. However, he knew that all he had to do was to bear off to the southwest until he crossed the ridge and then dropped down the slope to Horse Creek. Down that valley a few miles he would come to Owl Creek crossing. Then by heading straight out across the prairie towards Rattlesnake Butte he'd come into the old road again and follow it on to the roundup camp.

When he came to a fence with no gate he

took the wire pinchers off his saddle and pulled the staples to let the wire down. After leading Spot across he carefully fastened the wires back and rode on.

When he had started out he had figured on getting into camp by the middle of the forenoon, at the latest. But as so often happens on a nice day there were a number of things that delayed him.

First, there was the ground squirrel business. Whitey heard the little varmint whistle and saw him as he dived into a nearby burrow. It occurred to Whitey that it might be worth while to snare the beast, just in case the state should decide to start paying a bounty on ground squirrels as they do on coyotes.

So he climbed down from his horse, dug a

length of string out of his pocket and made a slip noose in one end. Arranging the noose carefully around the mouth of the burrow, he backed off, paying out the string as he went. Squatting behind a low sage bush he waited a little time, then whistled.

The ground squirrel popped his head up to see what the fuss was about, and Whitey twitched the noose tight about his body. It was like roping calves, almost. Or snaring tigers. Reeling the little fellow in, Whitey admired the stripes and rows of dark dots on the shiny fur, and finally decided to turn him loose. There was still nothing definite about the bounty, and besides, it would be a chore to look after the pelt while he was on the roundup.

So while the ground squirrel scurried back to his burrow, probably marveling at his narrow escape, Whitey clambered back on his horse and rode off.

Later in the morning, while he was letting

Spot drink at the edge of a little slough, he heard a strange harsh squalling from the high grass. Getting off his horse and going cautiously closer, Whitey found a striped garter snake swallowing a frog. Just the head of the frog and his front legs were sticking outside the snake's mouth. It was difficult to tell if the snake had grown a pair of legs, or if the frog was wearing a whale of a long tail. At any rate, the frog was complaining at the top of his voice as he slowly disappeared. But before Whitey could do anything about it the snake slithered away into the higher grass, taking his dinner with him.

It did seem to be an unhappy situation for the frog, but the snake had probably worked hard for his meal. If the frog had been mind-

ing his business he probably wouldn't have
gotten caught anyway, Whitey figured. So,
after a half-hearted search of the high grass,
he got on his horse again and rode on towards the roundup.

He'd ridden only a mile or so when he
noticed an old buffalo wallow. Quite often
there are old Indian arrowheads to be found
in such places, so he got off to take a look. A
few minutes' searching convinced him there
were none here, and he decided he'd better
be on his way. But Old Spot was gone!

Whitey had been riding with his bridle
reins tied together, and when he got off he'd
forgotten to throw them over the horse's
head and drop them on the ground. Now, a
Western horse is trained to stand and wait

if the reins are dropped on the ground, but if they are left over his neck, he'll go away.

Here was a pickle, for sure. The horse would head back towards the ranch, Whitey knew. There was nothing to do but follow. So he hitched up his belt and started walking. From the top of the first rise he saw Old Spot just going out of sight over the next ridge, already half a mile away.

After that Whitey was alone in the middle of the prairie. He stomped along, madder than a hornet, and tried to remember some of the terrible things he'd heard Waccapominy mutter to his horses. Here it was Whitey's first day on the roundup and already he'd let himself be set afoot like any greenhorn.

Then his feet started to hurt. His high-heeled boots were fine for riding, but they were never made to walk in. Before he'd gone a mile he had blisters on both heels. It was still a long way home.

As if that wasn't trouble enough, when Whitey limped up over a little knoll he came face to face with a bunch of range cattle. So now, besides being angry and footsore, he was also scared. For he knew that wild cattle won't bother a man on a horse, but he didn't know what they'd do to one that was on foot.

There were no trees for him to climb, nor any fences to get behind, so he stood still and wondered what in the world he should do.

The cattle threw up their heads and started slowly edging his way. He didn't dare run.

He tried to yell at them, but found that for some reason he couldn't make a sound.

The cattle came up and stood in a half circle watching him. And he watched them. Now and again, one of the critters would give a low bellow and paw dirt in the air.

Whitey would gladly have given his Stetson hat with the rattlesnake skin hatband, and his fancy stitched boots to have been some place else.

But standing there was getting him nowhere. So, perhaps to take them by surprise, he suddenly shied his hat at them, waved his arms, and yelled at the top of his voice.

The trick worked. The cattle turned and lumbered off a short distance.

While they were still moving Whitey hur-

ried back the way he'd come, over the knoll,
until the slope hid him. Then he made a
circle round the cattle, following low ground
where he could keep out of their sight. When
he was well past the danger he headed in the
direction he thought Old Spot had taken.
After crossing another low ridge he came on
the horse, grazing unconcernedly along a
drift fence that had barred his way.

Back in the saddle at last, Whitey lost no
more time on the way to the roundup camp.
He didn't even stop to look over the old pile
of sun-whitened buffalo bones he found at
the foot of a high cut-bank.

Ready for Work

WHEN WHITEY came to the top of the hogback overlooking the wide, flat Hay Creek valley he saw the chuck wagon in the shade of some cottonwood trees a half mile away. Farther off, a good-sized bunch of cattle was scattered out grazing. The men were eating their dinners.

Riding up, Whitey climbed off Spot and tied him to a nearby cottonwood. Then he went up to the cook fire.

"Come and git a plate, kid," Mr. Waccapominy hollered, opening up the Dutch oven sitting beside the cook fire.

When Whitey's plate was filled with beef, potatoes, and biscuits he sat on the grass and started his meal.

He expected a good many questions about why he'd been so long on the way. But what little talk there was dealt with the morning work, and of the cattle that had been found. While Whitey ate, the cowboys finished and

got up one by one to throw their plates and cups into a tub of water standing by the fire.

Some rode off to comb the brushy country they'd missed during the forenoon, and others rummaged in the wagon for branding irons.

Whitey was hurrying with his eating so as to be ready to help. He hoped he'd be one of the riders picked to rope calves and drag them to the branding fire. That was a much more exciting job than throwing and holding them down for the iron and the ear marking. But Uncle Torwal dashed his hopes.

"When you finish you can help Waccapominy," he said.

"All afternoon?" Whitey squalled. "I thought you'd need me to help with the branding."

"Maybe after he gets done with you we can use you," Uncle Torwal answered, "but he'll need wood and water first."

"Yessir!" Whitey said, but without any enthusiasm. He hadn't thought he'd end as a pot-walloper for a roundup cook.

When he took his eating tools to the tub he said, "Uncle Torwal told me I was to help you, Mr. Waccapominy."

"All right, kid," Mr. Waccapominy grunted. "First thing, you take your horse and drag some wood over to where those dudes are building their branding fire. Otherwise they'll be comin' up here an' stealin' mine—they're too lazy to git up if they was layin' in a cactus bed."

"Yessir, Mr. Waccapominy."

As Whitey trudged off to get Spot Mr. Waccapominy called, "When you git what they need start draggin' some wood up here."

"Yessir!"

While Spot drank at the creek, Whitey got his rope down and searched along the banks for driftwood and dry cottonwood branches lying on the ground. When he had collected a bundle he fastened the rope around it. Then, getting back in the saddle, he took a dally around the horn with the other end of the rope and dragged the bundle off to where the branding crew waited. Perhaps it was good practice for dragging calves, but Whitey couldn't see much excitement to it.

For an hour or more he went back and forth between the chuck wagon and the cottonwoods, dragging load after load until it seemed to him that there was enough to last a washerwoman a week. But at last Mr. Waccapominy was satisfied. "Now take the ax and bust a bunch of it up," he directed.

Whitey did as he said. After that he carried a dozen buckets of water from the creek to the water barrel, and filled the two washtubs besides. By that time the blisters on his feet from the morning's adventure were hurting, and he wondered what kind of chore Mr. Waccapominy would think up next.

About that time the cook looked up. He was mixing biscuit dough in a dishpan on the dropped-down front of the chuck-box. "That'll do 'er, kid!" he remarked. "Come over and set a bit. Roundup's kinda hard

work, eh?" he asked, with the nearest thing to a grin Whitey had seen him wear.

"It isn't quite like I thought it would be," Whitey admitted, sitting down on a box.

"I know how it is," the cook agreed, "but somebody has to do these squaw jobs."

Wiping his hands on the dirty flour sack he used for an apron, the cook picked up a spoon and walked to the tub of clean dishes for a plate. Lifting the lid of a big kettle on the edge of the fire, he ladled out a plateful of dried apricots that had been stewing there for hours, and replaced the lid. While Whitey watched, he put the plate on the work table and spooned on sugar, then he poured in milk from the can on the shelf.

"Here," he said, handing Whitey the plate.

"When you get done you might as well go on down to where they're branding. You're all caught up here."

"Thanks, Mr. Waccapominy," Whitey said. "These apricots taste good."

"You work good for me, I feed you good," Mr. Waccapominy told him, brushing flour out of his scraggly mustache.

Scraping the last bits from the plate and licking the spoon, Whitey was glad he was on the roundup after all. The wind felt good, and he liked the smells of cooking and of the cottonwood smoke mixed with the dust stirred up by the bawling cattle.

He rode down to the branding fire and sat on his horse, waiting for Uncle Torwal to notice he was there and put him to work.

While he'd been working for Mr. Waccapominy another small bunch of cattle had
been brought in, and now the branding was
going full swing. A cowboy would ride
into the herd and, after some maneuvering,
would flip his noose around a calf's hind legs
and drag him out to the branding fire. The
mother would follow anxiously behind.

"Quarter Circle Z!" the cowboy would
sing out, or "Hashknife!" or "Turkey
Track!" depending on what brand the old
cow wore. Uncle Torwal would make a mark
in the tally book under the proper brand.
Birdlegs Smith and another cowboy would
grab the calf and stretch it on the ground.

Then Uncle Torwal would pick an iron
out of the fire and press it carefully on the

calf's side or hip–depending on what brand it would wear. The calf would bellow, more surprised than hurt. And a few minutes later he'd be up and tearing across the flat, looking for his mother and indignant at having his owner's mark put on him. While the calf and the old cow were talking it over, a rider would drive them off into the bunch that had already been branded and tallied.

At the first lull in the work Uncle Torwal called Whitey. "How about taking over the tally book for me?" he asked.

"Sure," Whitey answered, "be glad to."

Uncle Torwal showed him how the different ranches' brands were arranged in the book, and how to put a tally mark under the proper one for each calf that was branded.

For the rest of the afternoon, Uncle Torwal oversaw the branding and watched that the irons didn't get cold or too hot, and Whitey kept the tally. It wasn't as exciting as roping or throwing calves, perhaps, but he figured it was a good start. Maybe tomorrow he would be put on one of those jobs.

The sun was still fairly high when the last calf was branded. The men stood around the branding fire a little while, beating the dust from their clothes and letting their sweaty shirts dry. Then, being as it was still early, they mounted to bunch the grazing cattle.

Riding with the others, Whitey helped gather the scattered cattle into a herd and start them moving back towards their home ranges. Cows were still bawling and searching for calves that had gotten separated from them in the confusion. Calves, in their turn, bawled for their mothers or galloped clumsily about in short rushes, excited by the strange goings-on. But little by little they all got themselves sorted out and moved slowly along without excitement. Riding along the flank of the herd, flipping his rope end to encourage laggards, Whitey wouldn't have traded jobs with anybody.

After the cattle had been driven through the drift fence, and the wire put back up, Whitey and the other riders returned to camp at a lazy trot.

With no herd to be held, there was no need to keep the horses up. So they were watered and unsaddled and turned loose to graze with the extra mounts. Old Spot had a reputation of being a bunch-quitter, likely to leave the others and sneak off for home at the first opportunity, so Whitey picketed him on good grass close to the wagon. The night wrangler had his horse saddled and tied to the wagon ready to go out to herd the saddle horses.

While Mr. Waccapominy finished cooking supper the cowboys rummaged in the wagon for their bedrolls and threw them down a little distance from the fire. After they'd eaten they sprawled on the grass with the bedrolls for backrests watching Mr. Waccapominy working at the chuck-box while they waited for bedtime.

Kangaroo Court

"I KINDA think maybe the Kangaroo Court has some business to take care of tonight," Birdlegs Smith remarked to no one in particular.

"If you think so, call her to order," Highwater agreed. "You're the Judge."

"All right, Kangaroo Court is now in session. Mr. Highwater, you are Prosecuting Attorney. Bring your prisoner up to this here bar."

"Who's the prisoner, yer honor?" Highwater asked. "And what's he to be tried for?"

"The kid is the prisoner," Birdlegs told him. "And what it is he's done is your business—I'm just Judge."

"That's right, Judge," Highwater said. "Now I think of it there are several things he should be tried for. Come up here to the bar, kid!"

Whitey had heard of these Kangaroo Courts. They served to entertain the men in the short time between supper and bedtime after a hard day's riding. They were also used to initiate newcomers or greenhorns. Just what the cowboys had in mind he didn't know, but he did know that no matter what it was he'd better take it with a grin. Any man who lost his temper when being tried by a Kangaroo Court was in for a hard time afterwards.

Whitey looked over at Uncle Torwal who was sitting off a little to one side. But he seemed to be busy with his tally book, paying no attention to what was going on. So Whitey got up and walked over to stand beside Highwater.

"Take off your hat when you are in court, kid!"

"Yessir!" Whitey said, respectfully, and took off his hat.

"You got a lawyer to defend you, kid?" Birdlegs asked, settling himself more comfortably against his bedroll.

"No, sir."

"Well, the Court will have to appoint

one," Birdlegs said. "We don't want it said this Court don't give a fair trial. Flyspeck, you are now Attorney for the Defense."

"I don't know any law," Flyspeck complained. "Even Kangaroo law."

"You can make it up as you go along," Birdlegs told him. "Now, what's this here prisoner charged with?"

"Well, Judge," Highwater told him. "He's a nefarious character and has committed several and various crimes. One, he couldn't catch his horse this morning and didn't get to work until afternoon. Two is that before supper he flung his saddle down beside the wagon, in territory that belongs by long custom to the cook. And three, he talked while everybody was eating."

"Those are all pretty serious crimes, for a fact," Birdlegs said. "A man could get strung up in lots of camps for less. What does the prisoner say about it?"

Before Whitey could decide what he should do Flyspeck spoke up for him. "The Attorney for the Defense admits his man is guilty, but pleads circumstances that alters cases—such as ignorance, bad companions, and acts of Providence, your honor."

"As Prosecuting Attorney of this Court I want to say right now that those excuses don't hold water. I say if a man wants to be ignorant he should at least be smart about it, so no one finds out. And these are mighty serious crimes this cowboy is accused of. What would the business come to if cowboys started coming to work any old time of day just because they couldn't catch their horses? In a little while nobody would be working more than eight or ten hours a day, instead of twelve to eighteen like they should.

"And this business of flinging a saddle or other traps down in the cook's territory not only endangers the life and limb of the cook, but the stomachs of every man working here. Even if the cook isn't put out of business with a busted leg from falling over such, you all know how touchous a roundup cook's temper is. Supposin' he just stumbles without being hurted, but gets into a temper and quits? Where'd we all be then, I respectfully ask you, Judge? The slop he feeds us is bad enough, but—"

"Slop, is it?" Mr. Waccapominy squalled, fumbling around in his sack of tools for a cleaver or some other weapon. "I'll learn you to call my cookin' slop, you uneducated hyenas, you."

"Now look what you went and caused, kid," Birdlegs said, scrambling to his feet ready to run. "You got him on the warpath!"

"I didn't do anything, honest!" Whitey objected, wondering what would happen next.

"Now, now! Hold your fire, Waccapominy," Highwater said. "We was just trying to show this here Court what a dangerous thing it is to have a jigger in camp that didn't know no better than to put his traps where the cook could fall over them and get hurted.

We didn't mean nothing against your cookin'—we was just speaking of ordinary kinds of cooks like Ol' Greasy over to the Mill Iron for instance."

"Well, if you was trying to say something nice you sure took a mighty queer way to do it," Mr. Waccapominy grumbled, hefting a heavy iron spoon in his hand.

"The Prosecuting Attorney was just trying to make the kid understand that a good cook like you is a valuable piece of property," Birdlegs told him. "We wanted to teach him to treat a cook kind and respectful like the President of the United States or the King of England, that's all. He didn't mean no offense."

"Well, get on with your fool Court," Waccapominy answered, "but watch how you talk about my cooking."

"Now, Judge," Highwater said after the cowboys had edged back to their bedrolls, and Mr. Waccapominy to banging his pots around, "besides these heinous crimes—"

"You didn't say anything before about him using hyenas in his crimes, and as his attorney I deny it!" Flyspeck objected.

"That doesn't mean anything to do with hyenas," Highwater explained. "It's a word commonly used by lawyers and newspaper writers to describe crimes that are out of the misdemeanor class."

"I wonder how he knows," Mr. Waccapominy muttered in a loud voice from back of his cook fire.

"Quiet, or I'll clear this here Court—cook or no cook!" Birdlegs said. "Go on with your case, Mr. Prosecuting Attorney."

"Well, like I was saying," Highwater continued, "besides these things I spoke of, the prisoner talked while he ate. Everybody knows this isn't no hotel Rockefeller where folks have time to set around and toy with their vittles. Cowboys are supposed to eat and git! Judge, I ask for the maximum sentence!"

"I think you're being too hard on this kid," Flyspeck objected. "You can't give him the maximum sentence, young as he is, for a first offense."

"It isn't one offense," Highwater replied. "It's three crimes, committed one after the other, and in plain sight of everybody! I say the maximum sentence is less than he deserves!"

By this time Whitey wasn't sure whether this was all a joke or not. Everybody seemed to be taking it awfully serious. Then Birdlegs spoke to him.

"Kid, this looks pretty serious for you," he said. "Got anything to say for yourself?"

"Well, sir, your honor," he stammered, "I guess it's like Mr. Highwater said—but I didn't do those things a-purpose. I just didn't think."

"Anybody else got anything to say before I sentence this pore feller for his crimes?" Birdlegs asked.

"I have," Mr. Waccapominy said. "He

hauled wood and toted water for me this afternoon without grumblin' like he was being disgraced. And that's more than any of you unregenerate polecats ever did!"

"After considering the evidence in this here case," Birdlegs said, "it is my opinion that this is a mighty grave situation, and ordinarily I'd give him the maximum sentence. On the other hand, I've had to take into account his extreme youth, and the cook's flowery testimonial as to his character. Besides, we're not fixed to give him the proper care he'd need if we gave him the maximum."

While Whitey fidgeted nervously in the firelight and the cowboys leaned forward to hear what the Judge would decide, Birdlegs lay back, closed his eyes, and thought.

"Prisoner, stand up to receive sentence," he said at last.

"I am standing up, your honor," Whitey gulped.

"Oh, so you are. Well, I sentence you to be chapped. The Prosecuting Attorney will be execut—I mean will do the deed. Deputies, seize the prisoner! Court is adjourned."

And before Whitey realized it he was being dragged through the dark towards the wagon. What was going to happen to him he didn't know, but he bit his lip and told himself that no matter what they did to him he wasn't going to let them know he was scared.

In silence the men bent him over a bedroll, holding his hands and feet so he was

powerless to move. One of the men offered
a pair of chaps to Highwater.

"Not those," he said. "We don't want to
cripple him with those heavy conchos. Gim-
me that pair there."

Highwater braced his feet, spit on his
hands, and took a firm grip on the tops of
the chaps. "Stand back now, in case blood
spatters," he said. "You ready, kid?"

"Yessir, I guess so," Whitey quavered.

There was a swish as Highwater swung
the heavy leather chaps and brought them
down across the seat of Whitey's pants. He
was so startled he almost cried out, then he
discovered that most of the noise was from
the leather striking the wagon tongue, and
that he wasn't really hurt at all!

Out in the darkness somebody counted "One!" and Highwater swung the chaps again. At "Four!" the voice said, "Guess that's enough."

The men holding Whitey let loose and helped him to his feet. All of a sudden he discovered that everybody seemed to be in a fine humor.

"How you feelin', kid?" Birdlegs asked with a grin.

"Fine," Whitey answered, limping just a little.

"Learned your lesson, eh?"

"Yessir!" Whitey told him. "I'll be more careful after this."

After more talk about the trial and other matters everybody started unrolling beds.

"Looks like it might rain a little before morning, kid. You better fold the edges of your tarp under your bed," Birdlegs remarked from where he was bedding down close by.

A bed canvas is usually six or eight feet wide by sixteen feet long. The bedding is arranged in the middle of one end, a foot or so down from the top. Then the long end at the bottom is hauled up for a top cover. The canvas being considerably wider than the bedding leaves wide flaps on either side. If there promises to be rain or wind these flaps are folded under the bed to make a wind- and rain-tight envelope. The extra length of the top canvas is ordinarily folded back out of the way. But in case of rain it is brought up over

the head of the bed to form a miniature tent to protect the sleeper's head and clothes.

When Whitey had finally gotten his bed arranged, his boots and clothes made into a bundle for a pillow, and had slipped down into his quilts, the sky was clear and bright with stars. For a little while he watched them, enjoying the smell of the grass mixed with the curious smell of the well-used bed tarp.

The next he knew, rain was spattering on his face as Birdlegs had predicted. He drowsily reached out for the loose fold of canvas and pulled it over his head, punching it up to make an air space. He could hear some of the men stirring about, folding their tarps under, but the patter of rain on the canvas so close to his face put him to sleep again.

Riding Circle

I T W A S still full dark next morning when Mr. Waccapominy beat on a dishpan to wake the men for breakfast.

Throwing back his bed canvas, Whitey found that the rain had stopped and the sky was already clear. All around him men were sitting up in their bedrolls, putting on their hats before beginning to dress. One by one they rolled their beds, threw them on the wagon, and headed for the creek to wash. Whitey did the same, stopping on the way to get Old Spot and lead him to water.

As Whitey splashed water on his face, Uncle Torwal, who was washing nearby, said, "You want to work for Waccapominy today, or go out on circle with us?"

"I'd like to go out on circle," Whitey answered, "if it's all right with you."

"All right, be saddled up when we are ready," Uncle Torwal told him.

They walked back to the wagon.

By this time the nighthawk had brought the horses up and put them in the rope corral. The cook had been up for hours and had steak, hot biscuits, and fried potatoes ready in the Dutch ovens. The big black coffeepot was steaming, and a gallon can stood ready on the let-down lid of the chuck-box for anyone who wanted to finish off his breakfast with syrup poured over his biscuits.

Whitey ate only two helpings of every-thing, and remembered not to waste his time

talking; so he was finished as soon as the rest. While the men walked into the flimsy corral to rope their horses, he saddled Old Spot.

Whitey was ready and waiting when Uncle Torwal mounted and said, "Well, let's get moving. It'll be sunup before you know it."

Today they were to work the broken country on the far side of Hay Creek, and the whole crew rode in a group until they came to the divide marking the Squaw Creek watershed. This was a sort of natural range boundary, and Uncle Torwal led them to the left along the high ground. As he rode he dropped a man or two off every mile or so. Moving back towards the camp, each man would comb all the draws and thickets in his territory, pushing any cattle he found ahead of him. With riders strung out in a rough line several miles long and moving in towards the center, the roundup gathered cattle like a huge seine.

At Cedar Spring Uncle Torwal jerked a thumb at Birdlegs and said, "You take the boy and work down from here," and rode on to place the rest of the riders.

This time of day most of the cattle were out in the open, grazing, and easy to find.

From a ridge Whitey and Birdlegs would see eight or ten cows and calves quietly feeding in a draw and Birdlegs would say, "You go round them up, kid, and I'll take a look over on the other side."

Riding quietly so as not to spook them, Whitey would ride around behind the feeding cattle and start urging them into motion. The end of his rope encouraged stragglers, and before long they would be strung out along one of the hundreds of stock trails that laced the range.

Soon Birdlegs would come in sight with whatever he had found, and the combined bunch would be moved still farther down the slopes. If there was an open swale handy, where the stock would graze without scattering too much, they'd leave them.

Both riders would then check other possible hiding places. As they went they had to make sure that no draw or gulley between them and the riders on either side was missed. It was a matter of pride to make a clean sweep and not leave an animal behind.

Little by little Birdlegs' and Whitey's herd increased in size. As it did, it became more and more difficult to keep the cattle moving all together. Some old cow was everlastingly taking it into her head to cut back into the breaks, leading her small group with her. Then it took hard riding to turn the rebels and push them into the middle of the herd.

As the sun climbed higher, the cattle began to drift into the shade of the plum and boxelder thickets to rest and chew their cuds. This made them harder to find. And when they were found they were uncooperative about coming out of those tangled places. Often Whitey would think he had them all out, when a calf he'd missed would bawl from the bushes. Its mother would bawl in answer and wheel back to join it, and all the others would wheel too. Then the whole business would have to be gone through again.

Before the morning was more than half over Whitey had decided that the roundup was like most ranch business—more work than excitement. However, he said nothing about his discovery. He took his turn at holding the critters they'd gathered while Birdlegs searched a draw; then Whitey searched the next draw himself.

But it was Birdlegs, not Whitey, that let an old mossy-horn steer cut back and get clean away. Every range has a few like him— old steers that have lived far back in the brakes so long they are wild as elk. Birdlegs had brought him out of a steep-sided little

canyon with half a dozen cows and calves. As soon as the steer was out in the open he threw his tail up and headed straight back.

Once or twice Birdlegs almost turned him, but in the end he called to Whitey, who was trying to cut him off on the other side, "Let him go! If we fool with him we'll lose the rest."

So they went back to the slow work of getting the ones they had into more open country without losing any others.

As the circle of riders drew in towards the center, the small bunches of cattle gradually joined to form a single herd, so that the work went easier and faster. Even so, it was well past noon before the cattle were all gathered and bunched on the flat below the wagon.

Three men were left to hold the herd while the rest rode on to the wagon to eat.

Whitey had been riding a horse ever since he could remember. But this morning's work was the hardest he had ever done, and when he slid off Old Spot beside the chuck wagon he ached in every joint. So, much as he'd counted on getting to rope calves that afternoon, he made no objection when Uncle Torwal suggested that Old Spot needed rest after the morning's work.

"You don't have an extra horse," Torwal said, "so if it's all right with you, maybe you'd better help Waccapominy around the wagon for a while, and let the old horse rest."

"Yessir, that would probably be a good idea."

After everybody had eaten, Whitey hauled water and did other odd jobs for Mr. Waccapominy. He helped make a huge dried apple pie for supper, and learned how to make biscuit dough. The sack of flour already had lard, salt, and baking powder mixed with it. By pouring water a little at a time into a hollow scooped in the flour, he mixed lumps of dough right in the top of the sack.

When Whitey had finished the chores he rode Old Spot down to where the last of the calves were being branded. Sitting on his horse, he watched the ropers catch the calves and bring them to the fire.

He could see now that he really needed a good deal of practice before he was ready to try it himself.

First, the calf had to be worked quietly out of the middle of the mass of cattle into the less crowded fringes. The rope had to be swung so that the noose fell around in front of the calf's hind feet in just a certain way. Then it had to be flipped just right, and at exactly the right time to tighten as the calf's legs came into it.

A difficult thing to do out in the open, but doubly hard with so little room to work. However, it was some comfort to know that a good many of the regular cowboys never did learn the trick. Some were good ropers and some were not. Maybe by next year he would have had practice enough to be one of the few chosen as ropers.

While Whitey was thinking of these

things, Uncle Torwal put the branding iron onto a black calf that let out a roar you could hear half a mile. At that his mother gave an answering bawl and headed for the branding fire with her head down and her tail up. It was plain she was not traveling for pleasure.

Now a bull usually shuts his eyes and charges blind, so it's not too hard to dodge him. But an old cow doesn't make that mistake; she watches where she is going. Uncle Torwal and the men were scrambling to get out of there quick. Except for Whitey, there didn't happen to be anyone on a horse near enough to stop her.

To get to the fire and the men she had to pass Whitey and Spot. When he looked back and saw her coming, he swung his loop to turn her, and accidentally caught her head in the noose. Spot was about half asleep, but when the rope went past his head he remembered his cow-horse days and braced himself. The cow hit the end of the rope with a crash and turned head over heels, landing on her side almost in the branding fire. By the time she gathered her wits, more men had ridden up to drive her off.

Naturally, the cowboys admired Whitey's quick work with his rope, and he didn't tell them it was an accident. As a matter of fact, he really had roped her, whether he'd meant to or not.

After the last calf was branded and the cattle were moved through the drift fence, the camp settled down for the evening as it

had the night before. But now there was no talk of Kangaroo Court. They spoke of Whitey's roping of the old cow, and of what probably would have happened if he hadn't stopped her.

"Reckon Torwal would still have been running, looking for a tree to climb," Birdlegs remarked.

"Highwater passed me so fast I thought I was standing still," Uncle Torwal said. "He seemed truly to be in a terrible hurry to get somewhere else."

"Reminded me a lot of the time the weasel got in the henhouse back home," someone else added.

And so the talk went. Whitey lay back against his bedroll listening, as was proper for a new man in the outfit. But he no longer felt like an outsider.

CONTENTS

SO-DRD-603

Contact: All inquiries and correspondence should be sent to Indian Chief Publishing House, P.O. Box 1814, Davis, CA 95617, or *info@indianchief.net*.

Book data: The Complete Big Island of Hawaii Guidebook, 2nd edition, ISBN 0-916841-79-0.

Contributors to this book: B. Sangwan, David J. Russ, Nikhi Sangwan, Frédérique Lamort

Printed in the U.S.A.

HOW TO USE THIS GUIDEBOOK

This guidebook is divided into five chapters: Overview, History, and an *Exploring the Island* chapter entitled Oahu. The *Exploring* chapter is subdivided into sections, areas, segments, and points of interest (see below).

Section: **KONA COAST**

Area: **Kailua-Kona**

Segment: *Aliʻi Drive*

Point of Interest: *Huliheʻe Palace*

What the Icons and Numbers Mean:

This guidebook is sectioned, and entries in it cross-referenced, to enable you to quickly and easily find what you are looking for, a lot like links on web pages on the Internet. And that is where the icons and numbers come in—as a link.

 Icon: This ubiquitous icon is a prod for you to reference a corresponding map for orientation or, if you are already looking at a map in the book, to reference a corresponding section or area where you will find more information.

Numbers are of three different kinds:

1 **Section Reference:** At the start of each section, such as Kona Coast or Hilo, a small island map with a rectangle defining the area covered in the section appears, together with a number that corresponds to the number-coded section on the larger island map at the start of the chapter. This is designed to enable you to reference the section on the map for orientation and an overview.

Entries Between Rules: Also, where sections are lengthier, a list of areas covered in the section appears between parallel rules directly beneath the section heading. This is designed to enable you to quickly find the area relevant to your interest.

2 **Area Reference:** At the start of most areas, such as Waikiki or East Honolulu, a gray box with a number appears. This corresponds to the number-coded area map relevant to the text. This is designed to orient you with the area.

3 **Point of Interest Reference:** Alongside several entries in the book, a black box with a number appears in the side bar. This corresponds to the point of interest located on the referenced area map (described above, in Area Reference). This will enable you to find the relevant points of interest quickly and easily.

Arrows: An arrow in the side bar alongside an entry indicates a point of interest that is not referenced on a map.

Alternatively, if you choose to use this book as a traditional guidebook, a quick and easy way into it is the *Index* at the end.

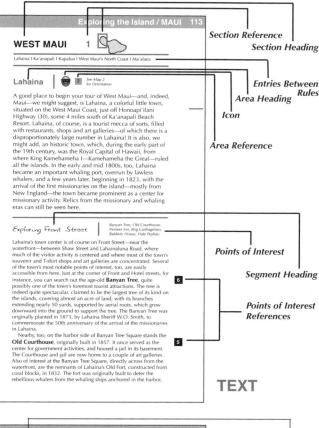

Section Reference

Section Heading

Entries Between Rules

Area Heading

Icon

Area Reference

Points of Interest

Segment Heading

Points of Interest References

TEXT

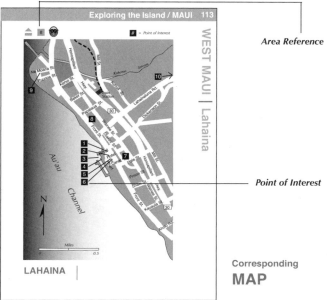

Area Reference

Point of Interest

Corresponding
MAP

HOW TO USE THIS GUIDEBOOK | Icons and Numbers

OVERVIEW

The Islands | Getting There | Getting Around | Tourist Information

The Islands

The Hawaiian islands lie approximately 2,400 miles southwest of the west coast of mainland USA, smack in the middle of the Pacific Ocean. The archipelago includes well over a hundred atolls, reefs, shoals and tiny islands spread out over some 1,600 miles of ocean, but there are only eight major islands in the chain: Oahu, Hawaii (the Big Island), Kauai, Ni'ihau, Maui, Molokai, Lanai and Kaho'olawe.

In this book, we cover the island of Hawaii.

Hawaii   *See Map 1 for Orientation*

Hawaii, the island, alternately known as "The Big Island" and "The Orchid Isle," is the largest island in the Hawaiian archipelago, more than twice as large as all the other Hawaiian islands combined, encompassing 4,028 square miles. It comprises five volcanic land masses, those of Mauna Kea, Mauna Loa, Hualalai, Kohala and Kilauea (currently one of the world's most active volcanoes), joined together by lava flows that form the island's fertile valleys and plateaus. The island lies approximately 35 miles southeast of Maui, or 170 miles southeast of Oahu.

The Big Island has a population of more than 150,000, and is a popular destination in Hawaii, drawing approximately 1.5 million visitors annually. It has over 9,400 hotel rooms, rental condominiums and bed and breakfast accommodations, nearly 150 restaurants, and offers a wealth of recreational opportunities, including swimming, snorkeling, scuba diving, surfing, windsurfing, sailing, biking, hiking, horseback riding, golfing, beachcombing and sport fishing. It also boasts a supremely enjoyable, temperate climate, with temperatures ranging from 45°F-55°F in January in the higher elevations to around 75°F-85°F in August in the coastal areas.

OVERVIEW | Getting There

Getting There | *Airports and Airlines*

The good thing about going to the Big Island is that you have the option of either flying there directly from mainland USA, or traveling through the busy hub at Honolulu International Airport on the island of Oahu, and from there on an inter-island flight to the Big Island of Hawaii.

Airports

The Big Island's principal airports are the Kona International Airport, located on the Kona Coast, just north of Kailua-Kona, and the Hilo International Airport, located in Hilo, on the island's east coast. A smaller commuter airport, the Waimea-Kohala Airport, is located at Waimea, in North Kohala.

Airport Contacts:
Hilo International Airport, Honolulu; (808) 934-5838/934-5840
Kona International Airport, Kailua-Kona; (808) 329-3423

Traveling Direct to Hawaii

The following airlines fly direct to Hawaii's Big Island from the continental U.S.:
Aloha Airlines, (808) 484-1111/(800) 367-5250/www.alohaairlines.com
American Airlines, (800) 433-7300/www.aa.com
United Airlines, (800) 864-8331/241-6522/www.united.com

Traveling Via Honolulu

Domestic Airlines flying to Honolulu:
Aloha Airlines, (808) 484-1111/(800) 367-5250/www.alohaairlines.com
American Airlines, (800) 433-7300/www.aa.com
America West Airlines, (800) 235-9292/www.americawest.com
Continental Airlines, (808) 532-0000/(800) 523-3273/www.continental.com
Delta Airlines, (800) 221-1212/www.delta.com
Hawaiian Airlines, (808) 871-6132/(800) 367-5320/882-8811/www.hawaiianair.com
Island Air, (808) 833-0122/www.islandair.com

Northwest Airlines, (800) 225-2525/*www.nwa.com*
United Airlines, (800) 864-8331/241-6522/*www.united.com*

International Airlines flying to Honolulu:
Air New Zealand, (800) 262-1234/*www.airnewzealand.com*
Air Canada, (888) 247-2262/*www.aircanada.com*
All Nippon Airways Co., (808) 838-0190/(800) 235-9262/www. ana.co.jp/eng
China Airlines, (800) 227-5118/*www.china-airlines.com*
Harmony Airways, (866) 868-6789/www.harmonyairways.com
Japan Airlines, (800) 525-3663/*www.japanair.com* or *www.jal. co.jp/en*
Korean Air, (800) 438-5000/*www.koreanair.com*
Philippines Airlines, (800) 435-9725/*www.philippineairlines.com*
Qantas Airways. (800 227-4500/*www.qantasusa.com*
Singapore Airlines, (800) 742-3333/*www.singaporeair.com*

Inter—Island Flights

There are two Hawaii-based airlines offering daily flights between Honolulu, Oahu, and the Big Island of Hawaii. Typically, fares for travel between Honolulu and either Kona or Hilo on the Big Island range from $79-$129 one-way to $158-$258 round-trip.

Airlines flying from Honolulu to the other Hawaiian Islands:
Aloha Airlines, (808) 484-1111/(800) 367-5250/*www.alohaairlines.com*
Hawaiian Airlines, (808) 871-6132/(800) 367-5320/882-8811/ www.hawaiianair.com*

Getting Around | *Car Rentals, Taxis, Bus*

Taxis are available on the island for point to point travel as well as island tours, and an island-wide bus service links all the population centers along the main routes of travel. But the best and most convenient way to get around the island is still by car, with rentals ranging from around $30-$190 per day to $130-$550 per week.

Car Rentals:
Affordable Car Rental, (808) 329-7766/*www.konarentalcars.com*
Alamo Rent a Car, (800) 327-9633/*www.alamo.com*

Avis Rent a Car, (808) 327-3000/(800) 321-3712/831-8000/ www.avis.com

Budget Car Rental, (808) 329-8511/(800) 527-0700/www. budget.com

Dollar Car Rental, (800) 800-4000/(800) 342-7398/www.dollar. com

Harper Car Rental, (808) 969-1478/(800) 852-9993/www. harpershawaii.com

Hertz Rent a Car, (808) 329-3566/(800) 654-3131/654-3011/ www.hertz.com

National Car Rental, (808) 329-1674/(800) 227-7368/www. nationalcar.com

Thrifty Car Rental, (800) 847-4389/www.thrifty.com

Oahu Taxis:

Air Taxi, (808) 883-8166; Aloha Taxi, (808) 329-7779; Alpha Star Taxi, (808) 885-4771; Hilo Harry's Taxi, (808) 935-7091; Kona Airport Taxi, (808) 329-7779; Laura's Taxi, (808) 326-5466, Marina Taxi, (808) 329-2481/329-6388; Marshall's Taxi, (808) 936-2654; Paradise Taxi, (808) 329-1234; Percy's Taxi, (808) 969-7060; and Speedi Shuttle, (808) 329-5433.

Typically, taxi fares from the Kona Airport to Kailua-Kona and the Keauhou area are $25-$35, and to Waikoloa, around $48-$60; and from Hilo International Airport to the Hilo area, $15-$20.

Bus:

Hawaii's Hele-On bus links virtually all of the island's principal communities, providing public transportation all around the island, journeying almost everywhere on the Big Island. Bus service is available free on all scheduled routes, with $1.00 charged for luggage and bicycles. A schedule of the route, stops and times can be obtained by calling the Hawaii County Mass Transit Agency, Hilo, at (808) 961-8744 or (808) 961-8745; or visit www.hawaii-county. com/mass_transit/heleonbus.html.

Tourist Information

Visitors Bureaus,
Division of Parks and Recreation,
Weather and Time

Visitors Bureaus

Hawaii Visitors and Convention Bureau (HVCB). Waikiki Business Plaza, 2270 Kalakaua Ave., Suite 801, Honolulu. HI 96815; (808) 923-1811/(800) 464-2924/*www.hvcb.org* or *www.gohawaii.com*. This is Hawaii's principal, one-stop source for visitor information, both for published materials and online information. The "gohawaii" web site has all the reference materials you could want, including listings for accommodations, restaurants, events, tours and recreation. The bureau also offers a free, cover-all publication in its visitor package, *The Islands of Hawaii: A Vacation Planner,* with a wealth of tourist information on places of interest on the islands, recreational opportunities and a wide selection of tours.

Hilo Big Island Visitors Bureau. 250 Keawe St., HI 96720; (808) 961-5797/(800) 648-2441/*www.bigisland.org*. Wealth of tourist information available, including directory of accommodations and restaurants and a calendar of events. Also maps, and the Big Island's premier, free tourist publication, *Hawaii's Big Island: Official Vacation Planner*. Open 8am-4.30pm, Mon.-Fri.

West Hawaii Big Island Visitors Bureau. 250 Waikoloa Beach Dr., Suite B-15, Waikoloa, HI 96738; (808) 886-1655/(800) 648-2441/*www.bigisland.org*. Good source for visitor information, including area accommodations, restaurants, tours and activities, events, and maps. Open 8am-4.30pm, Mon.-Fri.

Chamber of Commerce

Hawaii Island Chamber of Commerce. 106 Kamehameha Ave., Hilo, HI 96720; (808) 935-7178/*www.gohilo.com*. Visitor information brochures, including lodging, restaurant and tour company listings. Open 8am-4.30pm, Mon.-Fri.

Division of Parks and Recreation

Department of Parks and Recreation - County of Hawaii. 25 Aupuni St., Hilo, HI 96720; (808) 961-8311/*www.hawaii-county.com/parks/parks.htm*. Good source for information on Hawaii recreational facilities, including camping. Camping permits for county campgrounds are also available here . Hours: Mon.-Fri. 7.45am-4.30pm.

Department of Land and Natural Resources - Division of State Parks. P.O. Box 936, 75 Aupuni St., #204, Hilo, HI 96720; (808) 974-6200/961-7200/*www.state.hi.us*. Camping permits and information on State Park campgrounds on Hawaii. Hours: Mon.-Fri. 8am-3.30pm.

Weather, Time and Volcanic Activity

Weather:

For current weather conditions and forecasts for Hawaii, call (808) 961-5582.

Time:

For current Hawaiian Time, call (808) 961-0212.

Volcanic Activity:

(808) 985-6000

Marine Conditions:

(808) 935-5055

Camping Permits:

National Parks, (808) 985-6000
State Parks, (808) 974-6200
County Parks, (808) 961-8311

STORY OF HAWAII | A Brief History

Hawaii, the Big Island, is Hawaii's youngest island. It began form-
ing approximately a million years ago, when a series of eruptions
on the ocean floor created five adjacent, shielded volcanoes. This,
with the accumulation of molten lava over a period of time, finally
emerged as Mauna Kea—the highest point on the island, with an
elevation of 13,796 feet—Mauna Loa (13,677 feet), Hualalai (8,271
feet), Kohala (5,480 feet) and Kilauea (4,093 feet). Then, nearly
60,000 years ago, Kohala became extinct, and about 5,000 years
ago Mauna Kea became dormant, followed by Hualalai which last
erupted in 1801 and then also became dormant. Mauna Loa and
Kilauea remain active, with the latter now considered to be one
of the most active volcanoes in the world, continuing to erupt and
continually changing the island by adding to its land mass.

An ancient Hawaiian myth, however, endures that Hawaii and
the other Hawaiian islands are the offspring of Wakea, the divine
embodiment of the sky, and Papa, the earth deity, who arrived in
this part of the Pacific from Tahiti. Wakea and Papa first conceived
Hawaii, the big island, followed by Maui. Wakea then conceived
with Kaulawahine (another deity) the island of Lanai, and with
Hina, the island of Molokai. Papa, for her part, thoroughly infuri-
ated, then conceived with Lua (a male deity) the island of Oahu.
And finally, Papa and Wakea reconciled and together conceived
Kauai and the nearby island of Ni'ihau.

Hawaii's earliest inhabitants were the Marquesans, a Polynesian
people who journeyed to Hawaii from the Marquesas and Society
islands between 500 A.D. and 750 A.D., followed some years later,
around 1000 A.D., by the Tahitians. The Marquesans, who journeyed to Hawaii in large outrigger canoes, navigating by the stars
across several thousand miles of open ocean, introduced to Hawaii
and the other Hawaiian islands the first domestic animals, plants
and fruit; and the Tahitians, for their part, brought with them their
religion and their gods and goddesses, notable among them Kane,
the god of all living creatures; Ku, god of war; Pele, goddess of fire;
Kaneloa, the god of the land of the departed spirits; and Lono, god
of harvest and peace. The Tahitians also introduced to the islands
the *kapu* system, a strict social order that affected all aspects of life
and formed the core of ancient Hawaiian culture.

The first white man to sight the island of Hawaii was Captain
James Cook, a British explorer in search of a northwest passage
from the Pacific Ocean to the Atlantic Ocean. He first sighted
Hawaii in 1778, during his second expedition to the Pacific and the
Hawaiian islands, but did not land on the island until the following year, in February, 1779, dropping anchor off Kealakekua Bay. It
was also here, only a few weeks later, during his second visit to the

area to make necessary repairs to his ship, the *Resolution*, that Cook was killed, stabbed and clubbed to death by angry islanders. In any case, in the ensuing years, others followed, including Nathaniel Portlock and George Dixon—who had served under Cook—as well as Captain George Vancouver, another British explorer. These early Europeans, however, also brought with them to Hawaii and the other Hawaiian islands the white man's disease. Hawaiians had little or no resistance to Western diseases, and over a period of some 100 years following Cook's first contact with the islands, nearly 80% of the indigenous Hawaiian population was wiped out.

The mid and late 1700s also ushered in Hawaii's era of monarchy. Kamehameha I—also known as Kamehameha the Great—was born on the Big Island of Hawaii, near the northern tip of the island, in the late 1750s, and by 1791 he had wrested control of the island. In 1794, following the death of King Kahekili of Maui, he conquered Maui, as well as the nearby islands of Lanai and Molokai. The following year, in 1795, he also subdued Oahu. Then, in 1810, Kamehameha extended his dominion, through diplomacy, to include Kauai, thus unifying the island chain under his rule.

On April 4, 1820, the first missionaries arrived in the Hawaiian islands, on the island of Hawaii, at Kailua-Kona, on board the brig *Thaddeus*. Among them were Asa and Lucy Thurston, who built the stone Mokuaikaua Church there in 1837. The Thurstons were followed by others: in 1832, Reverend David Lyman and his wife, Sarah, sailed to Hilo and established there the Hilo Mission and the Hilo Boys Boarding School; also in 1832, Dr. Dwight Baldwin, together with his wife Charlotte, arrived in Waimea (Kamuela) in North Kohala, where he founded the Waimea Health Station; and in 1835, Reverend Lorenzo Lyons, who later wrote one of Hawaii's most memorable ballads, "Hawaii Aloha," arrived on the Big Island and established a series of churches, including the Imiola Church at Waimea and the Hokuloa Church at Puako. Among other notable early-day missionaries was Elias Bond, who arrived in Waimea in 1841 and established there, in 1855, the Kalahikiola Church, and who later on also became famous as the "King of Kohala."

The mid-1800s witnessed the birth of Hawaii's sugar industry. Large sugarcane plantations were developed throughout the islands, mostly by descendants of the early missionaries. Among Hawaii's largest sugar companies were Castle & Cooke, C. Brewer, American Factor and Theo H. Davies, which became charter members of Hawaii's Big Five—the islands' five largest corporations that produced and marketed nearly 96% of the islands' sugar and controlled Hawaii's economy and politics for more than half a century. Hawaii now produces approximately 1 million tons of sugar annually, although the Big Island contributes only a small portion to it.

The late 1800s and early 1900s also brought to the Hawaiian islands waves of immigrants—mostly Chinese, Japanese, Filipino.

Portuguese and other Europeans—drawn to Hawaii's growing sugar and pineapple industries. Over time, the number of these new immigrants turned Hawaii's indigenous population into a minority. On the island of Hawaii, in fact, pure-blooded, native Hawaiians now comprise only 2% of the population.

The late 19th century was also a period of transformation for the Hawaiian monarchy. In 1872, following the death of Kamehameha V, the last of the kings of the Kamehameha dynasty, the custom of electing a king was established, and in 1873, William Lunalilo became Hawaii's first king to be elected to the throne. Lunalilo died the following year, in 1874, and was succeeded by David Kalakaua, the "Merrie Monarch," who ruled until his death in January, 1891. Kalakaua was succeeded by his sister, Queen Liliuokalani. By then also, with the rapid growth of Hawaii's sugar industry, American interests on the islands had become deeply entrenched, and in 1892, upon the start of open rebellion, the *USS Boston* landed on the island of Oahu an armed force to protect American interests. A year later, in 1893, a more or less bloodless revolution deposed Liliuokalani and brought to power, at the head of a provisional government, Sanford B. Dole. The following year, Hawaii was declared a republic by the Hawaiian legislature, and on June 14, 1900, Hawaii was annexed, under the Organic Act, by the United States, and a territorial form of government established.

In 1902, Prince Jonah Kuhio Kalanianaole, born of royal parentage, and the last heir to the throne, became the first Hawaiian delegate elected to the U.S. Congress. Kuhio led the Hawaiian congressional delegation for the next two decades, and despite not having an official vote in the legislature—as Hawaii was only a territory of the United States at the time—he forged important legislation for the betterment of Hawaii and its people. Among his triumphs: the landmark Hawaiian Homesteads Act of 1910 and the Hawaiian Homes Commission Act of 1921, whereby public lands were made available to native Hawaiians for homesteading. He also obtained funding for such important projects as Pearl Harbor in Oahu, and in 1919 and 1920, he introduced two successive bills for statehood for Hawaii in the U.S. Congress. In 1922, Kuhio died at the age of 50.

On August 21, 1959, Hawaii finally gained statehood, becoming the 50th state of the nation—the "Aloha State." That same year, the first commercial jet, a Boeing 707, landed in Hawaii, at Honolulu, greatly reducing travel time from the continental U.S. to Hawaii to under 4½ hours. This, effectively, signaled the beginning of tourism in Hawaii.

In the following decade, Hawaii's tourist era began in earnest. On the island of Hawaii, in the 1960s, the Kona and Kohala coasts began developing into premier resort areas, starting with the construction of the Mauna Kea Beach Hotel, the Kona Village Resort and the Kona Hilton in 1965. In the 1970s, resort development continued along the island's Kohala and Kona coasts, with the opening, in 1972, of the prestigious, 3,200-acre oceanfront Mauna Lani Resort—which now includes the Mauna Lani Bay Hotel and the Fairmont Orchid—and the landmark King Kamehameha Hotel, built in 1975 in the resort town of Kailua-Kona. In the 1980s, the Waikoloa resort was developed, also on the south Kohala Coast, to include the Royal Waikoloan Sheraton Hotel (now the Waikoloa Beach Marriott), built in 1981, and the Hyatt Regency Waikoloa (now the Hilton Waikoloa Village) built in 1988 at a cost of $360 million. The most recent addition to the Kohala Coast is the luxury Hapuna Prince Hotel, built in 1994, overlooking Hapuna Beach.

The latter years have also witnessed the creation and preservation of a series of state parks and sanctuaries. In 1961, for instance, the 207,643-acre Hawaii Volcanoes National Park was first established, and in the same year, Pu'uhonua O Honaunau (City of Refuge) was designated a national historic park. In 1967, the 100-acre Kalopa State Recreation Area and the 16.4-acre Wailuku River State Park were established along the Wailuku River; and in 1971, the Kealakekua Bay Marine Life Conservation District was created to include 315 acres of an undersea ecological reserve, just offshore from Captain Cook in South Kona. Among others, in 1973 the 262-acre Laupakahi State Historical Park was established at the site of an early Hawaiian Settlement; in 1981, the Mauna Kea Ice Age Natural Area Reserve was formed, covering 3,894 acres on the Mauna Kea summit, to include an aeolian desert, an alpine lake and an area of Pleistocene glaciation; and in 1983, three natural area reserves, Manuka, Laupahoehoe and Kipahoehoe, were set aside as public lands, encompassing 25,550 acres, 7,894 acres and 5,583 acres, respectively.

The island of Hawaii is now positioned as a premier destination resort, with an abundance of excellent hotel and condominium accommodations and restaurants and other visitor facilities, and a wealth of recreational opportunities, including swimming, surfing, windsurfing, snorkeling, scuba diving, waterskiing, kayaking, sailing, sportfishing, hiking, horseback riding, camping, golf, tennis, helicopter touring, and more.

1 = Area Segment

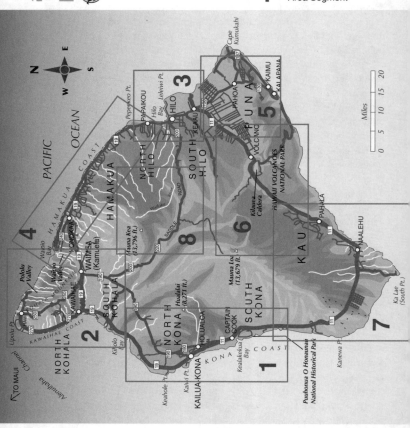

HAWAII

Area segments,
numerically coded,
are described on the
EXPLORING pages
as indicated below:

1 Kona Coast
[p 16–38]

2 Kohala [p 38–56]

3 Hilo [p 57–67]

4 Hamakua Coast
[p 67–72]

5 Puna [p 72–75]

6 Hawaii Volcanoes
National Park
[p 75–82]

7 Kau [p 83–88]

8 Saddle Road
[p 88–90]

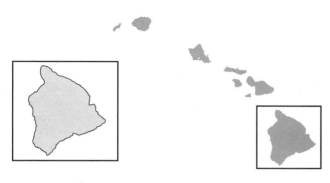

Hawaii | Exploring the Island

Hawaii, the island, is Hawaii's "Big Island." It is more than double the size of all the other major Hawaiian islands combined—and still growing! It is an island of superlatives: it is home to two of Hawaii's tallest mountains Mauna Kea and Mauna Loa, and one of the world's most active volcanoes, Kilauea. It is an island of grandeur, of contrast, of power, and, ultimately, it is the birthplace of Hawaii's first absolute monarch, Kamehameha the Great.

The Big Island encompasses 4,028 square miles and is made up of five merged volcanic land masses, those of Mauna Kea, Mauna Loa, Hualalai, Kohala and Kilauea. Kohala is at the north end of the island, at the heart of the Kohala district; Hualalai is in the west, the backdrop for the Kona Coast; Kilauea lies near the southeast, at the heart of the Hawaii Volcanoes National Park; and Mauna Kea and Mauna Loa rise near the center of the island, with Mauna Loa located to the southwest of Mauna Kea. Along the east coast of the island is Hilo, Hawaii's largest "city," and just to the north of there the lush Hamakua Coast. At the southeast and south of the island are the Puna and Kau districts, respectively.

For the purposes of exploring the island, we have divided Oahu into eight logically-grouped, geographically-distinct sections:

1   **Kona Coast**, the island's sun-drenched west coast, which includes Kailua-Kona and the South Kona and North Kona districts;

2   **Kohala**, which is made up of the northernmost portion of the island, and takes in the Kohala Coast and Kohala Mountain;

3   **Hilo**, the island's largest city, located on its east coast;

4   **Hamakua Coast**, the lush coastal stretch along the northeast of the island, which extends northward from Hilo to North Kohala;

5   **Hawaii Volcanoes National Park**, which comprises the southeastern preserve centered around the active volcano, Kilauea;

6   **Puna**, the district between Hilo and Hawaii Volcanoes Park;

7   **Kau**, the southernmost portion of the island;

8   **Saddle Road**, which takes in Mauna Kea and surrounding area.

[The numbers in the sidebar correspond to those in the number-coded map of the island.]

THE KONA COAST | 1

Kailua-Kona | South Kona | North Kona

The Kona Coast comprises the central portion of the west coast of the Big Island, from Kiholo Bay south to Kailua-Kona, Captain Cook and the Kipahoehoe Natural Area Reserve, stretching some 50 miles. This is of course one of the premier resort areas of the island, dry, sunny, and with good, sandy beaches. It has, together with the Kohala Coast just to the north, the majority of the island's hotels, restaurants, shops and other visitor facilities, and one of the island's only two commercial airports, the Keahole Airport.

Kailua-Kona

See Map 2 on Page 17

A good place to begin your tour of the Kona Coast—and the Big Island itself—is Kailua-Kona, a colorful little seaside town, situated along the northern part of the Kona Coast, at the foot of Mount Hualalai—the 8,271-foot volcanic mountain, on the slopes of which world-famous Kona coffee is grown. Kailua-Kona is of course a tourist mecca of sorts, filled with restaurants and shops, including several major shopping centers for serious shoppers. This also is an historic town, where in 1812 King Kamehameha I—or Kamehameha the Great—established his residence after shifting it from Honolulu, and where he lived until his death on May 8,1819. It was also here, on April 4, 1820, that the first American missionaries to the Hawaiian islands landed, at a point near present-day Kailua Pier. Relics from both the Hawaiian monarchy and missionary eras can still be seen here.

Aliʔi Drive

King Kamehameha Hotel, Kailua Pier
Huliheʻe Palace, Mokuaikaua Church,
Kealaokamaiamaiama Church

Kailua-Kona's chief interest, by most measures, lies in its main street, Ali'i Drive, which runs 7½ miles northwest-southeast, from Palani Road at the north end of town to the Kona Country Club and Holua Slide site in the south. Most of the town's restaurants, shops, boutiques and art galleries are concentrated here. Some of the town's most notable points of interest, too, are located along this street, with many others easily accessible from it. Here, for instance, at the top (north) end of the street, near the corner of Palani Road, **1** you can search out the landmark **King Kamehameha's Kona Beach**

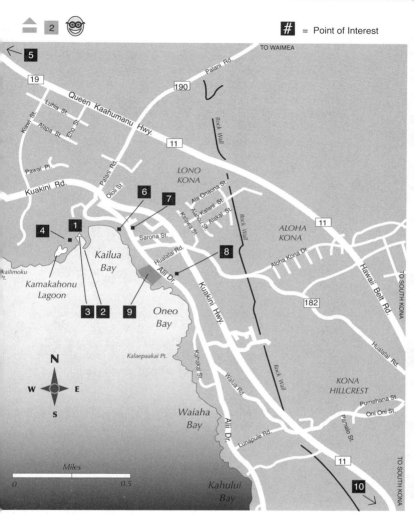

 # = Point of Interest

KAILUA-KONA

1. King Kamehameha Hotel
2. Kailua Pier
3. Kamakahonu Beach Park
4. Ahuena Heiau
5. Old Kona Airport Beach Park
6. Hulihee Palace
7. Mokuaikaua Church
8. St. Michael's Church
9. Hale Halawai Beach Park
10. White Sands Beach (Disappearing Sands)

3 **Hotel** (also known as King Kamehameha Hotel, or simply "King Kam"). It fronts on the glorious, white-sand **Kamakahonu Beach** at the head of Kailua Bay, which has good swimming and snorkeling possibilities. The hotel, built in 1975, comprises two identical buildings, boasting 460 guest rooms, three restaurants, a swimming pool, tennis courts, and even an adjoining shopping mall with over 30 specialty shops and boutiques and a museum exhibiting assorted Hawaiian artifacts. The hotel offers visitors (including non-guests) scheduled, complimentary tours of the museum as well as the hotel's historic grounds.

2 Directly below the Hotel King Kamehameha, adjacent to Kamakahonu Beach and also of interest, is the old **Kailua Pier**, built in 1915 at the site of the historic landing of the first missionaries to Hawaii in 1820. The pier is now a hub of activity centered around water sports and recreation, and also a staging point for local canoe clubs, fishing charters and boat excursions. And since 1959, Kailua Pier has been the site of the Hawaiian International Billfish Tournament, the popular, annual amateur marlin fishing competition, in which winning catches typically weigh in at over 1,000 pounds each!

4 Another place of interest, also on the grounds of King Kamehameha Hotel, situated on a lava outcropping adjacent to Kamakahonu Beach, is the ancient **Ahu'ena Heiau**, rebuilt and restored by King Kamehameha I in 1812, and more recently by the Hotel King Kamehameha interests. The *heiau*, which once was a temple for human sacrifice, comprises a complex of thatched huts, with a main structure, Hale Mana—or "House of Spiritual Power"— which in the early 1800s served as both a place of worship as well as a pulpit from where Kamehameha the Great ruled his kingdom, the Hawaiian islands. There is also a stone house here, Hale Pohaku, located adjacent to Hale Mana, where Kamehameha's body, upon his death, was prepared for burial.

5 Of interest, too, just to the northwest of the Hotel King Kamehameha, at the northern end of Kuakini Highway (11), lies the **Old Kona Airport Beach Park**, encompassing some 120 acres along the coast, and developed at the site of the old Kona Airport. The beach park comprises a sandy-grassy stretch, bordered by a rocky shoreline with abundant coral and tide pools. It offers some snorkeling possibilities in a small, sheltered cove at its north end, and also good bodysurfing and fishing. Park facilities include tennis courts, baseball fields, pavilions, picnic tables, restrooms and showers, as well as on-duty lifeguards.

6 Southeast of King Kamehameha Hotel, a little way on Ali'i Drive, on the *makai* (ocean) side, overlooking Kailua Bay and well worth visiting, is the historic **Hulihe'e Palace**, a vestige of the Hawaiian monarchy era. The two-story Victorian structure was originally built in 1838 by the Big Island's governor, John Adams Kuakini, brother of Queen Ka'ahumanu—the favorite wife of Kamehameha I—and served as a vacation home for Hawaii's monarchs and royalty until 1916. The palace was restored in 1927, and now houses a museum with a good collection of Royal Hawaiian *koa* furniture and other Hawaiian artifacts.

Also try to see **Mokuaikaua Church**, situated directly across from Hulihe'e Palace, on the *mauka* (inland) side of Ali'i Drive. The steepled, 112-foot-high church has the distinction of being the tallest structure at Kailua-Kona, as well as the oldest Christian church in the islands, dedicated in 1825 by Queen Ka'ahumanu, one of Hawaii's earliest and most important converts to Christianity. The church, however, constructed from coral taken from the ocean nearby, was largely rebuilt in 1837, following a fire that virtually destroyed the original structure. The interior of the church now features antique *ohia* wood beams and *koa* wood pews and pulpits. There is also an exhibit room here, with a scale model of the historic brig *Thaddeus*, the ship that brought to the Hawaiian islands the first American missionaries on April 4, 1820.

South still, a little way from Mokuaikaua Church and the Hulihe'e Palace on Ali'i Drive, just past Hualalai Road—directly across from the Waterfront Row shopping center—stands the historic **St. Michael's Church**, housed in a bright pink structure and claimed to be the oldest Catholic church on the Big Island, dating from 1850. Yet another church of interest, situated on the south side of St. Michael's, is the wood-frame, multi-level **Kealaokamaiamaia-ma Church**, which dates from the early 1900s.

Close at hand, too, just to the southwest of Ali'i Drive and Hualalai Road, lies the **Hale Halawai Beach Park**, a small, rocky beach that once was the site of an old prison and courthouse. The beach, in all fairness, is not particularly suitable for swimming, although it does have restrooms facilities and a pavilion.

Holualoa Bay to Kahalu'u Bay

Holualoa Bay, St Peter's Church, Kuemanu Heiau, Kahalu'u Beach

Southward from Hale Halawai Beach Park, strung along the coast on the *makai* (ocean) side of Ali'i Drive, are the resort hotels Kona Hilton, Hale Kona Kai, Kona Reef, Sea Village, Royal Sea Cliff and Kona-By-The-Sea; and farther, some 2 miles from Hale Halawai Beach, is **Holualoa Bay**, one of the best surfing spots at Kona. There are actually two major surfbreaks at Holualoa Bay: "Banyan's," which is more or less directly opposite a large banyan tree located on the ocean side of Ali'i Drive; and "Lyman's," which breaks near the southern end of the bay, just off Kamoa Point, and is named for the nearby home of the Lyman family, one of the early-day missionary families.

Just to the south of Holualoa Bay, another three-quarters of a
10 mile on Ali'i Drive, is **White Sands Beach Park**, variously known as
Magic Sands and Disappearing Sands for the sand's disappearing
quality—seasonal erosion—during the winter months. The beach is
quite popular with bodysurfers as well as surfers, and is notable as
the site of the annual Magic Sands Bodysurfing Championship. The
beach park also has restrooms and showers, a volleyball court, and
a lifeguard.

Well worth investigating, too, a mile or so south of White
Sands Beach, on the *makai* (ocean) side of Ali'i Drive, overlooking
Kahalu'u Bay, are the ancient **Kuemanu Heiau**, which comprises a
50-foot-wide, 100-foot-long stone platform where Hawaiian chiefs
4 15 once prayed for good surf, and **St. Peter's Church**, a picturesque
little blue-and-white church, popularly known as "The Little Blue
Church by the Sea." The church was originally built in 1880.

Also at Kahalu'u Bay, you can visit **Kahalu'u Beach**, one of
Kona's most popular swimming and snorkeling beaches, which also
attracts some surfers and an increasing number of fishermen. The
beach itself is palm-fringed and features gray sand; it is bordered
by a coral reef and a protective, 3,900-foot-long breakwater known
as Pa Oka Menehune, or "menehune breakwater," believed to have
been built by the legendary *menehune*, Hawaii's mysterious little
people who accomplished several engineering feats in the islands,
working only at night. At any rate, beach facilities at Kahalu'u include a lifeguard, picnic tables, pavilions, showers and restrooms.

Keauhou to Holualoa | *Keauhou Beach Resort, He'eia Bay,*
Keauhou Bay, Holua Slide,
Daifukuji Buddhist Temple

At Kahalu'u Bay, too, situated at the southern end of the bay is the
Keauhou Beach Resort, which has on its grounds several ancient
house sites, *heiaus* and other points of historical interest. Here, just
to the south of the hotel, you can search out the site of the historic
Hapaiali'i Heiau, and immediately to the south of there the Ke'eku
Heiau, which once was a place of human sacrifice. Another *heiau*
site is that of Kapuanoni Heiau, located adjacent to the Keauhou
Beach Resort swimming pool; it was once a place of worship for
ordinary Hawaiians as well as a fishing temple. Nearby, on the
mauka (inland) side of the hotel swimming pool is the site of the
former Big Island governor John Adams Kuakini's summer home,
Halau O Kuakini; and adjacent to that is the old, 150-foot-long
and 75-foot-wide King's Pond, fed by a freshwater spring, and once
regarded as sacred, reserved for the recreation of the reigning *ali'i*
(Hawaiian nobility). Also on the grounds is the historic beach house
of King Kalakaua, a New England-style wood-frame house with a
small lanai, dating from the late 1800s.

Southward a little way from Kahalu'u Bay and Keauhou Beach Hotel lies **He'eia Bay**, a small, picturesque cove, lined with boulders and sheltered from the open ocean, offering good swimming and snorkeling possibilities; and adjoining to the south of there is historic **Keauhou Bay**, notable as the **birthplace of Kauikeaouli**— Kamehameha III—born to Kamehameha I and Queen Keopuolani. It is believed that Kauikeaouli was stillborn, and brought to life by a *kahuna* (Hawaiian priest) at a nearby rock that is located near the head of the bay, directly inland, and where there is now a bronze plaque commemorating this miraculous event. Keauhou Bay, like He'eia Bay, is also lined with boulders, but offers excellent swimming and snorkeling possibilities, and also volleyball courts, picnic tables, showers and restroom facilities.

Yet another place of note, just east of Keauhou Bay, on the *mauka* (inland) side of Ali'i Drive, at the Kona Country Club Golf Course, is the site of the historic **Holua Slide**, now a national historical landmark, where a *holua* (sled run) was built on Kaneaka Hill, commissioned by Kamehameha I, in the early 1800s. The run is believed to have been a mile long, beginning on Kaneaka Hill and ending at the shoreline below, at He'eia Bay. Typically, the early-day *ali'i* would race their sleds—12 to 16 feet long, with hardwood runners—down the smooth, stone ramps of the run, to the bay. The *holua*, however, is not easily visible now, largely covered by the golf course.

Just south of the Holua Slide National Historic Landmark and Keauhou Bay, Ali'i Drive finally ends. From here, you can either return to Kailua-Kona northward, or, for the purposes of our tour, cross over on Kamehameha III Road to Kuakini Highway (Highway 11), which continues southeastward to South Kona, and which also has along it a few places of visitor interest.

At any rate, on Kuakini Highway (11), some 2 miles south from the intersection of Kamehameha III Road—approximately 7 miles south of Kailua-Kona—near the junction of Highways 11 and 180, is a **scenic overlook** that offers sweeping, panoramic views of Keauhou Bay and the Kona Coast. From here, some 4 miles northward on Highway 180 lies the little village of Holualoa, situated on the slopes of the Hualalai mountain at an elevation of 1,400 feet, overlooking Kailua-Kona; and to the south, approximately 1¾ miles and 2¼ miles from the intersection of highways 11 and 180, are the towns of Honalo and Kainaliu, respectively. At Honalo, you can visit the **Daifukuji Buddhist Temple**, a large, ornate temple with two altars, located on the inland side of the highway; and at Kainaliu, there is a theater, the **Aloha Theatre**, housed in an early 1900s building, which schedules performances by a local theater group, the Kona Community Players.

KONA COAST | South Kona

South Kona

  3

See Map 3
on Page 23

South Kona adjoins to the south of North Kona and the Kailua-Kona area. It can be reached directly on Highway 11, approximately a half mile south from Kainaliu (or 9 miles south from Kailua-Kona). South Kona is less populated than North Kona and Kailua-Kona, but has a couple of important towns and a few places of supreme tourist interest.

Captain Cook

Captain Cook Monument, Manago Hotel, Mauna Loa Royal Kona Coffee Mill & Museum, Kealakekua Bay, Napo'opo'o Beach

Northernmost in South Kona, some 8 miles from Kailua-Kona, is Kealakekua, a bustling town with shops, eateries, one or two churches, and a locally-popular flea market located on Haleki'i Street, held on Tuesdays, Thursdays and Saturdays. There is also a museum of interest here, the **Kona Historical Society Museum**, housed in the old, 19th-century Greenwell Store on Highway 11, a half mile south of mile marker 112. Museum displays are of artifacts and memorabilia centered around the history of the Kona area, as well as historical photographs depicting ranch life in the Kona district. Kealakekua, by the way, is Hawaiian for "pathway of the god," named for a nearby cliff, down the face of which, according to local lore, a god slid down, leaving an imprint.

South from Kealakekua on Highway 11, another mile or so, lies the town of Captain Cook, situated on a steep slope of the Mauna Loa mountain, at an elevation of 1,200 feet, overlooking Kealakekua Bay. The town is of course named for Captain James Cook, the English navigator who first charted the Hawaiian islands. In Captain Cook you can visit the **Greenwell County Park**—a public park named for pioneer rancher and businessman H.N. Greenwell, who also built the historic Greenwell Store in Kealakekua in **4** 1875—and the old **Manago Hotel**, situated along the highway (11) through town. This last, the Manago Hotel, is housed in a rustic, wood-frame structure dating from 1929; it now offers good overnight accommodations, a worthwhile restaurant, and superb views of Kealakekua Bay.

South still, lies Kealakekua Bay, reached by way of Napo'opo'o Road, which dashes off the highway (11) just to the south of Captain Cook, more or less directly southward to the little town of Napo'opo'o, situated at the southern end of the bay. But before Kealakekua Bay, there are one or two points of interest well worth investigating. Just to the west of Highway 11, for instance, some 200 yards or so on Napo'opo'o Road, on the *makai* (ocean) side of the road, you can search out the trailhead for the Captain Cook Monument Trail, which leads, at the end of a strenuous, 2½-mile

= Point of Interest

TO KAILUA-KONA

11

KEALAKEKUA

CAPTAIN COOK

1

Keawakaheka Bay

Kealakekua Bay

2

3

4

NAPOOPOO

5

HONAUNAU

160

6

Honaunau Bay

KEOKEA

Alahaka Bay

7

KEALIA

Puuhonua O Honaunau National Historical Park

HOOKENA

Kauhako Bay

8

11

Kapilo Bay

Kau Loa Pt.

N

W E

S

KIPAHOEHOE NATURAL AREA RESERVE

Kipahoehoe Bay

Papa Bay

Milolii Bay

MILOLII

9

Okoe Bay

10   **11**

Kapua Bay

Hawaii Belt Rd.

Mamalahoa Hwy.

TO NAALEHU

11

Miles

0   5

SOUTH KONA

1. Captain Cook Monument
2. Kealakekua Bay Marine Life Conservation District
3. Napoopoo Beach Park
4. Manago Hotel
5. Royal Kona Coffee Mill and Museum
6. St. Benedict's "Painted" Church
7. Lookout
8. Hookena Beach Park
9. Milolii Beach Park
10. Hauoli Kamana o Church
11. Macadamia Nut Orchard

1 hike with a 1,400-foot drop, to the shoreline and the **Captain Cook Monument**—a 27-foot white pillar, erected in 1874 at the site of the English explorer's death in 1779. As an added bonus, the coastal strip here offers excellent swimming and snorkeling.

5 Another place of interest along Napo'opo'o Road, three and a quarter miles west of the Highway 11 intersection, is the **Mauna Loa Royal Kona Coffee Mill & Museum**. Here, at the small museum-cum-gift shop, you can sample the famous, locally-grown Kona coffee and view artifacts, including old roasting equipment, as well as old photographs from the early 1900s and a brief film centered around coffee picking and coffee production.

▶ Finally, some four miles southwestward from the Highway 11 intersection on Napo'opo'o Road and we are at **Kealakekua Bay**, a sweeping, mile-wide bay, encompassing some 315 acres. The bay is **2** now largely preserved as the **Kealakekua Bay Marine Life Conservation District**, originally established in 1969 and quite popular with scuba divers and snorkelers for its abundant marine life. Typically, you can see a wide array of tropical fish in the waters here, as well as Spinner Dolphins. Kealakekua Bay is also the site of Captain James Cook's landing on the island on January 17, 1779, when he was at once revered, albeit mistakenly, as the reincarnation of the Hawaiian god, Lono. A month later, on February 14, 1779, when he returned to the bay to make some necessary repairs to his ship, he was clubbed to death in knee-deep water by the newly-wary Hawaiians who feared he was not, after all, Lono.

3 At Kealakekua Bay, you can also visit **Napo'opo'o Beach**, situated at the head of the bay. The beach has mainly pebbles and large boulders, but it offers good swimming and snorkeling possibilities.

▶ Directly above the bay sits the historic **Hikiau Heiau**, an engineering feat of no small measure, some 200 feet long and 100 feet wide. The *heiau* is significant in that it was here that Captain Cook, upon his first landing at Kealakekua Bay in 1779, during the Makahiki Festival, was brought for traditional ceremonies and heralded as the god Lono. In any case, from Napo'opo'o Beach, you can also see the Captain Cook Monument, the 27-foot obelisk, toward the north of the bay.

▶ Also of interest, just to the south of Kealakekua Bay is **Moku'oahi Bay**, at the northern end of which, near Palemano Point, you can search out the site of the historic Moku'oahi Battle, fought between Kamehameha I and rival island chief Kiwala'o in 1782. In the battle, which was a classic power struggle for control of a large part of the island, Kiwala'o's forces were defeated and Kiwala'o killed. It was Kamehameha's first victory, culminating, eventually, in his domination of all the Hawaiian islands. Incidentally, the only access to this area is by way of Ke'ei, located at the south end of Kealakekua Bay, southward along the shoreline.

South to Pu'uhonua O Honaunau

Approximately 7 miles south of Captain Cook on Highway 11 is Honaunau, a village, no more, with a post office and a small market. Of interest here, close to Honaunau, is the historic **St. Benedict's Painted Church**, one of the oldest Catholic churches on the island, situated on Highway 160—which goes westward off Highway 11 at Keokea—just south of mile marker 104. The church was originally built in 1902 by Belgian priest John Berchman Velghe, who arrived in Hawaii in 1899, and who painted much of the interior with biblical scenes such as "The Handwriting on the Wall," "Temptation of Jesus," "Cain & Abel," and "Hell." There is also a cemetery at the front of the church, which has commanding views of the coastline, from the Pu'uhonua O Honaunau National Historic Park just to the southwest, to Kealakekua Bay farther north.

Journeying westward, a little way from St. Benedict's Painted Church on Highway 160, three quarters of a mile west of mile marker 2, is a **scenic overlook** with superb, sweeping views of the Kona Coast and, directly below, of Pu'uhonua O Honaunau.

And so to **Pu'uhonua O Honaunau National Historic Park**—or "City of Refuge"—a place of supreme tourist interest, situated along the coast between Honaunau and Alahaka bays, at the end of Highway 160, roughly three and one-half miles west of Highway 11 and Honaunau. Pu'uhonua O Honaunau is one of the best-preserved relics of ancient Hawaii, when the *kapu* system, a strict social order that affected all aspects of life in Hawaii, was prevalent and at the core of Hawaiian culture. Typically, *kapu* breakers were punished by death, unless they swiftly sought sanctuary in a *pu'uhonua* (place of refuge), where, with the help of a *kahuna* (priest), they could redeem themselves and be rehabilitated. Pu'uhonua O Honaunau, thus, was once such a place.

In any event, **Pu'uhonua O Honaunau National Historic Park**, which was originally established in 1920 and designated a national historic site in 1961, encompasses some 180 acres, and has in it three ancient *heiaus*, several *tikis* (carved, wooden idols), petroglyphs, thatched Hawaiian huts, and, most impressive of all, the Great Wall—a massive lava-rock wall, 1,000 feet long, 17 feet wide and 10 feet high, built without the use of mortar, and dating from the mid-1500s. The wall encloses a coastal, peninsular tract, the *pu'uhonua* compound, where two of the *heiaus* are located: an old, unnamed *heiau* and the **Ale'ale'a Heiau**, the latter with a large, stone platform, approximately 150 feet long, 75 feet wide and 10 feet high. On the *mauka* (inland) side of the Great Wall are the old palace grounds, and at its north end, the Hale O Keawe Heiau, built around 1650, and which contains the remains of more than 20 Hawaiian chiefs, including one Keawe-i-keka-hi-ali'i-o-ka-moku, spiritually the most powerful of them all, for whom the *heiau* is named. The Hale O Keawe Heiau is surrounded by a wooden fence and features a thatched structure, which is in fact a mausoleum containing the remains of the chiefs, with several *tikis* (idols) at the front of it to protect the sacred site. Swimming, sunbathing and picnicking at the park are not encouraged due to the sanctity of the site. However, there is a picnic area a quarter mile or so south of the park, bordered by palm trees, and with restroom facilities.

Ho'okena, Kipahoehoe, Miloli'i

Ho'okena Beach, Miloli'i Beach Park, Hau'oli Church

From Pu'uhonua O Honaunau National Historic Park, we suggest you return to Highway 11 by way of Highway 160, roughly 4 miles. At the intersection of Highways 11 and 160 lies the little community of Keokea, and south of there, another 2½ miles or so, from a point approximately midway between mile markers 102 and 101, a steep, narrow road dashes off Highway 11 toward the ocean, some 2½ miles to Ho'okena. **Ho'okena** is a small, fishing village, which in the late 1800s was a busy little port where steamers and cargo ships called regularly. In 1889, during his travels in the South Pacific in the final years of his life, noted author Robert Louis Stevenson spent an entire week here, in his quest for the perfect climate. At any rate, the only place of interest at Ho'okena is the **Ho'okena Beach Park**, situated at the head of Kauhako Bay. The beach features gray sand and pebbles, and offers good swimming and snorkeling possibilities, with a protective coral reef just offshore. Beach facilities include showers and restrooms.

South from Ho'okena, some 13 miles or so on Highway 11, lies **Kipahoehoe Natural Area Reserve**, a 5,583-acre preserve that extends from approximately 5 miles east of Highway 11 to the coast, its shape resembling the ancient land divisions of Hawaii, known as *ahupua'a*—which also extended from the uplands to the coast. Kipahoehoe, which in Hawaiian means "much smooth lava," incorporates the 1919 lava flow from Mauna Loa, parts of which, particularly along the coast, were smoothed out by villagers, by filling in the cracks, crevices, holes and depressions with stones, to provide a smooth landing for their canoes.

South still, some 7 miles from Kipahoehoe Natural Area Reserve (30 miles south of Kailua-Kona) lies **Miloli'i**, an old Hawaiian fishing village. Miloli'i is reached by way of a small, narrow, one-lane road that goes west off Highway 11 at mile marker 89, roughly 4½ miles, passing by a macadamia nut orchard, and over the most recent (1926) lava flow from Mauna Loa. Miloli'i means "fine twist," a name derived from the community's old, established trade of weaving fine ropes and fishing nets from fiber from locally grown plants. It must also be noted that at Miloli'i the ancient practice of fishing for *opelu* (mackerel) by first feeding and fattening the fish, before catching them, is still prevalent.

In any case, there is a beach at Miloli'i, the **Miloli'i Beach Park**, made up mostly of lava outcroppings with small, natural pools, some with sandy bottoms, and sheltered coves that offer safe swimming conditions. The beach is bordered by ironwood trees, and has picnic tables, play equipment for children, and restroom facilities. There is also a church of interest here, **Hau'oli Kamana'o Church**, located directly inland from the beach park and housed in an old, wood frame building that dates from the turn-of-the-century.

Finally, 3 miles or so south of the Miloli'i turnoff on Highway 11 are the sprawling **MacFarms of Hawaii**, a 3,800-acre macadamia nut orchard, formerly co-owned by the late actor Jimmy Stewart and actress Julie Andrews. The orchard, however, is not open to public tours.

 (KONA COAST | North Kona)

North Kona

  See Map 4 on Page 29

North Kona, as the name suggests, takes in the northern portion of the Kona district, including the resort town of Kailua-Kona and, north of there, Honokohau, Ka'upulehu and Kiholo Bay. North Kona, not unlike South Kona, is mostly dry, sunny, and blessed with good beaches and picturesque bays, offering excellent fishing and snorkeling possibilities.

Honokohau Bay

Kaloko-Honokohau National Historical Park, Kamehameha Burial Site, Kaloko Fishpond. 'Aimakapa Fishpond, 'Alula Beach

The first place of interest in North Kona, journeying up the coast from Kailua-Kona, is the **Kaloko-Honokohau National Historical Park**, situated along Honokohau Bay, some 3 miles or so from Kailua-Kona, and reached by way of an unmarked dirt road that dashes off the highway (19) westward, a half-mile north of mile marker 97, directly to the park entrance. The park was first established in 1978, and comprises approximately 1,200 acres, including the long, sandy **Honokohau Beach** which curves around Honokohau Bay, sloping steeply down to the ocean. The beach is bordered by coral and tide pools, and backed by *kiawe* trees. It has some swimming possibilities, but is primarily frequented by nudists, surfers and fishermen. The beach can also be reached by way of an access road that goes west off the highway (19), roughly a half-mile north of mile marker 98—2½ miles north of Kailua-Kona—to intersect with another small road that heads northward a little way to the head of a trail, which, in turn, leads more or less directly to the beach.

▶   At the park, too, is **Honokohau Harbor**, originally built in March, 1970, to alleviate the excessive usage of nearby Kailua Pier, located at Kailua-Kona. The harbor has a small, sandy cove just to the south of it, known as **'Alula Beach**, and the 'Alula Bay Complex where several archaeological sites have recently been unearthed. There are no facilities at 'Alula Beach.

The Kaloko-Honokohau National Historical Park also has two well-visited fishponds, an early-day fish trap, and more than 200 historical sites, including shelters, *heiaus*, ancient Hawaiian platforms, petroglyphs, and burial sites. The two fishponds are the **Kaloko Fishpond**, located just to the north of the park's parking lot, covering roughly 11 acres and featuring a 750-foot-long seawall; and the **'Aimakapa Fishpond**, which encompasses nearly 20 acres and has the distinction of being the largest fishpond in the area, located directly *mauka* (inland) from the Honokohau Beach, a mile or so south of Kaloko Fishpond. The fish trap, the **Ai'opio Fish Trap**, which comprises roughly 1.7 acres and has no sluice gate, thereby making it a fish trap rather than a fishpond, is located at the north end of Honokohau Harbor, just south of the Kaloko and 'Aimakapa fishponds. Interestingly, this is also believed to be the **burial site of King Kamehameha I**, who died on May 8, 1918, at Kamakahonu in nearby Kailua-Kona, and whose bones are thought to be hidden in a secret cave near the Kaloko Fishpond.

▶   Also of interest at the Kaloko-Honokohau park is a section of the old **Mamalahoa Trail**, or "King's Highway," built between 1822 and 1855, and which runs parallel to the coastline, between the Kaloko Fishpond and Honokohau Harbor. The trail heads south from Kaloko Fishpond, passing through stretches of lava flow and a thicket of brush and trees, to lead to, besides 'Aimakapa Fishpond (1 mile), the ancient "Queen's Bath"—a small, spring-fed natural pool, some 20 feet in diameter, where Queen Ka'ahumanu, Kamehameha I's favorite wife, once bathed. The "Queen's Bath" is located approximately a quarter mile southeast of Kaloko Fishpond.

North from Keahole Point | Wailoli Beach, Pine Trees Beach, Onizuka Space Center, 'Opae'ula Pond, Kona Coast State Park

North from Kaloko-Honokohau National Historical Park, approximately 3 miles, is Keahole Point, reached by way of an access road that goes off the highway (19) seaward, a quarter mile south of mile marker 42 (5¾ miles north of Kailua-Kona). There are two well-liked beaches here, Wawaloli and Pine Trees, and also a facility for

▶   the **Natural Energy Laboratory of Hawaii** that was established in 1974 to study ocean thermal energy conversion—a project simply known as "OTEC"—whereby the difference in temperature between

= Point of Interest

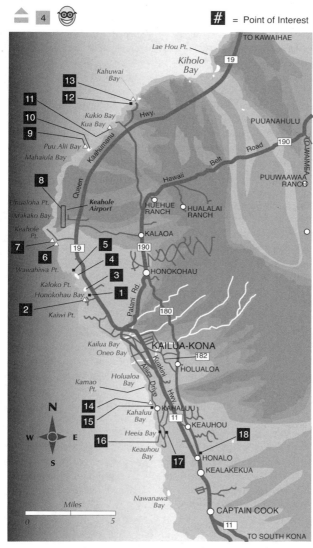

KONA COAST | North Kona

NORTH KONA

1. Kaloko-Honokohau Historical Park
2. Alula Beach
3. Aimakapa Fishpond
4. Kaloko Fishpond
5. King Kamehameha I Burial Site
6. Wawaloli (OTEC) Beach
7. Pine Trees Beach
8. Ellison S. Onizuka Space Center
9. Makalawena Beach
10. Opaeula Pond
11. Maniniowali Beach
12. Kona Village Resort
13. Kaupulehu Beach
14. White Sands Beach
15. St. Peter's Church
16. Birthplace of King Kamehameha III
17. Holua Slide
18. Daifukuji Buddhist Temple

the warm surface water and the cold water in the depths of the ocean may be used to generate electricity. In any case, **Wawaloli Beach Park**—also known as OTEC Beach due to its proximity to the natural energy facility—has no sandy beach, only a rocky shoreline, but is quite popular with picnickers and fishermen; while **Pine Trees Beach**—named for its grove of mangrove trees that are frequently mistaken for pine trees—is situated roughly a mile from OTEC Beach, and has a sandy beach. Pine Trees Beach is also one of the most popular surfing spots in the area. Both Pine Trees Beach and OTEC Beach are open to the public, although swimming is not recommended at either of them due to adverse ocean conditions.

Another mile north of Wawaloli (OTEC) Beach Park on Queen Ka'ahumanu Highway (19), and we are at Keahole Airport, the principal airport on the Kona Coast. The airport also has something to interest the visitor: the **Astronaut Ellison S. Onizuka Space Center**, where several space exhibits are on display, including a moon rock, as well as a variety of educational films and participatory and audio-visual exhibits centered around NASA'S manned space flight program. The space center is named for, and dedicated to, Hawaii's first astronaut, Ellison S. Onizuka, who was born in Kona and who died in the 1986 Challenger space shuttle tragedy, together with six other crew members.

North still, another half mile or so, just past mile marker 92, on the *mauka* (inland) side of the highway (19), is a lava tube, some 50 feet in diameter; and north of there, approximately midway between mile markers 91 and 90, a dirt road dashes off the highway through a *pahoehoe* (smooth lava) field, roughly one and one-half miles, to the coastal **Kona Coast State Park**, situated above Mahai'ula Bay. There is a lovely, white-sand crescent-shaped beach here, curving around the bay to the north, bordered by palms and *kiawe*. The beach has good swimming and snorkeling possibilities, and also a popular surfbreak just off Kawili Point, at the north end of the bay. Interestingly, there are also several old stone platforms and rock walls here, remnants of a small, early-day fishing village.

Two miles farther north on Queen Ka'ahumanu Highway (19), at a midway point between mile markers 89 and 88, an access road heads off southwestward one and one-half miles to the shoreline and **Makalawena Beach**. Makalawena is a long, curving, sandy beach, backed by shallow sand dunes and ironwood trees, with a series of coves and inlets separated by lava outcroppings. Approximately halfway down the beach, and just inland from there, is the 12-acre **'Opae'ula Pond**, one of the island's most important waterbird sanctuaries, where you can observe stilts, coots, ducks, and other such birds. The beach has excellent swimming, snorkeling and surfing possibilities, as well as good fishing; and just over the sand dunes, situated in the lava flow, there is a small, freshwater pool that is ideal for a refreshing dip. There is also a section of an ancient trail to be found here, the Ala Kahakai—or "Trail by the Sea"—just to the south of the beach. The trail leads south from here to the Kona Coast State Park; it once journeyed across the island, from the southeast part of the Hawaii Volcanoes National Park to Upolu Point in the north, covering a distance of nearly 200 miles.

Another beach, **Manini'owali Beach**, lies just to the north of Makalawena Beach, reached on a dirt road that branches off the highway (19), just past mile marker 88, and leads to a well-worn trail that, in turn, journeys a quarter mile or so to the beach. Manini'owali Beach—also known as Kua Bay—is situated on the north side of Pu'u Kuili, a 342-foot cinder cone, to the south of which is Makalawena Beach. Manini'owali Beach is a white-sand crescent-shaped beach, lying largely between two lava outcroppings, and bordered by *a'a* (rough lava) fields and ancient rock walls. The beach offers good, safe swimming and body surfing during calm weather, in clear, turquoise waters. The beach, however, has no facilities or shade trees.

11

Kona Village Resort and Kiholo Bay

A little way from Manini'owali Beach, with an entrance just south of mile marker 87 on Queen Ka'ahumanu Highway (19)—which is to say, 13 miles north of Kailua-Kona—lies the **Kona Village Resort**, one of the loveliest of Hawaii's all-Hawaiian luxury resorts. The resort is nestled on an 82-acre beachfront estate, at the site of an ancient fishing village, Ka'upulehu. It was originally developed in 1965, and boasts 125 authentic, thatched-roof *hales* (huts or, in this case, bungalows), representing a variety of Polynesian architectural designs, including Hawaiian, Tahitian, Fijian, Marquesan, Samoan and others from the South Pacific, and clear lagoons. There is also a swimming pool at the resort, a glass-bottomed catamaran for guests' use, three tennis courts, and a superb restaurant, Hale Samoa.

The Kona Village Resort fronts on **Ka'upulehu Beach**, a black lava beach, at the site of the ancient fishing village of Ka'upulehu. Ka'upulehu, in Hawaiian, means "roasting breadfruit," a name supposedly derived from an old tale in which the Hawaiian goddess of fire, Pele, met two young girls here, who were roasting breadfruit. When she asked the girls to share some of the breadfruit with her, only one of them offered to do so. And so, the following day, in her fury, Pele sent rivers of lava flowing through the village, destroying it almost entirely, save for the home of the girl who had shared her breadfruit with her. In any case, in 1946, a *tsunami* (tidal wave) destroyed what was left of the village. Nevertheless, there are still several ancient home sites and **petroglyphs** here—approximately 85 units—that are well worth touring.

From the Kona Village Resort, it is another 6 miles to Kiholo Bay, passing by a scenic overlook located a mile or so to the south of the bay, near mile marker 82, on the *makai* (ocean) side of the highway (19), which offers sweeping view of the bay. **Kiholo Bay** itself is reached by way of a three-quarter-mile trail that goes off the highway (19), approximately 250 yards south of mile marker 81. At the north end of the bay is a small peninsular tract, formed by the 1859 lava flow from Mauna Loa, which has two black-sand beaches and offers excellent swimming and snorkeling possibilities; and at the south end of the bay, you can search out the spring-fed, freshwater Luahinewai Pond, a delightful natural pool, ideal for a refreshing swim when journeying along the North Kona coast. There are, however, no facilities at Kiholo Bay.

Accommodations | Kailua-Kona, South Kona

Hotels and Condominiums

Four Seasons Resort Hualalai. *$625-$1,050.* 100 Ka'upulehu Dr., Kailua-Kona; (808) 325-8000/(888) 340-5662/(800) 819-5053/ *www.fourseasons.com/hualalai.* Luxury resort with 230 rooms and suites in 36 low-rise bungalows. TV, phones, air-conditioning; swimming pool, health club and spa, restaurant, tennis courts and golf course.

Keauhou Resort Condominiums. *$95-$125.* 78-7039 Kamehameha III Rd., Kailua-Kona; (808) 322-9122/(800) 367-5286/*www. sunquest-hawaii.com.* 28 one- and two-bedroom condominium units, with TV, phones, and ceiling fans, and kitchens with microwave ovens and dishwashers. Swimming pool. Maid service available upon request. Handicapped facilities. Minimum stay, 5 days.

King Kamehameha's Kona Beach Hotel. *$200-$250.* 75-5660 Palani Rd., Kailua-Kona; (808) 329-2911/(800) 367-6060/*www.konabeachhotel.com.* 455-unit hotel, situated on the beach overlooking Kailua Bay. TV, phones, air-conditioning. Swimming pool, tennis court, shops and beauty salon, restaurants, cocktail lounge. Daily maid service. Handicapped facilities.

Kona Bali Kai. *$105-$290.* 76-6246 Ali'i Dr., Kailua-Kona; (808) 329-9381/329-3333/(800) 244-4752/367-5004/*www.konahawaii. com* or *www.castleresorts.com/KBK.* 75 condominium units in oceanfront setting, with TV, phones and kitchens. Swimming pool, health club, spa. Daily maid service. Handicapped facilities. Minimum stay 3 days.

Kona Islander Inn. *$70-$100.* 75-5776 Kuakini Hwy., Kailua-Kona; (808) 329-3333/(800) 244-4752/622-5348/*www.konahawaii. com.* 58 units with TV, phones, refrigerators, and air-conditioning.

Shops. Daily maid service. Handicapped facilities.

Kona Magic Sands. *$105-$135.* 77-6452 Ali'i Dr., Kailua-Kona; (808) 329-3333/(800) 244-4752/622-5348/*www.konahawaii.com.* 37 units with TV, phones, refrigerators and kitchenettes. Swimming pool, restaurant and bar.

Kona Reef. *$220-$305.* 75-5888 Ali'i Dr., Kailua-Kona; (808) 329-2959/(800) 367-5004/*www.castleresorts.com/KRH.* Ocean-front condominium complex, with 1- and 2-bedroom suites. TV, phones, air-conditioning, kitchens. Also swimming pool and spa.

Kona Seaside Hotel. *$115-155.* 75-5646 Palani Rd., Kailua-Kona; (808) 329-2455/(800) 560-5558/*www.sand-seaside.com.* 225 units with TV, phones, air-conditioning, refrigerators. Swimming pool, restaurant.

Kona Village Resort. *$580-$1,050.* Queen Ka'ahumanu Hwy., Kaupulehu-Kona; (808) 325-5555/(800) 367-5290/*www.konavillage.com.* Full-service, luxury beachfront resort, with 128 Polynesian-style cottages, nestled on a 82-acre estate. Features tropical gardens, swimming pool, tennis courts, restaurants, cocktail lounge, and shops. Handicapped facilities.

Manago Hotel. *$33-$73.* 82-6155 Mamalahoa Hwy., Captain Cook; (808) 323-2642//*www.managohotel.com.* 64-room hotel, overlooking the South Kona coastline; housed in rustic, wood frame building, dating from 1929. Restaurant and cocktail lounge on premises; also beauty salon. Daily maid service. Handicapped facilities.

Outrigger Kanaloa at Kona. *$210-$390.* 78-261 Manukai St., Kailua-Kona; (808) 322-9625/(800) 688-7444/*www.outrigger.com.* Oceanfront condominium complex, with 118 1-, 2- and 3-bedroom units; TV, phones, kitchens. Swimming pool, tennis court. Restaurant and cocktail lounge on premises. Daily maid service. Handicapped facilities.

Outrigger Keauhou Beach Resort. *$140-$270.* 78-6740 Ali'i Dr., Kailua-Kona; (808) 322-3441/(800) 688-7444/*www.outrigger.com.* 310-room oceanfront hotel. TV, phones, air-conditioning. Swimming pool, health club, tennis courts; also shops, beauty salon, restaurants and cocktail lounge. Daily maid service. Handicapped facilities.

Outrigger Royal Sea Cliff. *$160-$355.* 75-6040 Ali'i Dr., Kailua-Kona; (808) 329-8021/(800) 688-7444/922-7866/*www.outrigger.com.* 148-unit oceanfront condominium complex with studios and I- and 2-bedroom units. TV, phones, air-conditioning; some kitchen units available. Swimming pool, spa, sauna, tennis courts, and shops. Daily maid service. Handicapped facilities.

ResortQuest Kona by the Sea. *$220-$445.* 75-6106 Ali'i Dr., Kailua-Kona; (808) 327-2300/(800) 321-2558/(877-997-6667/*www.resortquesthawaii.com.* Oceanfront condominium complex, with 78 units, including studios and one- and two-bedroom units. TV, phones, air-conditioning, kitchens. Swimming pool. Daily maid service. Handicapped facilities.

Royal Kona Resort. *$170-$570.* 75-5852 Ali'i Dr., Kailua-Kona; (808) 329-3111/(800) 919-8333/774-5662/*www.hawaiihotels.com.* 440-room oceanfront hotel. TV, phones, refrigerators. Swimming pool, tennis courts, beauty salon and shops; also restaurant and cocktail lounge on premises. Daily maid service. Handicapped facilities.

Sheraton Keauhou Bay Resort. *$190-$490.* 78-128 Ekuhai St., Keauhou; (808) 930-4900/(888) 488-3535/*www.sheratonkeauhou. com.* 530-room, full-service resort hotel. TV, phones, air-condition-ing. Swimming pool, spa, tennis courts, golf course and country club. Also shops, beauty salon, restaurants and cocktail lounge. Handicapped facilities.

Uncle Billy's Kona Bay Hotel. *$94-$99.* 75-5739 Ali'i Dr., Kailua-Kona; (808) 961-5818/(800) 367-5102/*www.unclebilly. com.* 145-room hotel, located in downtown Kailua. TV, phones, air-conditioning. Swimming pool, and shops. Restaurant and cocktail lounge on premises. Daily maid service. Handicapped facilities.

Bed and Breakfast

Aloha Guest House. *$140-$250.* Off Mamalahoa Hwy., Captain Cook, HI 96726; (808) 328-8955/(800) 897-3188/*www.alohaguest-house.com.* Situated on the slopes of Mauna Loa, overlooking the ocean and the Kona Coast. 5 rooms with private baths. TV, VCR, phones, refrigerators, coffee makers, internet access. Also hot tub and spa. Continental breakfast. Daily maid service.

Areca Palms Estate Bed & Breakfast. *$115-$145.* P.O. Box 489, Captain Cook, HI 96704; (808) 323-2276/(800) 545-4390/*www. konabedandbreakfast.com.* Two-story cedar home in tropical gar-den setting: ocean and garden views. 4 guest rooms. Full breakfast. Beach and snorkeling equipment available for guests' use. Spa.

Cedar House Bed and Breakfast. *$110-$135.* P.O. Box 823, Captain Cook, HI 96704; (808) 328-8829/(866) 328-8829/*www. cedarhouse-hawaii.com.* Situated on a coffee farm, amid mature tropical fruit trees. Offers 3 guest rooms, a suite and a cottage, all with ocean and coffee farm views. TV, VCR, snorkeling equipment. Also kitchen facilities. Buffet breakfast.

Dragonfly Ranch. *$100-$160.* P.O. Box 675, Honaunau, HI 96726; (808) 328-2159/(800) 487-2159/*www.dragonflyranch.com.* Ranch home in garden setting, with views of the Kona Coast. Offers 5 guest rooms with private entrances and oceanview lanais; TV and VCR, and kitchenettes. Daily maid service.

Hale Ho'ola. *$110-$150.* 85-4577 Mamalahoa Hwy., Captain Cook, HI 96704; (808) 328-9117/(877) 628-9117/*www.hale-hoola.*

com. Two-story plantation-style home with 3 guest rooms with private baths, TV, VCR, phones and refrigerators. Views of ocean and tropical gardens. Full breakfast buffet with freshly-ground Kona coffee and locally-grown tropical fruit.

Holualoa Inn. *$245-$375.* P.O. Box 222, Holualoa, HI 96725; (808) 324-1121/(800) 392-1812/*www.holualoainn.com.* Luxury bed and breakfast inn, situated in a coffee farming area, overlooking the ocean. Offers 7 individually-decorated rooms and suites with private baths, Gazebos, sitting rooms, living rooms, lanai, dining room, and pool on premises. Tropical setting.

Lion's Gate Bed and Breakfast. *$110-$180.* P.O. Box 761, Honaunau, HI 96726; (808) 328-2335/(800) 955-2332/*www.konabnb.com.* Two-story home on working macadamia nut and coffee farm. Offers 4 rooms and suites with private baths and lanais, and TV, DVD player, and internet access. Sitting room, and kitchen facilities. Outdoor jacuzzi. Tropical breakfast with baked goods, island fruit, macadamia nuts and Kona coffee.

Nancy's Hideaway. *$115-$135.* Kailua-Kona, HI; (808) 325-3132/(866) 325-3132/*www.nancyshideaway.com.* Private cottage and studio on 3 acres, overlooking the Kona coast. Private baths and lanais; kitchen facilities. Breakfast consists of breads, pastries, muffins, tropical fruit and juices, and Kona coffee.

Dining | Kailua-Kona, South Kona

[Restaurant prices—based on full course diner, excluding drinks, tax and tips—are categorized as follows: *Deluxe,* over $30; *Expensive,* $20-$30; *Moderate,* $10-$20; *Inexpensive,* under $10.]

Aloha Angel Café. *Inexpensive-Moderate.* Mamalahoa Hwy. (11), Kainaliu; (808) 322-3383/*www.alohatheatre.com.* Housed in the Aloha Theatre Building, dating from 1932, Open-air, garden setting. Serves primarily omelettes, salads, sandwiches, bagels, burgers and burritos for breakfast and lunch, and fresh island seafood, steak, chicken and pasta for dinner. Espresso bar. Open for breakfast and lunch daily, and dinner on weekends. Reservations suggested.

Bubba Gump Shrimp Company. Moderate. 75-5776 Ali'i Dr., Kailua-Kona; (808) 331-8442/(800) 913-2455/*www.bubbagump.com.* Waterfront setting. Menu features seafood, steak, prime rib and chicken. Good selection of smoothies. Open for lunch and dinner daily.

Don Drysdale's Club 53. *Moderate.* At the Keauhou Village Shopping Center, Keauhou, (808) 322-0070. Open-air eatery with bar, decorated with sports memorabilia and offering sports television coverage. Serves standard American fare: soups, sandwiches, fish and chips, burgers. Also cocktails. Open daily, 11am-11.30pm.

KONA COAST | Accommodations/Dining

Hale Moana Dining Room. *Deluxe.* At the Kona Village Resort, Queen Ka'ahumanu Hwy., Kailua-Kona; (808) 325-5555/(800) 367-5290/*www.konavillage.com*. Elegant setting, overlooking Kahuwai Bay. Features Pacific Rim cuisine. Specialties include Grilled Hawaiian Seafood, Loin of Lamb in Puff Pastry, Abalone and Shrimp Sauté, and Veal Medallion with Crab. Cocktails. Live entertainment. Open for dinner. Reservations required.

Hualalai Grille by Alan Wong. *Moderate-Expensive.* At the Four Seasons Resort Hualalai, 100 Kaupulehu Dr., Kailua-Kona; (808) 325-8000/(888) 340-5662/*www.fourseasons.com/hualalai*. Offers Hawaiian regional cuisine, blending Asian and European flavors, with emphasis on fresh local ingredients. Menu features creative seafood specialties, kalua pig, soups and sandwiches. Good selection of desserts, including chocolate mousse, and a special coffee menu. Open for lunch and dinner daily. Reservations recommended.

Huggo's. *Moderate-Expensive.* 75-5828 Kahakai Rd., Kailua-Kona; (808) 329-1493/*www.huggos.com*. Oceanfront setting, overlooking Kailua Bay. Continental cuisine. Menu features fresh seafood, Maine lobster, stuffed fish, spicy Korean shrimp, prime rib, grilled sweet chili chicken, and New York steak. Live entertainment. Open for lunch Mon.-Fri., dinner daily. Reservations suggested.

Jameson's By The Sea. *Moderate.* 77-6452 Ali'i Dr., Kailua-Kona; (808) 329-3195. Oceanfront restaurant in delightful setting, serving fresh fish, baked and stuffed shrimp, shrimp curry, lobster tail, New York steak, and filet mignon. Open for lunch Mon.-Fri., and dinner daily. Reservations recommended.

Kama'aina Terrace. *Moderate.* At the Outrigger Keauhou Beach Hotel, 78-6740 Ali'i Dr., Kailua-Kona; (808) 322-3441/(877) 532-8468/*www.ohanahotels.com*. Open-air setting; plantation atmosphere. Hawaiian regional cuisine, featuring fresh island seafood, including seafood curry, and lemongrass encrusted opakapaka, crab legs, steak, rack of lamb and chicken. Also seafood and prime rib buffets Fridays and lobster nights on Saturdays. Open for breakfast and dinner daily. Reservations suggested.

Kimo's Family Buffet. *Inexpensive-Moderate.* At Uncle Billy's Kona Bay Hotel, 75-5739 Ali'i Dr., Kailua-Kona; (808) 329-1393/(800) 367-5102/*www.unclebilly.com*. Open-air setting, with Polynesian decor. All-you-can-eat, buffet-style dinners, with meat loaf, barbecue chicken, mahi mahi and other fresh island fish, Cantonese pork, western-style ribs, chicken teriyaki, and salad bar. Open for dinner daily (except Sunday), 5.30pm-8.00pm.

Kona Beach Restaurant. *Moderate.* At King Kamehameha's Kona Beach Hotel, 75-5660 Ali'i Dr., Kailua-Kona; (808) 329-2911/(800) 367-6060/*www.konabeachhotel.com*. Large dining room, overlooking Kamakahonu Beach and Ahuena Heiau. Serves fresh seafood, prime rib, rack of lamb, barbecued baby back ribs, crispy oriental chicken, broiled Maine lobster, and pasta. Also cocktails, and entertainment. Open for breakfast, lunch and dinner daily. Reservations recommended.

Kona Inn Restaurant. *Moderate-Expensive.* Kona Inn Marketplace, 75-5744 Ali'i Dr., Kailua-Kona; (808) 329-4455. Housed in the historic Kona Inn, offering superb ocean views and spectacular sunsets. Menu features fresh island fish, lobster, and prime rib; also salads and pasta and stir-fry dishes. Cocktails. Open for lunch and dinner. Reservations suggested.

La Bourgogne. *Expensive.* At the Kuakini Plaza South, 77-6400 Nalani St., Kailua-Kona: (808) 329-6711. French restaurant; intimate setting. Menu features traditional French cuisine, including roast duck, rack of lamb and filet mignon. Also cocktails. Desserts include tarts and chocolate cake. Open for dinner, Tues.-Sat. Reservations recommended.

Manago Hotel Restaurant. *Inexpensive.* At the Manago Hotel, 82-6155 Mamalahoa Hwy., Captain Cook; (808) 323-2642/*www.managohotel.com*. Cozy, rustic restaurant, housed in historic hotel built in 1929. Offers standard local fare; house specialties include T-bone steak, fresh fish, teriyaki chicken, pork chops and hamburgers. Also cocktails. Open for breakfast, lunch and dinner. Reservations suggested.

Ocean View Inn. *Inexpensive.* 75-5683 Ali'i Dr., Kailua-Kona: (808) 329-9998. Overlooking Kailua Bay. Serves primarily American, Chinese and Hawaiian fare. House specialties are steak, laulau and poi, and kalua pig; also good selection of sandwiches, and chicken and vegetarian entrées. Soda fountain. Open for breakfast, lunch and dinner, Tues.-Sat.

Outback Steakhouse. *Moderate-Expensive.* At the Coconut Grove Marketplace, 75-5809 Ali'i Dr., Kailua-Kona; (808) 326-2555/*www.outback.com*. Casual setting with Australian outback theme. House specialties include fresh island fish, rack of lamb, steak, prime rib, and pasta dishes. Also good selection of appetizers and salads.Open 4.30pm-10.00pm daily. Reservations suggested.

Pahui'a. *Expensive-Deluxe.* At the Four Seasons Resort Hualalai, 100 Kaupulehu Dr., Kailua-Kona; (808) 325-8000/(800) 819-5053/*www.fourseasons.com/hualalai*. Elegant restaurant, overlooking the ocean. Menu features creative Hawaiian and European entrées, including prime ahi steak, macadamia nut crusted mahi mahi, guava glazed scallops, peppercorn steak, rack of lamb, potato gnocchi and risotto. Also good selection of desserts, including coconut tapioca, Grand Marnier cake, tarts and soufflé. Open for breakfast and dinner daily. Reservations required for dinner.

Quinn's. *Moderate.* 75-5655 A Palani Rd., Kailua-Kona; (808) 329-3822. Open-air, garden lanai setting amid tropical plants. Serves steaks, seafood, filet mignon, burgers and sandwiches. Cocktails. Open for breakfast, lunch and dinner. Reservations suggested.

Sibu Café. *Inexpensive.* 75-5695 Ali'i Dr., Kailua-Kona; (808) 329-1112. Casual, open-air restaurant, specializing in Indonesian cuisine. House specialties include Balinese chicken, spicy pork, ginger beef, stir-fry, and a variety of curries. Open for lunch and dinner daily.

Tres Hombres. *Inexpensive-Moderate.* 75-5864 Walua Rd. (Ali'i Dr.), Kailua-Kona; (808) 329-1292. Traditional Mexican fare and seafood, including lobster, fajitas, crab enchiladas, mahi mahi with Veracruz salsa. Open for lunch and dinner daily.

Tropics Café Restaurant. *Moderate-Expensive.* At Royal Kona Resort, 75-5852 Ali'i Dr., Kailua-Kona; (808) 329-3111/(800) 919-8333/*www.royalkona.com.* Open-air restaurant in Polynesian setting, overlooking Kailua Bay. Specializes in Euro-Asian cuisine, including lasagna, swordfish, teriyaki steak, prime rib, Pineapple smoked pork loin. New York steak, Hawaiian chicken, and filet mignon. Open for lunch and dinner. Reservation suggested.

KOHALA | 2

The Kohala Coast | North Kohala | Waimea

The Kohala Coast |

See Map 5
on Page 39

The Kohala Coast begins where the Kona Coast ends—at the north end, at Waikoloa Resort—extending northward to Kawaihae, taking in some 15 miles of glorious coastline. This is the premier resort area of the Big Island, with some of the island's most prestigious luxury hotels—among them the Royal Waikoloan Sheraton, Hilton Waikoloa Village, the Mauna Lani and the Mauna Kea Beach Resort—and also one of Hawaii's loveliest beaches, Hapuna. The Kohala Coast also, we might add, is the sunniest spot on the island, boasting a virtually-perfect 365 days of sunshine a year!

Waikoloa Beach Resort

Waikoloa Beach Marriott Hotel, Anaeho'omalu Beach, Petroglyphs, Hilton Waikoloa Village

Southernmost on the Kohala Coast—which is to say, directly north of the Kona Coast when journeying up the coast on the Queen Ka'ahumanu Highway (19), some 24 miles north of Kailua-Kona—lies the Waikoloa Beach Resort. It comprises two resort hotels, the Royal Waikoloan Sheraton Hotel and Hilton Waikoloa Village,

= Point of Interest

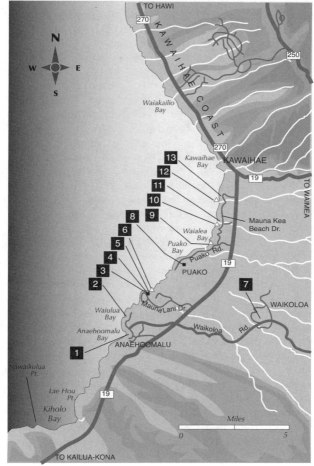

KOHALA COAST

1. Waikoloa Beach Marriott Hotel
2. Hilton Waikoloa Village
3. Historical Park
4. Mauna Lani Bay Hotel
5. Fairmont Orchid
6. Kalahuipuaa Beach
7. Waikoloa Golf Course
8. Petroglyphs
9. Waialea Beach
10. Hapuna Beach
11. Hapuna Beach Prince Hotel
12. Kaunoa Beach
13. Mauna Kea Beach Resort

KOHALA | The Kohala Coast

as well as two luxury condominium complexes, The Bay Club at Waikoloa Beach Resort and the Shores at Waikoloa. Waikoloa Beach Resort, developed mostly on former "Crown lands" that once belonged to the Kamehameha family, lies largely along Anaeho'omalu and Waiulua bays. At the head of the first of these, Anaeho'omalu Bay, stands the **Waikoloa Beach Marriott Hotel**, a 540-room, multiple-wing luxury hotel, situated on a 15-acre historical site, overlooking picturesque Anaeho'omalu Bay. The hotel was originally built in 1981, at a cost of around $70 million, and now boasts, besides a large pool with a cocktail and snack bar, three well-appointed restaurants, several good shops and boutiques, six tennis courts, and an 18-hole, championship golf course.

At the front of the Waikoloa Marriott, curving around Anaeho'omalu Bay, is the lovely, golden-sand, palm-fringed **Anaeho'omalu Beach**, gently sloping into the ocean and offering excellent swimming, snorkeling and windsurfing possibilities. The beach also has picnic tables, showers and restroom facilities. There are also, adjacent to the beach, two ancient fishponds, Ku'uali'i Fishpond and Kahapapa Fishpond, the latter featuring a *makaha* (sluice gate). The fishponds were once stocked with mullet, and reserved exclusively for the *ali'i* (Hawaiian royalty). Anaeho'oamalu, which is Hawaiian for "protected mullet," derives its name from these fishponds.

From the Waikoloa Marriott, too, a little way from Anaeho'omalu Beach, you can visit a field of **petroglyphs**, reached by way of a three-quarter-mile drive along Waikoloa Drive, from the entrance to the Waikoloa Beach Resort to the head of a paved, well-marked pathway—which is actually part of the ancient "King's Trail" that once circled the island, and which leads another one-third mile northward, directly to the petroglyphs. The petroglyphs are believed to date from the 15th century, and comprise one of the largest and most easily accessible such concentrations of petroglyphs on the island, covering roughly two acres of *pahoehoe* (smooth) lava. There are several thousand petroglyph figures here, depicting primarily humans and animals, with some evidence of the western alphabet as well. Besides the petroglyphs, there are several cave and rock shelters and also a few ancient house sites here, among them the Hale Noa and Hale Mua sites, the two best known, each comprising a 30-foot-wide and 100-foot-long rock platform. Interestingly, this area was first inhabited as early as the 800s.

Of interest, too, just to the northwest of the Royal Waikoloan is the **Anchialine Pond Preservation Area**, reached by following Waikoloa Beach Drive approximately a half mile past the Royal Waikoloan Hotel, to an unmarked two-lane road that dashes off a short distance toward the ocean, leading to a parking lot, from where a paved, sign-posted pathway journeys past ponds and on to the shoreline. The ponds here are essentially brackish-water pools in the lava flow terrain, filled with tiny red shrimp—or *opae'ula*—

and clear glass shrimp—or *opae'huna*—which are indigenous to Hawaii. The Anchialine Pond Preservation Area derives its name from the Greek word, "anchialos," meaning "near the sea." The park has no facilities.

Adjoining to the north of Anaeho'omalu Bay is Waiulua Bay, at the head of which stands the **Hilton Waikoloa Village**, a sprawl-   **2**
ing, luxury resort hotel, nestled on 62 lush, landscaped acres, originally developed in 1988 by Hawaii's celebrated developer, Chris Hemmeter, at a cost of approximately $360 million. The hotel comprises three 6-story towers, with 1,240 guest rooms—more than in the entire city of Hilo!—and 9 restaurants, 9 tennis, squash and racquetball courts, and a large shopping complex. The resort also features an extensive system of waterways, consisting of canals and lagoons, with boats and gondolas to ferry guests around; a tramway connecting the different hotel towers; a mile-long, covered museum walkway, lined with original Hawaiian and Oriental art and an-tiques, valued at more than $5 million; a three-quarter-acre swim-ming pool with waterfalls, water slides and a bar; and an abun-dance of exotic birds such as flamingos, parrots and swans, which roam the resort's tropical grounds and lagoons freely, as well as some endangered native Hawaiian Nene and Koloa ducks. There is also an 8-million-gallon saltwater lagoon here, where you can view Atlantic bottlenose dolphins, and learn all about dolphins through educational and interactive programs called "Dolphin Encounters." Additionally, you can see the remains of an ancient fishing village, the **Nawahine Rock Settlement**, quite close to the hotel—just to the   ◀
north of Waiulua Bay—where several stone walls and house sites are still visible.

Mauna Lani Resort

Fairmont Orchid, Mauna Lani Bay Hotel, Kalahuipua'a Beach, Historical Park, Puako Petroglyphs

North from the Hilton Waikoloa Village, a mile or so, lies the Mauna Lani Resort. It can be reached more or less directly on Mauna Lani Drive, which dashes off the highway (19) westward, approximately a half mile north of mile marker 74. The Mauna Lani Resort takes in some 3,200 acres that were once part of the 12th-century Hawaiian settlement of Kalahuipua'a, and later on part of the Crown lands. The resort itself began developing in 1972, and now includes the Mauna Lani Bay Hotel and Bungalows, the **Fairmont Orchid**, some exclusive condominiums, a world-class   **5**
golf course, an historical park with a series of ancient fishponds and preserved petroglyphs, and a beautiful white-sand beach, **Kalahuipua'a Beach**.   **6**

At the heart of the Mauna Lani Resort is of course the **Mauna**   **4**
Lani Bay Hotel (and Bungalows), situated on the beach and com-prising 345 hotel rooms and 5 lavish bungalow suites, with pools

and spas, and a personal butler and cook! Built in 1983 at a cost of around $80 million, the hotel features a large atrium with waterfalls and lush, tropical foliage, and three superb restaurants and an 18-hole, championship golf course. The beach at the front of the hotel at Nanuku Inlet, is the **Kalahuipua'a Beach**, a lovely, white-sand beach, bordered by a protective coral reef at the inlet, offering excellent swimming and snorkeling possibilities. A smaller, adjacent beach, the Keiki Beach, was only recently developed along the south side of the Nanuku Inlet, with white sand and shallow waters, ideally suited to children. The beach has showers and restroom facilities.

Also worth visiting at the Mauna Lani Resort is the **Historical Park**, accessed from a parking lot situated just off Mauna Lani Drive, a little over a mile west of Queen Ka'ahumanu Highway (19). A paved, well-marked trail, the Kalahuipua'a Trail, sets out from here and loops through the park. The park itself is a 27-acre preserve, with fishponds, shelter caves, petroglyphs, burial sites, and other archaeological sites of interest to the visitor. There are, in fact, five fishponds—including the 5-acre Kalahuipua'a Fishpond, the largest—where mullet and milkfish are still being raised. Also in the park, along the trail, is the ancient Keawanui Landing, which was once used by Kamehameha I and where you can now see a thatched canoe shed with an outrigger canoe at the water's edge.

Yet another point of interest, quite close to the Mauna Lani Resort, is the **Puako Petroglyphs** field, reached by way of Mauna Lani Drive west from the highway (19), about a mile, to North Kaniku Drive; then north a half mile on North Kaniku Drive to a parking lot, where there is a Hawaii Visitors Bureau marker, and from where a marked trail leads another three-quarter mile north to the petroglyph fields. There are approximately 3,000 petroglyphs here, carved into a field of *pahoehoe* (smooth lava). These are some of the oldest on the Big Island, and comprise one of the largest concentrations of petroglyphs in the islands.

Waialea, Hapuna and Kauna'oa Beaches

North from the Mauna Lani Resort on Queen Ka'ahumanu Highway (19), a half mile or so past mile marker 70, Puako Road dashes off westward one and one-quarter miles, to the historic **Hokuloa Church**, a small, white stucco church, built by early-day missionary Reverend Lorenzo Lyons, and dedicated in March, 1859. Reverend Lyons is well-remembered for the many songs he wrote, most famous among them, "Hawaii Aloha."

Nearby, too, is **Waialea Beach**, accessed from Puako Road, which goes off the highway (19) and heads west toward the ocean, to the little village of the same name, Puako; then north on a dirt road, a half mile from the highway, to the beach access road that leads to the beach about a half mile down. Waialea Beach, also known as "Beach 69"—a name derived from the public utility pole located near the dirt road leading to the beach—is a small, undeveloped beach, backed by *kiawe* trees and private homes. It has some swimming and snorkeling possibilities during calm weather, but there are no facilities at the beach.

A little way from Puako, a quarter mile or so north—which is to say, 7 miles north from the Waikoloa Beach Resort—just off the highway (19), lies **Hapuna Beach**, one of the loveliest, sunniest, most glorious white-sand beaches on the island. The Hapuna Beach Park comprises approximately 61 acres, with the beach itself stretching a half mile between two lava outcroppings. This, by the way, is also the site of the annual Rough Water Swim, a one-mile swimming event, held on the Fourth of July every year. The beach has good bodyboarding and bodysurfing possibilities, and a cove at the north end of the beach offers safe swimming and snorkeling conditions as well; during high surf, though, swimming is not advisable due to the dangerous ocean conditions here. Beach facilities include on-duty lifeguards, picnic tables, a snack bar, showers and restrooms.

Overlooking Hapuna Beach, too, situated on the low cliffs at the north end of the beach park, is the **Hapuna Beach Prince Hotel**, one of the newest resort hotels on the island, built in 1994. The hotel is situated on a 32-acre oceanfront estate, and boasts 350 guest rooms, five restaurants, and an 18-hole, Arnold Palmer and Ed Seay-designed golf course.

Yet another resort in the area, a mile or so north of Hapuna Beach, is the **Mauna Kea Beach Hotel**, situated at the end of Mauna Kea Beach Drive—which goes off the highway (19)—at the head of Kauna'oa Bay, overlooking a beautiful white-sand beach. Mauna Kea Beach Hotel is the Big Island's oldest resort hotel, originally developed—and designed—by millionaire Laurance S. Rockefeller in July, 1965. The resort is nestled on a sprawling, 400-acre estate, surrounded by lush gardens with more than 500,000 plants. It includes an 18-hole, Robert Trent Jones-designed championship golf course, a 13-acre tennis park, and nearby stables, offering guests horseback rides as well. The hotel has 310 guest rooms, six restaurants and dining areas, and a 6-Story atrium filled with tropical plants. The hotel also features a priceless art collection, the Rockefeller Pacific Rim Collection, consisting of over 1,600 objects of art and rare artifacts, including a 7th-century pink-granite Buddha from India, a 700-year-old sculpted Buddha head, a series of bronze statues from the Pacific Rim, and several centuries-old treasures from Hawaii, Pacific Polynesia, Japan, China, Thailand and Sri Lanka.

The beach fronting Mauna Kea Beach Hotel is the **Kauna'oa Beach**, one of the most beautiful beaches on the island, lying largely along the bay of the same name. Interestingly, the crescent-shaped, palm-fringed white-sand beach is an ancient nesting site for sea turtles, and it also has, at its north end, a manta ray lookout where a lighted area attracts manta rays at nighttime. The beach offers excellent swimming and snorkeling possibilities, with the southern portion of the beach especially suitable for children. It also has showers and restroom facilities.

North from Mauna Kea Beach Hotel, roughly a mile, Highway 19 dashes off eastward—inland—toward Waimea, while Highway 270 continues northward another one and one-half miles to the town of Kawaihae, at the southern end of the Kawaihae Coast, and, consequently, North Kohala.

North Kohala

  6

See Map 6
on Page 45

North Kohala, for all practical purposes, comprises the north-ernmost portion of the island, the peninsular tract that juts out northeastward into the ocean at the top end of the island. It takes in two distinct areas: the Kawaihae Coast, which is largely dry, arid, and undeveloped, stretching some 13 miles north from Kawaihae to Mahukona; and the Kohala Mountain which rises farther inland, between the town of Hawi in the north and Waimea in the south, and lies in sharp contrast to the coast, characterized by lush, green pasture lands.

Kawaihae Coast

Pu'ukohola National Historical Site, Mailekini Heiau, Spencer Beach Park, Lapakahi State Historical Park, Koaie Cove

The first place reached on the Kawaihae Coast, at its southern end, is Kawaihae, a small town situated at the head of Kawaihae Bay, roughly one and one-half miles north of the intersection of highways 19 and 270. Kawaihae itself has little to interest the visitor, save for a handful of gift and souvenir shops, a restaurant or two, and a deep-water harbor that is the second-largest on the island, after the Hilo Harbor, and dates from 1959. Additionally, Kawaihae Bay offers some canoe-paddling, fishing and windsurfing possibilities.

Just to the southwest of Kawaihae, however, or a quarter mile or so to the northwest of the intersection of Highways 19 and 270, you can search out the **Pu'ukohola National Historical Site**, a 77-acre park, established in 1972. At the center of the park is the historic Pu'ukohola Heiau, 224 feet long and 100 feet wide, built in 1791 by Kamehameha I. The *heiau* is important in that its erection marked the beginning of the ascendancy of Kamehameha, culminating in his dominion over all the Hawaiian islands. According to

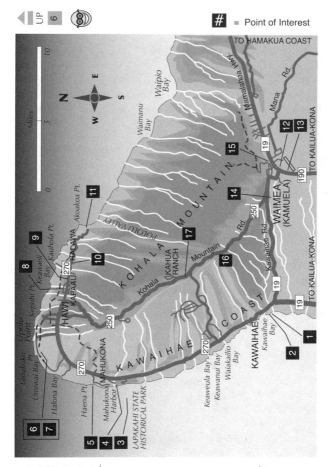

= Point of Interest

NORTH KOHALA

1. Spencer Beach Park
2. Puukohola Heiau National Historical Site
3. Koaie Cove Marine Life Conservation District
4. Mokuhona Beach Park
5. Kapaa Beach
6. King Kamehameha I Birthplace Memorial
7. Mookini Heiau
8. Kamehameha I Statue
9. Kalahikiola Church
10. Kamehameha Rock
11. Pololu Valley Lookout
12. Parker Ranch Visitor Center
13. Mana Hale
14. Kamuela Museum
15. Imiola Church
16. Lookout
17. Ironwood Avenue

legend, it was Kapoukahi, a *kahuna* (priest) from Kauai, who first prophesied that if Kamehameha built a *heiau* atop Pu'ukohola— "Hill of the Whale"—and dedicated it to the war god, Kuka'ilimoku, he would go on to conquer and rule all the Hawaiian islands. And so the *heiau* was built, on the orders of Kamehameha, and upon its completion, Keoua, Kamehameha's cousin and rival chief of the Big Island's Kau district, was invited to the dedication ceremony. Predictably, as Keoua approached Kawaihae, he was killed by Kamehameha's warriors and his body sacrificed at the *heiau* to the war god. And with this act, control of the Big Island passed to Kamehameha, eventually leading to his conquest of all the Hawaiian islands in 1810.

Of interest, too, approximately 100 feet offshore from the Pu'ukohola Heiau and now submerged in the ocean, is the Haleokapuni Heiau, dedicated to the shark gods; and located below Pu'ukohola Heiau, just to its west, is the ancient **Mailekini Heiau**, built by ancestors of Kamehameha. Interestingly, in the early 1800s, Mailekini Heiau was converted into a fort by an Englishman named John Young, one of Kamehameha's top foreign advisers, who also governed the Big Island from 1802 until 1812.

1 Try to also visit the nearby **Spencer Beach Park**, situated off Highway 270, approximately one-quarter mile west of the intersection of Highway 19. Spencer Beach, also known as Ohai'ula Beach, is a popular, sandy beach, bordered by *kiawe* trees and backed by a grassy area, ideally suited to vacationing families with children. The beach has good, safe swimming, snorkeling and bodysurfing, and also some camping possibilities. The beach also has a lifeguard, basketball and volleyball courts, picnic tables, barbecue pits, showers and restrooms.

From Spencer Beach—and Kawaihae—Highway 270 heads more or less directly north along the coast, some 13 miles, to Mahukona. But before Mahukona, just to its south and with an entrance at mile marker 14, is **Lapakahi State Historical Park**, a 265-acre park, strung along the Kawaihae Coast. From here, you can see breaching whales just offshore during the winter and spring months. Also, a short, one and one-half mile walking trail loops through the park, leading past a recreated, old working Hawaiian village, and various historic house sites, canoe sheds, animal pens, salt pans, and fishing shrines. Lapakahi, by the way, was once a fishing village, inhabited as early as the 1300s.

3 Also of interest, offshore from Lapakahi State Historical Park is the **Koaie Cove Marine Life Conservation District**, a 262-acre marine preserve, created in 1979. However, be forewarned, that the removal of any marine life, shells, rocks or coral is prohibited at the preserve.

4 A little way to the north of Lapakahi State Historical Park, there is yet another place of interest: **Mahukona Beach Park**. It is reached by way of Highway 270, a mile or so north of Lapakahi, then *makai* (toward the ocean) on a paved access road, another half-mile, directly to the beach. The park is located along the south side of Mahukona Harbor, which once served as the principal port for the sugar mills and plantations of North Kohala, used by the Kohala Sugar Company and the Hawaii Consolidated Railway Company, among others. The beach is somewhat rocky, but with crystal clear waters, offering excellent snorkeling possibilities. The beach also affords good views, across the Alenuihaha Channel, of East Maui. Facilities here include restrooms, showers, picnic tables, and also some campsites.

North from Mahukona Beach, another one and one-quarter miles, off Highway 270, is **Kapa'a Beach Park**, bordered by *kiawe* trees, and quite popular with fishermen. Kapa'a also has a small, rocky cove on the south side of the park, with some swimming possibilities. Besides which, the beach park offers good views, looking northward across the Alenuihaha Channel, of Mount Haleakala on the island of Maui. Beach facilities include picnic tables and restrooms.

5

Upolu Point | *Upolu Point, Mo'okini Heiau,*
Kamehameha I Birthplace State Memorial

Some five miles north of Kapa'a Beach Park is **Upolu Point**, the northernmost point on the island of Hawaii, reached by way of Highway 270, approximately four miles north of Kapa'a, to mile marker 20, then off on a side road northward, another two miles or so, passing by the Upolu Airport—a small, 1930s airport—to Upolu Point. Needless to say, there are good, sweeping views from here, of the open ocean and the island of Maui.

Close at hand also, one and one-half miles west of Upolu Point, accessed from a dirt road that heads off westward from Upolu Point, is the ancient **Mo'okini Heiau**, one of the most famous *heiaus* on the island. The *heiau* is believed to have originally been built in 480 AD, and rebuilt in the 1100s in the course of a single night by Hawaii's legendary little people, the *menehune*, under the direction of Pa'ao, a great *kahuna* (priest) from Tahiti. Interestingly, the *heiau* was built from boulders taken from Pololu, some 12 miles to the east, and passed from hand to hand. The *heiau* is 280 feet long, 140 feet wide and 25 feet high, and was once the exclusive domain of the *ali'i* (Hawaiian nobility), who worshipped and offered human sacrifices to their gods here. More recently, in 1963, Mo'okini Heiau was designated a national historic landmark and opened to the public.

7

Also at Mo'okini Heiau, a quarter mile to the west of it, and accessed on the same dirt road that leads to the *heiau*, you can visit the **King Kamehameha I Birthplace State Memorial**, where the great

6

Kamehameha, Hawaii's first supreme monarch, was born, around 1758. The approach to the actual birth site is on the south side of the memorial, where, at the center of an enclosing rock wall, 240 feet square and 4½ feet high, you can see the ancient birthstones.

Kohala Mountain

| Kamehameha Statue, Kalahikiola Church, Kamehameha Rock, Keokea Beach, Polulu Valley Lookout, Ironwood Avenue

Northernmost in the Kohala Mountain area is Hawi, a remote village situated at the junction of Highways 270 and 250, some four miles or so east of Mo'okini Heiau. Hawi was once a thriving sugar plantation town, and home to the Kohala Sugar Company from the 1880s until the 1970s, when the sugar mill finally closed. There is little to interest the visitor here now.

Two miles east of Hawi on Highway 270, however, lies the little town of Kapa'au, where, directly in front of the Kapa'au Courthouse, you can see the original, 9-ton bronze **statue of King Kamehameha I**—a duplicate of which stands in front of the Judiciary Building on King Street in Honolulu—cast in 1880 in Florence, Italy. Interestingly, the statue was once believed to have been lost at sea, when the ship transporting it sank in the Atlantic Ocean, just off Port Stanley in the Falkland Islands. A duplicate statue was subsequently commissioned and completed, and erected in Honolulu in 1883. But a year later, an American sea captain happened upon the original statue, which had been salvaged from the ocean, during a visit to the Falklands, and purchased it for a reported $500. He then transported the statue to Hawaii and sold it to the Hawaiian government, whereupon it was erected at Kapa'au, its rightful place, near the birthplace of the Hawaiian monarch.

Another place of interest at Kapa'au, a half mile or so east from the Kamehameha Statue, is the historic, wood-frame **Kalahikiola Church**, reached by way of a small road that goes off the highway *mauka* (toward the mountains), directly to the church. The church was originally built in 1855 by early-day missionaries Reverend Elias Bond and his wife, Ellen, who first arrived in Hawaii in 1841.

Approximately two miles east of the Kalahikiola Church, or half mile east of mile marker 25, situated just off the highway (270), is the **Kamehameha Rock**, measuring 3 feet by 1½ feet. It was this rock, according to legend, that Kamehameha single-handedly carried from the nearby beach to its present location, in a brash display of his strength. The beach, of course, lying one and one-half miles east of the legendary rock, is the **Keokea Beach**, part of a 7-acre beach park, and is largely rocky, situated at the head of picturesque Keokea Bay. The beach is frequented primarily by picnickers, with some camping permitted as well. Facilities include picnic tables, restrooms and showers.

Finally, some two miles from Keokea Beach—or 8 miles east of

Hawi—at the end of the highway (270), at mile marker 29, there is the **Pololu Valley Lookout**, with commanding views, looking south, of the northeastern coastline of the island and, directly below, the Pololu Valley—a mile long and one-third mile wide valley, where once a village flourished, surrounded by terraced *taro* patches. There are also several tiny islets just off the coast here, preserved as seabird sanctuaries. For the adventurous, there is a 4-mile trail that descends from the lookout into the valley, leading to a black-sand beach at the mouth of the valley. Swimming, however, is not recommended at the beach due to the dangerous undercurrents there.

From the Pololu Valley Lookout, we suggest you return to Kapa'au and Hawi, westward on Highway 270, then south from Hawi on Kohala Mountain Road (Highway 250), along a scenic route, to Waimea, some 20 miles distant. There are several good vistas to be enjoyed en route, of the Kawaihae Coast and the lush, upcountry Kohala Mountain pasture lands, dotted with grazing cattle and horses. Also, some 7 miles from the start of the Kohala Mountain Road, there is a lovely, 5-mile section, between mile markers 14 and 9, lined with ironwood trees, known as **Ironwood Avenue**; and a mile or so past Ironwood Avenue, at mile marker 8, there is a **scenic overlook**, with superb views of the Kohala and North Kona coastlines. The last part of the highway descends steadily for 6 or 7 miles to Waimea, offering along the way good views of both the South Kohala coast and, in the distance to the southeast, Mauna Kea.

Waimea (Kamuela)

Parker Ranch Visitor Center, Mana Hale, Pu'uopelu, Kamuela Museum, Imiola Congregational Church

Waimea lies at the foot of the Kohala Mountain, at an elevation of approximately 2,600 feet, some 20 miles south of Hawi or 8 miles east of Kawaihae, journeying directly inland (eastward) on Kawaihae Road (Highway 19). The town is at the center of the famous **Parker Ranch**, the largest privately-owned ranch in the country—larger than Texas' King Ranch!—encompassing 250,000 acres. The town itself is largely owned by the Parker Ranch interests, headed by Richard Smart, great-great-great grandson of John Palmer Parker, who originally founded the ranch in 1847. Several of the town's buildings and businesses continue to bear the family name: Parker Square, Parker Ranch Shopping Center, Parker Ranch Visitor Center and Museum, Parker School, Parker Ranch Lodge, Parker Ranch Broiler, and so on. Waimea, by the way, is also known as Kamuela, Hawaiian for Samuel, named for Samuel Parker, founder of the town and grandson of Parker Ranch founder, John Parker. In fact, Kamuela is the town's official name, and therefore also its postal address, to avoid any confusion with the townships of Waimea on the islands of Kauai and Oahu.

For visitors to Waimea, there are a handful of places well worth **12** investigating. The **Parker Ranch Visitor Center**, for one, situated at the Parker Ranch Shopping Center, at the intersection of highways 19 and 190, is a good place to begin a tour of the town. Here at the center, you can visit a small museum, and also take in a 23-minute film presentation which will give you an overview of the town and ranch, including the workings of the ranch, as well as a history of the area. The Visitor Center museum essentially comprises two rooms, one dedicated to Duke Kahanamòku, Hawaii's most famous surfer and swimmer, who won the gold medal in the 100-meter freestyle swimming event at the 1912 Olympic Games, and who was also a family friend of the Parkers; and the other filled with historical artifacts from the ranch, including old saddles and 19th-century photographs of the Parker family.

Nearby, too, on Highway 190, a half mile west of the intersection of Highway 19, are the **Parker Ranch Historical Homes**, comprising two 19th-century homes: Mana Hale and Pu'uopelu. **13** The first of these, **Mana Hale**, a New England-style structure with a beautiful, *koa* wood interior, was originally built in the 1850s, designed by John Palmer Parker, founder of Parker Ranch, and located on Mana Road, 7 miles east of Waimea. In the late 1800s, Samuel Parker, grandson of John Palmer Parker and member of King Kalakaua's (Kamehameha V's) cabinet, entertained several dignitaries and other notable guests here, including the king. In the 1970s, the building was dismantled and reassembled at its present location on Highway 190. There is a small, scale model of the original residence on display here now, as well as a family tree and several photographs of the Parker family.

Adjacent to Mana Hale, is **Pu'uopelu**, an elegant, 8,000-square-foot residence, originally built in 1862 as a smaller, L-shaped wood-frame house, and purchased in 1879 by John Palmer Parker II, uncle of Samuel Parker, who then established it as the Parker family residence. Pu'uopelu remained the Parker residence until the death of Parker Ranch owner, Richard Smart, son of Thelma Parker and Henry Gaillard Smart. At any rate, the residence boasts a French Provincial interior, and houses the late Richard Smart's art collection, including works of impressionists Monet and Renoir, as well as 18th-century Venetian paintings, rare art objects from the Ming Dynasty, and French and Italian antique furniture pieces. The house itself is of considerable interest, featuring, among other highlights, a living room that is 55 feet long and 35 feet wide, with 16-foot-high ceilings with skylights and ornate chandeliers. The grounds, too, are well worth touring, and include a picturesque rose garden and a small lake.

Another place of interest, situated a quarter mile east of Waimea, just off Highway 19, along a section known as Church

Row, is the old **Imiola Congregational Church**, originally estab- [15]
lished in 1832 by Reverend Lorenzo Lyons. The original stone
structure was destroyed in a storm in 1855, and rebuilt in 1857 as a
wood-frame, New England-style structure with a *koa* wood interior.
Reverend Lorenzo Lyons, who wrote several songs, including the
well-known "Hawaii Aloha," and who died in 1886, is buried in the
church courtyard.

Also of interest, a mile or so west of the Waimea township,
located on Kawaihae Road (Highway 19), is **Hale Kea**, a wood-
frame, plantation-style house, situated on a landscaped, 11-acre
estate, with a gazebo at the rear of the house, overlooking a
waterfall and groves of eucalyptus trees. Hale Kea—Hawaiian for
"White House"—was originally built in 1897 as the residence of
the manager of the Parker Ranch, and later purchased by Laurance
Rockefeller, when it became a favorite vacation spot for celebrities
such as Jacqueline Kennedy, Henry Kissinger and Gerald Ford. Hale
Kea now boasts a collection of boutiques and galleries, and also a
restaurant, Hartwell's.

Try to also visit the **Kamuela Museum**, located on highway 19, [14]
just to the west of the intersection of Highway 250, approximately a
mile west of Hale Kea. The museum was originally founded in 1968
by native Hawaiian Albert K. Solomon, Sr., whose wife, Harriett,
is the great, great granddaughter of John Palmer Parker, founder
of Parker Ranch. The museum houses an extensive collection of
artifacts, amassed over a period of some 65 years, rivaling most
museums in the islands. Displays include traditional *poi* pounders, *tapa* beaters, ancient war clubs, ceremonial salt pans, and old
Hawaiian mooring rocks and fish-hooks. There are also such rare
exhibits as dinosaur bones from the Jurassic era, tables inlaid with
abalone, an ivory carving of a Chinese temple, rare Chinese vases,
King Kalakaua's ivory domino set, and an original Royal Hawaiian
koa table from Iolani Palace in Honolulu.

From Waimea, you can return to Kawaihae on Kawaihae Road
(Highway 19), approximately 8 miles; or journey southwestward
on Mamalahoa Highway (190), 40 miles or so, to Kailua-Kona.
This last, the Kailua-Kona route, has a bonus: some 30 miles
from Waimea—or 10 miles northeast of Kailua-Kona—just off the
highway (190), between mile markers 28 and 27, there is a scenic
lookout, overlooking what is considered to be the last lava flow
from Mount Hualalai (which is now dormant) in 1801. Interestingly,
this last lava flow in this region filled in much of the area between
Keahole Airport, just north of Kailua-Kona, and Kiholo Bay, some 11
miles further to the north.

Accommodations | Kohala, Waimea

Hotels

The Fairmont Orchid. *$329-$1,399*. One North Kaniku Dr., Kohala Coast; (808) 885-2000/(800) 845-9905/*www.fairmont.com/ orchid*. Full-service, luxury hotel with 542 rooms and suites. Tennis courts, swimming pool, golf course, health club and spa, beauty salon, shops, restaurants, cocktail lounge. Handicapped facilities.

Hapuna Beach Prince Hotel. *$250-$1,250*. 62-100 Kaunaoa Dr., Kohala Coast; (808) 880-1111/(800) 882-6060/(866) 774-6236/ *www.princeresortshawaii.com*. Beachfront luxury hotel with 350 rooms and suites. Facilities include a swimming pool, jacuzzi and spa, beauty salon, fitness center, tennis courts, golf course, shopping arcade and restaurants. Handicapped facilities.

Hilton Waikoloa Village. *$200-$1,050*. 425 Waikoloa Beach Dr., Kohala Coast; (808) 886-1234/(800) HILTONS (445-8667)/*www. hiltonwaikoloavillage.com*. Full-service, 1,240-room luxury resort hotel, situated above Anaeho'omalu Buy on a 62-acre oceanfront estate. Facilities include swimming pools, health club, spa, tennis court, 18-hole golf course, shops, beauty salon, restaurants and cocktail lounge. Also features special children's programs, including a dolphin encounter. Handicapped facilities.

Kamuela Inn. *$59-$99*. P.O. Box 1994, Hwy. 19, Kamuela, HI 96743; (808) 885-4243/(800) 555-8968/*www.hawaii-bnb.com/ka-muela.html*. 31 units with TV, some with kitchenettes. Complimentary continental breakfast. Shops. Daily maid service.

Mauna Kea Beach Hotel. *$295-$595*. 62-100 Mauna Kea Beach Dr., Kohala Coast; (808) 882-7222/(800) 882-6060/(866) 774-6236/ *www.princeresortshawaii.com*. 310 rooms and suites in luxury, beachfront resort hotel. Hotel facilities include a swimming pool, health club and spa, sauna, tennis courts, golf course, and jogging and horseback riding trails. Also shops and beauty salon, and restaurants and cocktail lounge. Handicapped facilities.

Mauna Lani Bay Hotel & Bungalows. *$430-$5,900*. 68-1400 Mauna Lani Dr., Kohala Coast; (808) 885-6622/(866) 877-6982(800) 367-2323/*www.maunalani.com*. Luxury, beachfront resort hotel, with 372 rooms, suites and individual, 4,000-square-foot bungalows with private swimming pools and Jacuzzis. Hotel facilities include a swimming pool, tennis courts, golf course, health club and spa, beauty salon, shops, restaurants and cocktail lounge.

Shores at Waikoloa. *$285-$400*. 69-1035 Keana Pl., Kohala Coast; (808) 886-5001/(800) 922-7866/(877) 997-6667/*www. resortquesthawaii.com*. Beachfront condominium complex, with 72 one- and two-bedroom units with TV, phones, air-conditioning, and kitchen facilities. Swimming pool, health club, tennis court and golf course; also restaurant and shops. Daily maid service. Handicapped facilities.

Waikoloa Beach Marriott. *$240-$950.* 69-275 Waikoloa Beach Dr., Kohala Coast; (808) 886-6789/(800) 922-5533/*www.marriott. com*. 545-room full-service beachfront hotel. Swimming pool, health club, tennis courts, golf course, restaurant, cocktail lounge, and shops on premises. Handicapped facilities.

Waimea Country Lodge. *$105-$125.* 62-1210 Lindsey Rd., Kamuela, HI 96743; (808) 885-4100/(800) 367-5004/*www. castleresorts.com*. 21-room hotel in Hawaii's upcountry, located at an elevation of 2,500 feet. TV, phones, some rooms with kitchen facilities. Daily maid service.

Bed and Breakfast

Belle Vue Cottage and Suites. *$95-$175.* P.O. Box 1295, 1351 Konokohau Rd., Kamuela, HI 96743; (808) 885-7732/(800) 772-5044/*www.hawaii-bellevue.com*. Offers individually decorated cottage and suite, with views of the ocean and the Kohala coast. Private baths, TV, kitchenettes, deck and patio. Full breakfast, fruit basket and tropical flowers.

Hale Ho'onanea Bed and Breakfast. *$100-$130.* P.O. Box 44953, Kamuela, HI 96743; (808) 882-1653/(877) 882-1653/*www. houseofrelaxation.com*. Country setting on 3-acre estate at 900-foot elevation. Offers three guest rooms with ocean views. Private baths kitchenettes and lanais. Tropical breakfast.

Jacaranda Inn. *$159-$450.* 65-1444 Kawaihae Rd., Kamuela, HI 96743; (808) 885-8813/*www.jacarandainn.com*. Eight rooms and suites in six different cottages on historic, 12-acre ranch estate at 2,500 feet. Private baths and sitting areas. Also separate cottage with three bedrooms and three baths available. Full hot breakfast.

Waimea Gardens. *$150-$160.* P.O. Box 563, Kamuela, HI 96743; (808) 885-8550/*www.waimeagardens.com*. Offers two cottages with private baths, kitchenettes, patios and gardens. Also TV, VCR, phones, beach towels. Self-serve continental breakfast.

KOHALA | Accommodations

KOHALA | Dining

Dining | South Kohala, Waimea

[Restaurant prices—based on full course diner, excluding drinks, tax and tips—are categorized as follows: *Deluxe*, over $30; *Expensive*, $20-$30; *Moderate*, $10-$20; *Inexpensive*, under $10.]

South Kohala

Batik Room. *Expensive-Deluxe*. At the Mauna Kea Beach Hotel, 62-100 Mauna Kea Beach Dr., Kohala Coast: (808) 882-5810/(800) 735-1111/*www.maunakeabeachhotel.com*. Elegant decor, featuring art of Asian royalty, Sri Lankan batik tapestries and clay pottery animals, ocean views. Serves a variety of International dishes, including Maine and Hawaiian lobsters, Thai curries, and a wide selection of fresh island seafood. Entertainment. Open for dinner. Reservations recommended.

Bamboo Restaurant. *Moderate-Expensive*. Hwy. 270, Hawi; (808) 889-5555/*www.bamboorestaurant.com*. Offers creative Pacific Rim cuisine, emphasizing fresh island ingredients. Menu features fresh fish and island seafood, chicken and beef dishes, pork quesedillas, and salads. Open for dinner daily, except Mondays. Reservations recommended.

Bay Terrace. *Moderate-Expensive*. At Mauna Lani Bay Hotel and Bungalows, One Mauna Lani Dr., Kohala Coast; (808) 885-6622/(800) 356-6652/*www.maunalani.com*. Open-air setting, amid tropical foliage. Asian and American cuisine, featuring fresh fish, pasta, and steak. Also cocktails, and entertainment. Open for breakfast, lunch and dinner. Reservations suggested.

Brown's Beach House. *Expensive-Deluxe*. At the Fairmont Orchid, at 1 North Kaniku Dr., Kohala; (808) 885-2000/(800) 845-9905/*www.fairmont.com/orchid*. Menu features fresh island seafood, beef, chicken, pork chops, pasta and vegetarian dishes, soups and salads, foie gras, and soufflé and mousse for dessert. Nightly entertainment, including a hula performance. Open for lunch and dinner daily, Reservations suggested.

Café Pesto. *Moderate*. Kawaihae Shopping Center, 5 Hata Building, 130 Kain Ave., Kawaihae; (808) 882-1071. Contemporary decor. Offers a good selection of gourmet pizza, calzone, and pasta dishes. Espresso and wine bar. Open for lunch and dinner.

The Canoe House. *Expensive*. At the Mauna Lani Bay Hotel and Bungalows, 68-1400 Mauna Lani Dr., Kohala Coast; (808) 885-6622/(800) 356-6652/*www.maunalani.com*. Oceanfront setting, with views of Maui. Tropical, Polynesian decor. Seasonally changing menu, featuring regional and Pacific Rim cuisine, with emphasis on fresh island fish. Also steak, chicken, lamb and vegetarian dishes. Good selection of desserts. Cocktails. Open for dinner daily. Reservations recommended.

Donatoni's. *Moderate-Expensive.* At the Hilton Waikoloa Village, Waikoloa Beach Dr., Waikoloa; (808) 886-1234/(800) 445-8667/*www.hiltonwaikoloavillage.com.* Well-appointed restaurant with ocean views; tropical setting, featuring waterfalls. Authentic Northern Italian cuisine; wide selection of fresh fish, steak, and pasta dishes. Cocktails. Open for dinner. Reservations recommended.

Gallery Restaurant. *Expensive-Deluxe.* At the Mauna Lani Bay Hotel at Mauna Lani Resort, Kohala Coast; (808) 885-6622/(800) 356-6652/*www.maunalani.com.* Luxurious, well-regarded restaurant, serving gourmet International cuisine. House specialties include pork tenderloin, veal scaloppine, rack of lamb, grilled duck breast, filet mignon, lobster, and fresh fish. Cocktails. Open for dinner. Reservations recommended.

The Grill. *Expensive-Deluxe.* At the Fairmont Orchid at Mauna Lani, One North Kaniku Dr., Kohala Coast; (808) 885-2000/(800) 885-2000/*www.fairmont.com/orchid.* Elegant restaurant, with ocean views. Features Hawaiian regional cuisine, with emphasis on fresh island seafood and steak. Entertainment. Open for dinner. Reservations recommended.

Hawaii Calls. *Expensive-Deluxe.* At the Waikoloa Beach Marriott, Waikoloa; (808) 886-6789. Intimate atmosphere. Menu features fresh island seafood, New York steak, grilled chicken breast, pasta dishes, prime rib, sashimi, soups, salads, and chowder. Open for dinner. Reservations recommended.

Imari. *Expensive-Deluxe.* Hilton Waikoloa Village, Waikoloa Beach Dr., Waikoloa; (808) 885-1234/(800) 445-8667/*www.hiltonwaikoloavillage.com.* Large dining room in a Japanese tea garden setting, with a Japanese pond and waterfalls. Menu features Teppanyaki-style cuisine, including sashimi, tempura, sushi, jumbo shrimp, lobster tail, filet mignon and beef teriyaki. Cocktails. Open for dinner. Reservations suggested.

Kamuela Provision Company. *Moderate.* At the Hilton Waikoloa Village, Waikoloa Beach Dr., Waikoloa: (808) 886-1234/(800) 445-8667/*www.hiltonwaikoloavillage.com.* Situated on a bluff with panoramic ocean views and memorable sunsets. House specialties include kiawe smoked duck, stir fry chicken, lobster, fresh island fish, filet mignon, prime rib and lamb chops. Also cocktails. Open for dinner. Reservations recommended.

Knickers Bar and Lounge. *Moderate-Expensive.* At the Mauna Lani Bay Hotel at Mauna Lani Resort, 1 Kaniku Dr., Kohala Coast; (808) 885-6622/(800) 356-6652/*www.maunalani.com.* Open-air setting; overlooking ocean and resort golf course. Specializes in Continental cuisine. Menu features fresh fish. Chicken Mauna Lani, Top Sirloin, filet mignon, pork chops, lamb chops and prime rib. Cocktails. Open lor breakfast, lunch and dinner. Reservations suggested.

Norio's Sushi Bar and Restaurant. *Expensive.* At the Fairmont

KOHALA | Dining

Orchid at Mauna Lani, One North Kaniku Dr., Kohala Coast; (808) 885-2000/(800) 885-2000/*www.fairmont.com/orchid*. Well-regarded, traditional Japanese restaurant, offering fresh island seafood, including Hawaiian abalone and flounder; also teriyaki beef, assorted tempura, and good selection of sashimi and sushi platters. Open for dinner daily. Reservations recommended.

The Pavilion at Manta Ray Point. *Expensive-Deluxe.* At Mauna Kea Beach Hotel, One Mauna Kea Beach Dr., Kohala Coast; (808) 882-5810/(800) 735-1111/*www.maunakeabeachhotel.com*. Open-air setting; overlooking Kauna'oa Beach. Menu features Hawaiian regional cuisine and pasta, steak and fresh island seafood. Cocktails. Open for breakfast, lunch and dinner; also Sunday brunch.

Waikoloa Village Clubhouse Restaurant. *Moderate.* At the Waikoloa Village Golf Course, Waikoloa Village; (808) 883-9644. Open-air restaurant, overlooking golf course. Steak and seafood; also chicken, and prime rib. Cocktails. Open for lunch and dinner daily. Reservations suggested.

Waimea

Edelweiss. *Moderate-Expensive.* Hwy. 19, Waimea; (808) 885-6800. Housed in rough-hewn building with open ceilings; owned and operated by renowned German chef, Hans-Peter Hager. House specialties include pork roast with sauerkraut, wienerschnitzel, roast duck. New York steak, rack of lamb, and filet mignon. Cocktails. Open for lunch and dinner, Tues.-Sat. Reservations suggested.

Merriman's. *Expensive-Deluxe.* 1 Opelo Plaza, Opelo Rd. (Hwy. 19), Waimea; (808) 885-6822. Tropical, contemporary decor. Hawaiian regional cuisine, prepared by owner/chef, Peter Merriman. Menu features fresh fish, paella, wok-charred ahi, beef, Kahua Ranch lamb, Kahena natural veal, chicken, duck, vegetables, and steak. Cocktails. Open for lunch and dinner daily. Reservations suggested.

HILO | 3

Downtown Hilo | Around Hilo

Hilo is the largest city on the island, and fourth largest in the state of Hawaii. It is the seat of Hawaii county, and the commercial and political center of the Big Island, with a population of approximately 47.000. It also boasts some of the largest orchid and anthurium gardens and macadamia nut orchards in the state, and is smack in the middle of one of the wettest parts of the island, averaging nearly 140 inches of rainfall annually. The city itself is situated at the head of Hilo Bay, fanning out south and westward, surrounded by lush, green hills. It is, quite characteristically, filled with contemporary as well as turn-of-the-century homes and buildings, as well as abundant public parks and recreation areas, plant nurseries and flower gardens. It also has a couple of museums of interest, and fresh produce and fish markets, a handful of beach parks quite close at hand, and best of all, a tropical rainforest zoo, the only one of its kind in the country.

Downtown Hilo |

See Map 7
fon Page 58

Wailuku River Area | Maui's Canoe, Kalakaua Park

A good place to begin your tour of Hilo is its downtown section, which lies largely between the Wailuku River—which runs along the west side of the city—and the Waiakea Peninsula at the northeastern end. Starting out, at the west end of the city, by the mouth of the Wailuku River (on its south bank), you can see from the Pu'ueo Bridge, looking inland along the river, the landmark "**Maui's Canoe.**" The landmark is essentially a large rock that vaguely resembles a canoe. Legend endures that demigod Maui was once gallantly taming the sun from the top of Mount Haleakala on the neighboring island of Maui, when he was suddenly distracted by the realization that his mother, the goddess Hina, had become trapped in her home on the Big Island, directly beneath Rainbow Falls, just upstream on the Wailuku River, a mile or so inland from Hilo. Without a moment to spare, Maui jumped into his canoe and, with two mighty strokes, crossed the channel from the island of Maui to the island of Hawaii, and landed here, at the mouth of the River Wailuku, from where he dashed off upriver and saved his mother, Hina. And Maui's canoe has remained here ever since.

At any rate, a little way from the Wailuku River and Maui's Ca-

1

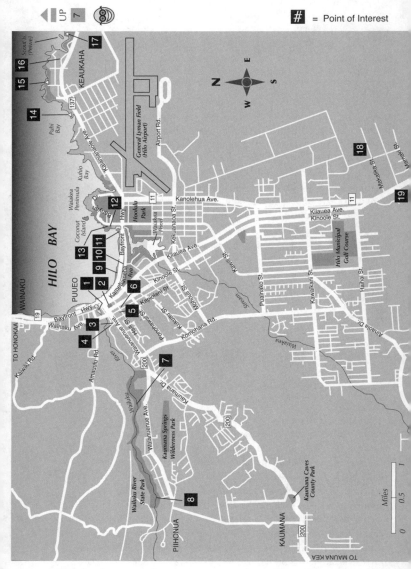

= Point of Interest

HILO

1. Maui's Canoe
2. Kalakaua Park
3. Naha and Pinao Stones
4. Hawaii Public Library
5. Lyman Museum and Mission House
6. Haili Church
7. Rainbow Falls
8. Boiling Pots
9. Hilo Bayfront Park
10. Mooheau Park
11. Wailoa River tate Park
12. Suisan Fish Market
13. Liliuokalani Gardens
14. Keaukaha Beach Park
15. Onekahakaha Beach Park
16. Hilo Tropical Gardens
17. James Kealoha Beach Park
18. Nani Mau Gardens
19. Panaewa Rainforest Zoo

noe, just to the south, lies **Kalakaua Park**, bordered by Kalakaua and Kino'ole streets and Waianuenue Avenue, with Keawe Street just to the north of it. The park is dedicated to Hawaii's King Kalakaua, the Merrie Monarch, with a bronze statue of him located here, in a large, grassy area. Also at the park are an old, spreading banyan tree, a nearby veterans' memorial situated adjacent to a small reflecting pool, and a large sun dial, located in the southwest corner of the park, dating from 1877.

Waianuenue Avenue

Hawaii Cultural Center,
Naha and Pinao Stones

Near the park, too, with some visitor interest, are a handful of older, early 1900s buildings: on Waianuenue Avenue, directly across from the park, is the **Old Federal Building**, dating from 1919 and featuring a neo-classical design; on Kalakaua Street, on the opposite side of the park, is the **Hawaiian Telephone Company Building**, with its hand-painted terra-cotta tiles, built in the 1920s and designed by renowned architect C.W. Dickey; and nearby, also on Kalakaua Street, is the old police station, now home to the **East Hawaii Cultural Center**, which houses a gallery-cum-gift shop.

Well worth investigating, too, are the ancient **Naha and Pinao stones**, located directly in front of the Hawaii Public Library on Waianuenue Avenue. The **Naha Stone**, some 12 feet long and 1½ feet high, is the larger of the two, weighing approximately 3½ tons. It also has its associations to Kamehameha I, who is believed to have displayed his strength and determination as a boy by moving this same rock, a feat of no small measure, which others had failed at. He then went on to fulfill its prophecy, becoming the first king of all the Hawaiian islands. The other, the **Pinao Stone**, which stands more or less upright, 4 feet or so high and 1½ feet wide, is believed to be one of the pillars to the entrance of the ancient Pinao Heiau.

Museums and Churches

Lyman Museum and Mission House,
St. Joseph's Church, Haili Church,
Central Christian Church

Close at hand also, on Haili Street, near Kapiolani Street, is the **Lyman Museum** and **Mission House**, especially interesting to history buffs. The Mission House is a New England-style wood-frame structure, built in 1839. It was originally the home of early-day missionaries David and Sarah Lyman, who arrived on Oahu from Boston in 1832, and on the island of Hawaii a few years later, in 1834. The restored missionary home features the original *ohia* wood beams that still support the roof, as well as *ohia* and *koa* wood floors and furniture.

The **Lyman Museum**, situated adjacent to the Mission House, is home to a wealth of exhibits and artifacts centered around the history and geology of Hawaii. The Island Gallery on the ground floor of the museum is devoted largely to the cultural aspect of the history of Hawaii, with displays including old Hawaiian tools, fish-hooks, bowls, jewelry, leis, and exhibits illustrating the ancient art of producing *kapa* (a native Hawaiian fiber), as well as examples of traditional Hawaiian games; there is also a large representative map here, detailing the origins of the diverse ethnic groups in the islands. On the upper floor are the Earth Heritage Gallery and Chinese Art Gallery. In the first of these, the Earth Heritage Gallery, you can learn all about the geology of Hawaii, and also delve into astronomy, referenced from Mauna Kea, the highest point in Hawaiian islands, located more or less at the center of the Big Island. While the Chinese Art Gallery is devoted entirely to Chinese art, featuring, among other exhibits, rare treasures from the Ching Dynasty and pottery dating from 2 BC.

Also on Haili Street, a little way from the Lyman Museum and Mission House, between Kapiolani and Keawe streets—a section of Haili Street popularly known as "Church Row"—are three historic churches: **St. Joseph's Church**, a Spanish mission-style church built in 1919, which also has the distinction of being the largest church in Hilo, located near the corner of Kapiolani Street; **Haili Church**, one of the oldest in Hilo, founded in 1824, and where services are still offered in Hawaiian, located to the east of St. Joseph's Church; and the **Central Christian Church**, with its Victorian architecture, dating from 1892, situated near the comer, on the east side, of Kilauea Street.

Around Hilo

See Map 7
fon Page 58

Wailuku River State Park

Wailuku River State Park, Rainbow Falls, Boiling Pots, Kaumana Caves County Park

Moving out from the city center, west from the Lyman Museum and Church Row, a mile or so along the Wailuku River, lies the **Wailuku River State Park**, reached more or less directly on Waianuenue Avenue and a little access road northward. The park encompasses roughly 16 acres, lying largely along the east-west Wailuku River, notably the longest perennial river in Hawaii, nearly 23 miles long. At the east end of the park are the well-visited **Rainbow Falls**, easily accessible from the parking lot alongside the small access road that goes off Waianuenue Avenue. The waterfalls plunge approximately 80 feet directly into a large, 100-foot-wide natural pool. The falls derive their name from the rainbows that form here at certain times in the morning, when the sun's rays strike at a certain angle. There is also a short trail that leads from the pool to the top of the falls, then heads back down, past a large banyan tree, to the parking lot.

At the west end of Wailuku River State Park, roughly one and one-half miles from Rainbow Falls, is an area known as "**Boiling Pots**," reached directly on Waianuenue Avenue and Pe'epe'e Falls Street. On Pe'epe'e Falls Street is a vista point that overlooks the Wailuku River, Pe'epe'e Falls, and the "boiling pots." The "boiling pots" are in fact depressions in the streambed, a result of the irregular formation of hot lava. A trail leads from here, along the right (east) side of the lookout, down to the river, where there is a large, grassy area, ideally suited for picnicking, as well as restroom facilities.

8

Another place of interest, away from the city center, some 5 miles southwestward on Kaumana Drive (Highway 220)—which goes off Waianuenue Avenue—is the **Kaumana Caves County Park**. Here you can visit the Kaumana Caves, formed by lava tubes from the 1881 lava flow from Mauna Loa. One of the caves is almost 200 yards deep, and the other approximately 100 feet. A series of stairs lead down to the caves. There are picnic tables and restrooms at the caves.

◄

Bayfront Park and Banyan Drive

Liliuokalani Gardens, Suisan Fish Market, Wailoa River State Park

From the Kaumana park and caves, however, let us return to the center of town and proceed northeast from the Lyman Museum and Church Row on Waianuenue Avenue and the Bayfront Highway, to the **Hilo Bayfront Park**, which borders Hilo Bay. Interestingly, this area was the main landing for ships until the turn of the century, when, following the construction of a breakwater, the port was moved a mile or so to the east of here. There is a half-mile-long gray-sand beach at the park, backed by ironwood trees, frequented primarily by fishermen, canoe paddlers, and windsurfers. The park also has good picnicking possibilities, and showers and restrooms.

9

Nearby, too, adjacent to Hilo Bayfront Park, is **Mo'oheau Park**, situated between the Bayfront Highway and Kamehameha Avenue, and also south of Hilo Bay. Mo'oheau Park is notable as the oldest public park in Hilo, consisting of large, grassy areas, and featuring a baseball diamond, two soccer fields, volleyball courts, and a bandstand where, until recently, regularly scheduled concerts were held, performed by the county band.

10

Eastward, a short distance from the Bayfront and Mo'oheau parks on Bayfront Highway—or Kamehameha Avenue—and we are on the **Waiakea Peninsula**, accessed on Lihiwai Street, or, just to the east of there, on Kanoelehua Avenue (Highway 11). In fact, both Lihiwai Street and Kanoelehua Avenue emerge to the north on **Banyan Drive**, a mile-long scenic drive that loops along the top end of the peninsula, and is lined with more than 50 banyan trees,

◄

◄

HILO | **Around the City**

planted, individually, by personages whose names the trees now bear, among them Amelia Earhart, Cecil B. DeMille, King George V, Franklin Delano Roosevelt, Babe Ruth, and Richard Nixon.

▶   Just offshore from the Waiakea Peninsula is **Coconut Island**, reached by way of Keli'ipio Place—which goes off Banyan Drive, along the west part of it—and a walkway that leads directly, some 150 feet or so to the island. Coconut Island was originally known as Moku Ola, Hawaiian for "healing island," a name derived from the spring waters that gush forth between the peninsula and the island and are supposedly endowed with healing properties. The island, during World War II, was overrun by the U.S. military, but was returned to the public in 1945. It is now preserved as a public park, with good swimming possibilities on the east side of the island, near the diving tower, where there are also one or two sheltered coves, ideal for children to swim in, and a large, grassy area at the center of the island. The park also offers good picnicking possibilities, and showers and restrooms.

Also, just off Banyan Drive, near the intersection of Lihiwai Street, are the **Liliuokalani Gardens**, named for Hawaii's Queen Liliuokalani. The gardens are in fact the largest Yedo-type gardens outside of Japan, comprising some 30 acres, dotted with pagodas, ornate stone structures, waterways, and ponds. The gardens also offer good views of Hilo Bay and Coconut Island.

Across from the Liliuokalani Gardens, also near the intersection of Banyan Drive and Lihiwai Street, is Hilo's well-known **Suisan Fish Market**, with its daily auction a cultural experience of sorts, much to be recommended to first-time visitors to the area. Here, the day's fresh catch—ahi, mahi mahi, ono, opah, hebi, tuna and swordfish—is publicly displayed and auctioned off to local wholesalers and restaurants, amid a smattering of locally-spoken languages, including the popular Pidgin, a blend of Hawaiian and English. The market is open to the public between 8am and 3.45pm, and the fish auction is conducted in the mornings, 7am to 9am.

Here also, just to the southwest of the Suisan Market and Banyan Drive, along the southern edge of Hilo Bay, is **Wailoa River State Park**, a 150-acre park, created as a *tsunami* (tidal wave) buffer zone, after the well-remembered *tsunami* of May 23, 1960, which devastated Hilo, killing 61 people and destroying 288 structures, with the cumulative damage in excess of $50 million. The park comprises large expanses of lawn, and also has a 27-acre pond, the Waiakea Pond. At the park, too, is the Wailoa Center, which serves as both a visitor center and an art center, offering information on *tsunamis*—with photographs of Hilo during and after the *tsunami* on display—as well as periodically featuring works of local artists. Two other memorials at the center, on either side of it, are the Shinmachi Tsunami Memorial and the Hawaii County Vietnam Memorial.

Kalanianaole Avenue Area | *Onekahakaha Beach Park,*
Hilo Tropical Gardens,
Kealoha Beach Park

East of Wailoa River State Park, near the corner of Manono and Pi'ilani streets, is **Ho'olulu Park**, the site of the annual Merrie Monarch Hula Festival, and which also has in it ball fields, tennis courts and other recreational facilities; and just to the east of there, situated along Puhi Bay, off Kalanianaole Avenue—a mile or so east of Kamehameha Avenue—is **Keaukaha Beach Park**, with a series of small coves, but no sandy beach.

East still, another half mile from Keaukaha Beach Park, lies **Onekahakaha Beach Park**, accessed from Onekahakaha Road, which goes off Kalanianaole Avenue. The park is quite popular with families, and ideally suited to children. It features a large ocean pool that is shallow and has a sandy bottom, and is protected by a breakwater. There is also an on-duty lifeguard here, and picnic tables, pavilions, showers and restrooms.

Just east of Onekahakaha Beach Park, situated off Kalanianaole Avenue, are the **Hilo Tropical Gardens**, a 2-acre garden where you can see orchids, anthuriums, heleconias, hibiscus, and other native Hawaiian flowers and plants, all labeled for easy identification. There are also some natural tide pools here, as well as a gift shop on the premises.

Continuing eastward along Kalanianaole Avenue, a half mile or so east of the Hilo Tropical Gardens, is the **James Kealoha Beach Park**, a popular beach park, also known as "4 Miles," for the distance from here to the Hilo Post Office at the western end of the city. The beach park is in fact situated at the head of a small bay, with a shaded, grassy area to the back of it. It also has at its eastern end some sheltered coves, ideal for swimming and snorkeling. Also near the eastern end of the bay, just offshore, is Peiwe Island (Scout Island), with a handful of ironwood and *hala* trees. The beach park, in any case, has showers and restroom facilities. It also has some camping possibilities, and surfing during favorable conditions.

Of interest, too, directly across from the James Kealoha Beach Park on the south side of Kalanianaole Avenue, is **Lokoaka Pond**, a 60-acre fishpond, used to raise trout and mullet; and a mile or so to the east of there, along Kalanianaole Avenue, at the Richardson Ocean Park Center, is **Richardson's Beach**, a small, black-sand beach, backed by a seawall and a grassy area. The beach has excellent swimming, snorkeling and bodyboarding possibilities, and an on-duty lifeguard. Beach facilities include showers and restrooms.

Farther Afield | *Nani Mau Gardens, Panaewa Rainforest Zoo,*
Mauna Loa Macadamia Nut Visitor Center,

Hilo has other places to delight the visitor, farther afield but well worth visiting. Just to the south of Banyan Drive and Kalanianaole Avenue, for instance, some 3 miles along Highway 11 and off on **18** Makalika Street, eastward, are the **Nani Mau Gardens**, one of the largest gardens in Hilo, taking in more than 20 acres. Here you can view a variety of sculpted floral displays of orchids, anthuriums and gardenias, and also a macadamia nut orchard. Trams whisk visitors around the gardens, and canopied golf carts are also available for rent for touring the premises. There is a gift shop here as well.

A mile or so south from Nani Mau Gardens on Highway 11, Mamaki Street goes off westward, approximately another mile, leading **19** to one of Hilo's great glories, the **Panaewa Rainforest Zoo**, the only tropical rainforest zoo in the country. The Panaewa zoo, established in September, 1978, encompasses some 40 acres, with 12 acres currently devoted to the zoo, and boasts more than 125 inches of rainfall annually. Zoo exhibits include more than 50 different species of birds and animals, among them African pygmy hippopotamuses, monkeys, tigers, and a variety of tropical birds. The zoo is open to the public daily, and there is no admission fee.

▶   South still, some 5½ miles from Hilo is the **Mauna Loa Macadamia Nut Visitor Center**, reached on Highway 11 and Macadamia Road, which goes eastward off the highway (11), another 3 miles, to lead to the visitor center. At the visitor center you can learn all about the macadamia nut, which was first brought to Hawaii from Australia in the 1870s, but which is now more or less synonymous with Hawaii, with more than 55 million pounds of the nut produced in the state annually. There are over a million macadamia nut trees here, and visitors can also get a first-hand look at the macadamia nut factory, and the processes of roasting and packaging the nuts. There is a video film presentation of the complete process, and free samples for tasting. A gift shop and snack bar are also located on the premises.

South from the Macadamia Nut factory and orchards, and consequently Hilo, Highway 11 heads off into the Puna district and on to the Hawaii Volcanoes National Park. And north from Hilo lies the scenic Hamakua Coast, accessed more or less directly on the Bayfront Highway, eastward from downtown Hilo, and Highway 19 north.

Accommodations | Hilo

Hotels

Dolphin Bay Hotel. *$79-$149*. 333 Iliahi St., Hilo; (808) 935-1466/(877) 935-1466/*www.dolphinbayhilo.com*. 18-unit hotel with studios and 1- and 2-bedroom apartments. TV, refrigerators, and kitchenettes.

Hawaii Naniloa Resort. *$130-$230*. 93 Banyan Dr., Hilo; (808) 969-3333/*www.naniloa.com*. 325-room hotel; TV, phones, air-conditioning. Also swimming pools, fitness center, jacuzzi and sauna, restaurants, bar.

Hilo Hawaiian Hotel. *$155-$415*. 71 Banyan Dr., Hilo; (808) 935-9361/(800) 367-5004/*www.hilohawaiian.com* or *www.castleresorts.com/HHH*. Luxury hotel with rooms and suites with ocean or city views. TV, phones, air-conditioning, refrigerators. Also swimming pool, restaurant, lounge, meeting rooms, and gift shop on premises.

Hilo Seaside Hotel. *$68-$98*. 126 Banyan Dr., Hilo; (808) 935-0821/(800) 560-5557/*www.hiloseasidehotel.com*. 135 rooms with TV, phones, air-conditioning, refrigerators, and kitchenettes. Also pool and restaurant.

Uncle Billy's Hilo Bay Hotel. *$89-$94*. 87 Banyan Dr., Hilo; (808) 961-5818/(800) 367-5102/*www.unclebilly.com*. 144-room oceanfront hotel. TV, phones, air-conditioning, refrigerators, and some kitchenettes. Also swimming pool, restaurant and general store on premises.

Bed and Breakfast

Bay House Bed and Breakfast. *$120*. 42 Pukihae St., Hilo; (808) 961-6311/(888) 235-8195/*www.bayhousehawaii.com*. Secluded wooded setting above Hilo Bay. Offers three guest rooms with private baths and private lanais with ocean views. Cable TV in rooms. Sitting room has refrigerator, microwave oven, coffee maker and phone. Buffet-style breakfast, with freshly-baked pastries, tropical fruit, and Kona coffee.

Emerald View Guesthouse. *$150*. 272 Kaiulani St., Hilo; (808) 961-5736/*www.emeraldview.com*. Two guest rooms with private bath and private decks with waterfalls views. Hawaiian tropical breakfast, consisting of home-baked banana or coffee cake, fresh fruit, and Kona coffee.

Hale Kai Hawaii Bed and Breakfast. *$105-$135*. 111 Honoli'i Pali, Hilo, HI 96720; (808) 935-6330/*www.halekaihawaii.com*. Oceanfront setting at Honoli'i Bay. 5 rooms, with TV. Swimming pool, Jacuzzi. Full breakfast. Daily maid service.

The Inn at Kulaniapia Falls. *$109*. P.O. Box 646, Hilo, HI 96721; (808) 935-6789/(866) 935-6789/*www.waterfall.net*. Situated at 850-foot elevation on a 22-acre estate, with a 120-foot waterfall. Offers five rooms and suites with private baths and balconies with ocean and waterfall views. Hawaiian breakfast.

Kia'i Kai Bed and Breakfast. *$95-$155*. P.O. Box 10064, Kea'au, HI 96749; (808) 982-9256/(888) 542-4524/*www.hawaii-ocean-retreat.com*. Situated on a cliff overlooking the ocean. Offers one room, one suite, and a cottage. Private baths and lanais; hot tub. Breakfast consists of pineapple muffins, fresh island produce and fruit, and Kona coffee.

Shipman House Bed and Breakfast. *$205-$225*. 131 Ka`iulani St., Hilo; (808) 934-8002/(800) 627-8447/*www.hilo-hawaii.com*. Historic mansion with five guest rooms with private baths. Fir floors, 12-foot ceilings, antique piano, rare travel books, oversized bath tubs. Continental buffet breakfast, with fresh island fruit, macadamia nut granola, breads, muffins, fruit juice and Kona coffee.

Waterfalls Inn. *$140-$190*. 240 Kaiulani St., Hilo; (808) 969-3407/(888) 808-4456/*www.waterfallsinn.com*. Historic home on 1½-acre property on Hilo's Reed's Island. Four guest rooms with private baths. Breakfast consists of breads and pastries, freshly-made granola, island fruit, and Kona coffee.

Dining | Hilo

[Restaurant prices—based on full course diner, excluding drinks, tax and tips—are categorized as follows: Deluxe, over $30; Expensive, $20-$30; Moderate, $10-$20; Inexpensive, under $10.]

Café Pesto. *Inexpensive-Moderate*. 308 Kamehameha Ave., Hilo; (808) 969-6640. Housed in the historic, Renaissance revival-style S. Hata Building, dating from 1912. Serves gourmet pizzas, sandwiches and salads, with island-grown produce and fresh fish. Also espresso and wine bar. Open for lunch and dinner, Mon.-Fri.

Ken's House of Pancakes. *Inexpensive*. 1730 Kamehameha Ave., Hilo; (808) 935-8711. Informal coffee shop, serving American and local fare, including pancakes, omelets, soups and sandwiches. Dinner menu features grilled fish, steak, prime rib, chicken and pasta. Open 24 hours.

Nihon Restaurant & Cultural Center. *Inexpensive-Moderate*. 123 Lihiwai St., Hilo: (808) 969-1133. Japanese restaurant with traditional Japanese decor, offering views of Hilo Bay and the Liliuokalani Gardens. Full sushi bar. Also steak, chicken, soups and salads. Cocktails. Open for lunch and dinner. Mon.-Sat. Reservations suggested.

Queens' Court Restaurant. *Moderate-Expensive.* At the Hilo Hawaiian Hotel, 71 Banyan Dr., Hilo: (808) 935-9361/*www.castleresorts.com/HHH*. Overlooking Hilo Bay and Coconut Island. Decor features historic photographs of Hawaiian royalty and old Hilo town. Varied cuisine, with both ala carte menu and buffets. Features Hawaiian specialties, seafood, and prime rib and Dungeness crab buffets. Cocktails. Entertainment. Open for breakfast, lunch and dinner daily. Reservations recommended.

Sandalwood Room. *Moderate.* At the Hawaii Naniloa Hotel, 93 Banyan Dr., Hilo; (808) 969-3333/*www.naniloa.com*. Open-air, oceanside restaurant. Features Continental cuisine, with emphasis on steak and seafood. Specialties include filet mignon. New Zealand lobster tail, Alaskan king crab, and fresh catch of the day. Also cocktails. Breakfast and dinner daily. Reservations suggested.

Ping How. *Moderate.* At the Hawaii Naniloa Hotel, 93 Banyan Dr., Hilo; (808) 969-3333/935-8888. Oceanfront setting. Offers a good selection of traditional Chinese dishes. Cocktails. Open for dinner. Reservations recommended.

Uncle Billy's Hilo Bay Restaurant. *Moderate.* At Uncle Billy's Hilo Bay Hotel, 87 Banyan Dr., Hilo; (808) 961-5818/(800) 367-5102/*www.unclebilly.com*. Open-air setting; Polynesian decor. Serves primarily Continental cuisine, including steak and seafood. Hula show and Hawaiian music and entertainment nightly; cocktails. Open for breakfast and dinner.

HAMAKUA COAST | 4

Honoka'a | Waipio Valley

The Hamakua Coast is one of the loveliest parts of the Big Island, largely unspoiled and remarkably picturesque, with lush mountains to its west and verdant valleys and the open ocean to the east. It lies largely to the north of Hilo, stretching northwestward some 48 miles to the Waipio Valley. It comprises, for the most part, the northeastern coastline of the island, taking in not only the coastal section of the Hamakua district, but also parts of the North Hilo and South Hilo districts which lie adjacent to one another, to the north of Hilo. The best way to access it is on Highway 19 north and northwestward from Hilo to Honoka'a, then Highway 240 directly north to the Waipio Valley, which marks the northern end of the Hamakua Coast. Alternatively, when journeying from the west, from Kailua-Kona and the Mauna Kea area, head east on Saddle Road (Highway 220) and Kaumana Avenue, then north on Highways 19 and 240.

HAMAKUA COAST | Exploring the Coast

North from Hilo

*Akaka Falls State Park,
Kolekole Beach,
Waipio Art Center*

 8 *See Map 8
on Page 69*

The first place of interest, heading out from Hilo on Highway 19
1 north, is **Honoli'i Beach Park**, which lies just outside Hilo, about
2 miles, and can be accessed on Kahoa Street which goes off the
highway (19), a quarter mile, to the beach. Honoli'i is one of the
most popular surfing spots in the vicinity of Hilo, and at the north
end of the beach, there is also a large pond that is ideally suited to
swimming. Beach facilities here include showers and restrooms.

2 North from Honoli'i Beach, 3 miles or so, **Pepe'ekeo Scenic
Drive** heads off *makai* (toward the ocean) from the highway (19),
and journeys some 4 miles along a scenic coastal route, past lush,
tropical vegetation and over a series of one-lane bridges, before
re-emerging on the highway. On Pepe'ekeo Drive, too, at Onomea
3 Bay, you can visit the **Hawaii Tropical Botanical Garden**, a 25-acre
garden where more than 1,800 species of plants indigenous to a
rainforest are on display. The botanical garden first opened to the
public in 1984, and is now visited by an estimated 30,000 people
every year.

Northward another 3 miles, Highway 220 branches off Highway
19 and heads westward through sugarcane fields and the small,
19th-century plantation town of Honomu, to lead to the **Akaka
Falls State Park**, situated at an elevation of 1,200 feet and encompassing some 66 acres. The park's principal attractions are its two
4 picturesque waterfalls: the **Kahuna Falls**, cascading some 100 feet,
and the higher, 420-foot Akaka Falls, for which the park is named.
There is also a worthwhile loop trail that winds through the park,
passing by lush vegetation, including bushes of philodendrons and
torch ginger, and groves of bamboo. The park has picnic tables and
restroom facilities.

North still on Highway 19, a half mile or so from the Highway
220 (or Akaka Falls) turnoff, just past mile marker 14, a small access
5 road dashes off the highway (19) to lead to **Kolekole Beach Park**.
The beach is situated near the mouth of Kolekole Stream, which is
fed by the Akaka Falls farther inland. There is also a small waterfall
near the beach, on Kolekole Stream, and a safe, natural pool for
swimming, located just inland from the bridge that crosses overhead, adjacent to the waterfall. Additionally, there are pavilions,
picnic tables, showers and restrooms at the beach, and also some
camping possibilities; swimming, however, is not recommended in
the open ocean here due to the adverse conditions.

Another six miles farther on Highway 19, a half mile north of
mile marker 20, stands the small, quaint, turn-of-the-century **Po-
6 hakupuka Congregational Church**, painted white, and with a brown
roof; and 7 miles or so beyond the church, just north of mile marker
27, a small road dashes off the highway (19) toward the ocean, ap-

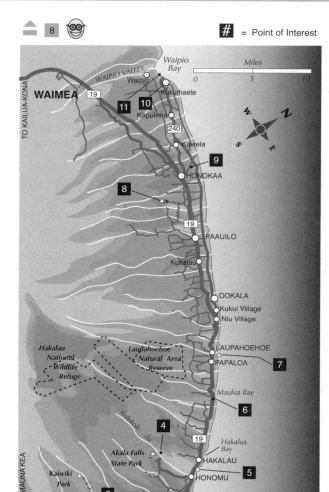

= Point of Interest

8

TO KAILUA-KONA

WAIMEA

19

WAIPIO VALLEY
Waipio

Waipio Valley

Waipio
Bay

Miles
0   5   10

N W E S

11

10

Kukuihaele

Kapulena

240

Kawela

9

HONOKAA

8

19

PAAUILO

Kukalau

OOKALA
Kukui Village
Niu Village

Hakalau
National
Wildlife
Refuge

Laupahoehoe
Natural Area
Reserve

LAUPAHOEHOE
PAPALOA   7

Maulua Bay

6

Kolekole Str.

4

19

Hakalau
Bay

Akaka Falls
State Park

HAKALAU

5

HONOMU

Kaiwiki
Park

2

Pepeekeo
Kawainui

Pepeekeo Pt.
Pepeekeo Mill

PAPAIKOU   3

Pueopaku

Kaiwiki

Onomea Bay

200

Paukaa

19

WAINAKU   1

HILO

Hilo Bay

HAMAKUA COAST

1. Honolii Beach Park
2. Pepeekeo Scenic Drive
3. Hawaii Tropical Botanical Garden
4. Kahuna Falls
5. Kolekole Beach Park
6. Pohakupuka Church
7. Laupahoehoe Beach Park
8. Kalopa State Park
9. Waipio Valley Art Center
10. Waipio Valley Overlook

7 proximately a mile, to Laupahoehoe Point and **Laupahoehoe Beach Park**. Laupahoehoe, which in Hawaiian means "smooth lava rock," is in fact situated on a flat sort of peninsula that was created by a lava flow from Mauna Kea. The beach itself is lined with ironwood and palm trees, and offers some picnicking possibilities as well as restroom facilities. It also offers good views, looking southward, of the Hamakua coastline. Interestingly, Laupahoehoe was once the site of a thriving little village, with several homes and a school; until on April I, 1946, a *tsunami* (tidal wave) destroyed the village, killing 32 people, including several children who, at the time, were in attendance at the Laupahoehoe School. There is now a memorial at the south end of the peninsula, dedicated to those who lost their lives in the *tsunami*.

8 Next up, some 13 miles farther, **is** the **Kalopa State Park**, reached more or less directly on Highway 19 north, a half mile or so past mile marker 39, then Kalopa Road *mauka* (inland) from the highway to Kalanai Road, which eventually, another 2¼ miles farther, leads to the park. Kalopa State Park is situated at an elevation of approximately 2,000 feet, and takes in some 100 acres of pristine, lush Hawaiian rainforest. There are several self-guided nature trails, of varying lengths and descriptions, meandering through the park, including the three-quarter-mile Native Forest Nature Trail, one of the most popular trails here, which sets out from a point just to the north of the cabins located near the park's parking area, and loops through the park. Trail guides-cum-maps are available at the trailheads for most of the trails here.

▶ Farther still, another three and one-half miles, at the intersection of Highways 19 and 240 (which goes northwestward off Highway 19 along the coast) lies **Honoka'a**, a small sugar plantation town with a population of around 2,000, which until 1993 was home to the Hamakua Sugar Mill, the sole employer of generations of Honoka'a residents.

From Honoka'a, it is another approximately 9 miles northwestward on Highway 240 and a small, side road that dashes *makai* (seaward) off the highway, to Kukuihaele, a small village with one or two shops, which is a good base from which to explore the nearby Waipio Valley, lying a mile or so farther along. At Kukui-
9 haele also, you can visit the **Waipio Valley Art Center**, which has on display wood-carvings, paintings and hand-crafted jewelry. The center also houses the offices of the Waipio Valley Shuttle, which offers guided tours of the Waipio Valley, as well as a shuttle to and from the valley.

Waipio Valley | *Waipio Valley Overlook, Hi'ilawe Falls, Kaluahine Falls, Waipio Beach, Waimanu Valley*

Waipio Valley is the gem of the Hamakua Coast, situated at the north end of the coastal stretch, some 48 miles from Hilo. But before Waipio Valley, directly above the valley at the end of Highway 240, approximately 9½ miles northwest of the Highway 19 intersection, or a quarter mile from Kukuihaele, is the **Waipio Valley** **10** **Overlook**. The vista point offers views of not only the Waipio Valley, but also of the switchback trail that leads to nearby Waimanu Valley, which lies to the northwest of Waipio Valley, and is visible as a giant "Z" on the north valley wall of Waipio Valley.

From the Waipio Valley Overlook, it is another three-quarter mile or so to Waipio Valley, journeying along a steep, narrow road with a 27% grade, passable only on foot or in a four-wheel-drive vehicle. Waipio Valley is one of the most famous and most beautiful valleys in Hawaii, a mile wide and 3 miles deep (receded inland from the ocean), surrounded by steep cliffs overlooking the ocean. At the southern end of the Waipio cliffs are the **Hi'ilawe Falls**, the highest waterfalls in Hawaii, cascading some 1,200 feet. Another waterfall here is the 620-foot **Kaluahine Falls**, located on the east side of the valley, along the cliffs directly beneath the Waipio Valley Lookout, and best viewed from Waipio Beach, near the mouth of the Waipio Stream. **Waipio Beach**, by the way, is notable as the longest black-sand beach in Hawaii, nearly a mile long, backed by ironwood trees. The beach is quite popular with fishermen and some dedicated surfers. Swimming is not recommended here due to the unsafe ocean conditions. There are also no facilities at the beach.

The Waipio Valley, interestingly, was once also known as the "Valley of the Kings," where in the early days the island's *ali'i* (chiefs) would retreat to, before or after a battle, and from where also, during the 1500s, the Big Island's King Umialiloa ruled the island. The valley, in fact, once supported a population of around 20,000, and boasted one of the largest *taro* acreages on the island. But by the early 1800s the valley's population dwindled to roughly 1,300, and in 1946, a *tsunami* (tidal wave) further devastated the valley. The valley now has fewer than 50 permanent residents.

Well worth visiting, too, northwest of the Waipio Valley, is **Waimanu Valley**, reached by way of a somewhat strenuous, 9-mile trail that sets out from the north end of the Waipio Valley, a hundred yards or so directly inland from Waipio Beach. The trail climbs approximately 1,200 feet, out of the Waipio Valley and to the top of the ridge, then threads through 14 gulches, before finally descending into the Waimanu Valley. The Waimanu Valley is of course considerably smaller than Waipio Valley, but in a similar setting.

From the Waipio Valley—or Waimanu Valley, if you have

ventured that far—we suggest you return to Kukuihaele, and then Honoka'a, from where you can proceed westward to Waimea (12 miles), or return on Highway 19 south to Hilo.

Accommodations | Waipio and Kukuihaele

The Cliff House. *$195*. P.O. Box 5045, Kukuihaele, HI 96727; (808) 775-0005/(800) 492-4746/*www.cliffhousehawaii.com*. Two-bedroom old Hawaiian house in spectacular, oceanfront setting atop a cliff, surrounded by 40 acres of pasture land. TV, VCR, phones, full kitchen. Fresh fruit and Kona coffee beans.

Mountain Meadow Ranch Bed & Breakfast. *$95-$135*. P.O. Box 1697, Honoka'a, HI 96723; (808) 775-9376/*www.mountain-meadowranch.com*. Ranch home situated at 2,200-foot elevation, surrounded by pasture land. Offers two guest rooms with TV, VCR and DVD. Also 2-bedroom cottage available. Pastoral views from rooms and cottage; also some ocean views. Continental breakfast. Daily maid service.

Waianuhea. *$195-$400*. P.O. Box 185, 45-3505 Kahana Dr., Honoka'a, HI 96727; (808) 775-1118/(888) 775-2577/*www.waianuhea.com*. Bed and breakfast with 5 individually-decorated rooms with private baths. Ocean and garden views. TV, phones, daily maid service. Gourmet breakfast, evening wine. Also great room on premises.

Waipio Wayside Bed & Breakfast Inn. *$99-$180*. P.O. Box 240, Honoka'a, HI 96727; (808) 775-0275/(800) 833-8849/*www.waipiowayside.com*. Restored plantation home, originally built in 1938. Tropical setting; old Hawaiian decor. Offers 5 guest rooms with private baths; TV. Continental Breakfast with organically-grown tropical fruit. Maid service upon request. Handicapped facilities.

PUNA | 5

The Puna district adjoins to the south of Hilo, sweeping southward to Kaimu and Kalapana, and southwestward to the Hawaii Volcanoes National Park—which has in it the presently-active Kilauea and Mauna Loa volcanoes. Puna is a largely flat area, encompassing some 300 square miles, characteristic in its lava flows and black-sand beaches. It is also, in many ways, wild and lawless, and intensely Hawaiian, one of the few places in the islands where Hawaiian is still widely spoken and Hawaiian lore is still a part of daily life.

Pahoa to Kaimu | Lava Trees, Isaac Hale Beach, Kehena Beach | 1 | See Map 1 on Page 14

Puna's principal towns are Kea'au and Pahoa, situated some 7 and 17 miles south of Hilo, respectively, on Highways 11 and 130 (which goes off Highway 11 at Kea'au). The first of these, Kea'au, is a small town, situated at the intersection of Highways 11 and 130, and the first place reached in Puna when journeying from Hilo. It is also, in some ways, the gateway to the Puna district, but with very little to interest the visitor.

At **Pahoa**, 10 miles or so farther south on Highway 130, there are a handful of places of interest in and around town, and a colorful little main street that is reminiscent of the Old West, with wood-frame buildings with western facades and a boardwalk. Pahoa dates from 1909, originally established as a lumber town by the Pahoa Lumber Company which logged the surrounding *ohia* forests to produce railroad ties—nearly 2.5 million ties!—for the Santa Fe Railroad on the mainland. At the time, the town also boasted one of the largest sawmills in the country. But beginning in 1918, lumber gave way to sugar as the area's primary industry, until in 1947, when a *tsunami* devastated nearby Hilo, including destroying the railroad tracks that linked Pahoa to Hilo, thus severing the main artery between the two centers and disrupting the transportation of sugar from the Puna district. Pahoa is now populated with gift shops and eateries, and it also has the island's oldest theater, the Akebono Theater, originally built in 1910.

A little way from Pahoa, 2 miles or so southeastward on Highway 132, which goes off Highway 130 at Pahoa, lies the **Lava Trees State Monument**, a 40-acre park filled with lava tree molds (vertical columns of black lava, rising in the place of trees). Interestingly, this area was once an *ohia* forest, which in 1790, during a volcanic eruption, was engulfed by lava—smooth lava, or *pahoehoe*—and as the lava progressed through the forest and came into contact with the trees, it hardened—due to the moisture and cooler temperature of the trees—into the vertical columns and shapes seen here now, known as the "lava trees." There is a short, ¾-mile loop trail that journeys through the park, and also shelters and restroom facilities.

Eastward still, another 4½ miles on Highway 132, you can search out the site of **Kapoho**, once a small town with more than 70 houses, a general store and a school, but which was buried in 1960 in a lava flow from Kilauea's east rift zone, when lava fountains reached heights of 1,500 feet.

Another two miles or so from the Kapoho site, and we are at **Cape Kumukahi**, the easternmost point on the island and, consequently, in the state of Hawaii. At Cape Kumukahi, which in Hawaiian means "first beginning," there is a lighthouse that, during a 1960 lava flow, was miraculously saved from destruction as the river of lava split into two just before reaching it, thus flowing around it as it entered the sea. Of course, according to popular belief, it was Pele, the goddess of fire, who, having appeared at the lighthouse on the eve of the eruption in the guise of an old woman, and having been showered with kindness and given food by the lighthouse keeper, mercifully spared the lighthouse.

At any rate, south of Cape Kumukahi, approximately 5 miles, lies **Isaac Hale Beach Park**, situated along the eastern end of Pohoiki Bay. It can be reached by way of Highway 132 west from the cape to the intersection of Highway 137, then 137 more or less directly south to the beach park; or, when journeying from the Lava Tree State Monument, follow Pohoiki Road southeastward 4½ miles, directly to the park. Isaac Hale is a well-liked beach park, comprising roughly 2 acres, and bordered by palm trees and lined with boulders. There is also a boat ramp here, and just inland from the beach, is a small, volcanically-warmed fresh-water pool, approximately 16 feet long, 8 feet wide and about 4 feet deep, believed to have been dug out by Pele, the goddess of fire. The beach, while popular with fishermen and surfers, also offers good swimming and snorkeling possibilities in calm weather. The beach has portable toilets.

From Isaac Hale Beach Park, it is another 2 miles southwest-ward on Highway 137 to the **MacKenzie State Recreation Area**, a 13-acre park, located on the *makai* (ocean) side of the highway. The recreation area is situated along low sea cliffs, nestled amid ironwood trees that were originally planted in the early 1900s by forest ranger A.J. MacKenzie, for whom the park is named. And for lovers of the supernatural the park is also known as a place of "night marches," for the nightly procession of Hawaiian spirits. The state park, in any case, is primarily frequented by picnickers and fishermen, as swimming is inadvisable due to the dangerous ocean conditions here. Park facilities include picnic tables, pavilions, and restrooms.

Southwestward still, approximately 5 miles on Highway 137—a few hundred feet west of mile marker 19—lies yet another beach, **Kehena Beach**. Kehena Beach is a long, narrow black-sand beach, bordered by palm and ironwood trees, which was originally formed by lava flows in 1955, and which dropped nearly three feet during an earthquake in 1979. The beach is quite popular with nudists.

Finally, 3 miles farther on Highway 137 is Kaimu, followed, an-other mile from there, by Kalapana. Sadly, though, the Kaimu-Kala-pana area, which was once fairly populated, was almost completely destroyed by lava from the Kilauea eruption in 1990. **Kaimu Beach**, too, which is one of the island's most popular and most photo-graphed black-sand beaches, was overrun by lava. Nevertheless, there is still a church here, the **Star of the Sea "Painted" Church**, which was moved by the residents of Kalapana just before the lava reached it, and later relocated at its present location, along Highway 130, at mile marker 20, a mile or so inland from Kaimu—or 8½ miles south of Pahoa. The church dates from 1929, and features stained-glass windows and murals of religious scenes on its interior walls.

HAWAII VOLCANOES NATIONAL PARK | 6

The Hawaii Volcanoes National Park is a 207,643-acre preserve that has in it the Mauna Loa and Kilauea volcanoes, Hawaii's only active volcanoes, with the latter boasting the longest, continuous eruptions (along its east rift zone) in Hawaii's documented history, averaging approximately 300,000 cubic feet of lava per day, covering more than 30 square miles and adding over 350 acres of land mass to the island. The park itself lies largely between the Puna and Kau districts, extending south to the ocean, with the snow-capped Mauna Kea looming farther to the north of it. It can be reached by way of Highway 11 from Hilo, approximately 59 miles southwestward, passing through the Puna district; or, when journeying from the west, some 36 miles from Na'alehu, or 96 miles from Kailua-Kona, also on Highway 11.

Kilauea and Crater Rim Road | *See Map 9 on Page 76*

The best of all places to begin your tour of the Hawaii Volcanoes National Park, we might suggest, is the **Kilauea Visitor Center**, located near the park entrance, along Crater Rim Road, which goes off Highway 11 and circles the Kilauea Caldera. Here you can obtain both information on eruption sites, hiking trails and campsites, as well as permits for hiking and camping in the park. The center also has a natural history museum, and features films on volcanic eruptions and educational lectures given by park rangers.

Adjacent to the Kilauea Visitor Center, and also of interest, is the **Volcano Art Center**, housed in the original **Volcano House** that was built in 1877 and relocated here in 1941. During the 19th century, the Volcano House hosted several well-known novelists, scientists, adventurers, and even heads of state, including Mark Twain, Theodore Roosevelt and Queen Lili'uokalani, the last Hawaiian monarch, among others. The art center was established in 1974, to support and promote Hawaii's visual and performing arts; it now houses the works of nearly 300 local artists, photographers and

HAWAII VOLCANOES NATIONAL PARK

= Point of Interest

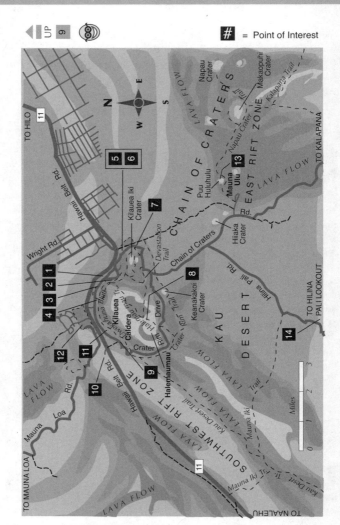

HAWAII VOLCANOES NATIONAL PARK

1. Visitor Center and Museum
2. Volcano House
3. Sulphur Banks
4. Steaming Bluff
5. Kilauea Iki Overlook
6. Thurston Lava Tube
7. Ohia Forest
8. Lookout
9. Jaggar Museum and Observatory
10. Namakani Paio Campground
11. Kilauea Overlook
12. Volcano Golf Course
13. Lookout
14. Kipuka Nene Campground

crafts people, and features workshops for painting, pottery, and music.

Here, too, across the street from the Volcano Art Center, is the present-day **Volcano House**, a lovely, rustic, 42-room lodge, situated on the rim of the Kilauea Caldera, at an elevation of roughly 4,200 feet, dating from 1941. The lodge, in addition to offering overnight accommodations and superb, unobstructed views of the Kilauea crater, also houses the well-regarded Ka Ohelo Dining Room, and an old, stone fireplace where the fire has burned continuously since 1866—a carry-over from the old Volcano House.

Directly below the Kilauea Visitor Center and the Volcano House and Art Center, is the **Kilauea Caldera**, ringed by the 11-mile-long Crater Rim Road, which offers excellent views to motorist-sightseers. The "caldera," which is a natural, crater-like formation that results from the collapse of the summit of a volcano when the magma drains out from below, is approximately 2 miles wide and 2½ miles long, and encompasses some 2,600 acres. Kilauea itself, which rises an estimated 20,000 feet from the ocean floor, is the youngest volcano in Hawaii. It is also, equally importantly, the most active volcano in the world, and one of only two active volcanoes in Hawaii. It has been erupting continuously along its south and east rift zones, since early 1983, averaging roughly 300,000 cubic meters of lava per day.

Kilauea's primary vent is the **Halemaumau Crater**, a collapsed crater located within the larger Kilauea Caldera, near its southern end. The crater is approximately 3,000 feet wide and 1,300 feet deep, which for more than a century—between 1823 and 1924—was a lava lake with a constant current of liquid lava, some 50 feet deep. However, on May 11,1924, a spectacular eruption blasted rocks out of the crater, sending rivers of lava down the southwest rift zone of Kilauea, and signaled an end to the lava lake. The lava lake has reappeared several times since, most recently in 1967 during an eruption. Halemaumau also, we are told, is the home of Pele, the Hawaiian goddess of fire, who, according to local legend, searched far and wide for a suitable home in the Hawaiian islands—on Ni'ihau, Kauai, Oahu and Maui—finally settling here, on the Big Island of Hawaii.

For the more adventurous, there are also a handful of **hiking trails** here, among them the 11.6-mile Crater Rim Trail which journeys along the rim of the Kilauea Caldera, alongside the Crater Rim Road, beginning and ending at the Kilauea Visitor Center; the Halemaumau Trail, which begins just to the northwest of Volcano House, then descends into the caldera, cutting across the floor of the caldera, to the Halemaumau Overlook, some 3.2 miles distant; and the Byron Ledge Trail, which actually begins at a point roughly a half-mile northeast of the Halemaumau Overlook, and offers in it an alternate return route from the overlook to the visitor center and

HAWAII VOLCANOES NATIONAL PARK

Volcano House, journeying 2.7 miles.

Of interest, too, just to the west of the visitor center, located on the north side of Crater Rim Road, are the **Sulphur Banks**, where you can see, amid yellow and orange mounds of dirt and rocks, gases—hundreds of tons of sulphur gases from Kilauea—rising from the hot magma below, amid water vapors, and escaping through the cracks in the earth. A trail leads approximately a third of a mile from the Kilauea Visitor Center to the steaming banks.

Also, a half mile or so west of the Sulphur Banks, located along a bluff on the south side of Crater Rim Road, is a series of **steam vents**—essentially cracks in the ground, where rainwater is trapped and heated by embedded rocks that, in turn, are heated by the magma below, thus releasing steam. A short, 150-yard walk leads from the vents to the "Steaming Bluff" along the rim of the crater, from where you can also enjoy good, all-round views of the Kilauea Caldera, Halemaumau, and the Volcano House. Another worthwhile trail that leads to the "**Steaming Bluff**" is the old Sandalwood Trail, which begins on the west side of the Volcano House and journeys approximately three quarters of a mile to the bluff.

Just west of the steam vents on Crater Rim Road, a little less than a mile to the west of the Sulphur Banks, is the **Kilauea Military Camp**, a 67-acre rest and recreation center for the armed forces personnel; and west of there, another one and one-half miles, situated along the Uwekahuna Bluff, off Crater Rim Road, is the **Hawaiian Volcano Observatory**, established in 1912 to observe and investigate seismic and volcanic activity, and to notify the park service and civil defense agencies of any impending dangers. The observatory is staffed by members of the U.S. Geological Survey, including seismologists, geochemists and geophysicists. Both the observatory and military camp, however, are closed to the public.

Adjacent to the Hawaii Volcano Observatory is the **Thomas A. Jaggar Museum**, named for Dr. Thomas Jaggar, a professor of geology at the Massachusetts Institute of Technology, and founder of the Hawaii Volcano Observatory, whose intent was to observe active volcanoes and study earthquake regions, and predict eruptions, in order to save human lives. The museum houses several informative exhibits, centered around the geology of the earth, eruption history, and the present seismic activity in the area. Also on display are examples of the different types of lava found in the park: "a'a," rough lava; "pahoehoe," smooth lava; "Pele's Tears," tiny, smooth volcanic rocks; "Pele's Hair," fine. glass-like volcanic strands; and "cinder," fragments of pumice thrown out in volcanic fountains. The museum also offers excellent, unobstructed views, from its strategic location atop Uwekahuna Bluff, of the Kilauea Caldera.

A little way from the Thomas A. Jaggar Museum and Volcano Observatory, 3 miles or so south and eastward along Crater Rim Road, is the **Halemaumau Overlook**, which has commanding views of the Halemaumau Crater. Also from here, a short walk leads to the rim of the crater for a close-up view; and 2 miles or so farther—eastward—near the intersection of the Crater Rim Road and the Chain of Craters Road, is the trailhead for a hiking trail known as **Devastation Trail**. Devastation Trail heads off down a paved walkway, a little more than a half mile, passing through an *ohia* **forest**, past the Pu'u Puai cinder cone and over a 1959 lava flow, offering at the end a glorious view of the Kilauea Iki Crater.

Another popular trail dashes off from a point approximately one and one-half miles east of the intersection of Crater Rim Road and the Chain of Craters Road, off Crater Rim Road, and leads along a loop, a third of a mile, passing through a lush, fern forest, to the **Thurston Lava Tube**. The lava tube is a 450-foot-long tunnel, nearly 20 feet high in places, formed as a result of the outer part of the lava flow cooling, and the inner portion continuing to flow, eventually draining to create a hollow tube.

Just to the northeast of the Thurston Lava Tube, a half mile, is the **Kilauea Iki Crater**, situated just off Crater Rim Road. Kilauea Iki—meaning "little Kilauea"—is memorable for its 1959 eruption, when a series of lava fountains, including one that reached a height of approximately 1,900 feet, could be seen along a 1,200-foot-long stretch. There is an **overlook** at the crater, with excellent views of it, and a trail, the Kilauea Iki Trail, which begins near the top—north—end of the parking lot at the Thurston Lava Tube, then descends some 400 feet into the crater. The trail is a 4-mile-long loop trail, and quite strenuous, suitable for early morning or late afternoon hikes.

Chain of Craters Road

See Map 9 on Page 76

Southeastward from the Kilauea Caldera and Crater Rim Road, some 3 miles south of the park entrance, the **Chain of Craters Road** sets out, journeying southeastward, past a series of craters, lava flows, and with other points of interest and hiking trails, to eventually lead, some 21 miles farther, to the **current eruption site** where lava is presently flowing into the ocean.

In any case, some 2 miles south from the Crater Rim Road and Chain of Craters Road intersection, Hilina Pali Road goes southwestward off the Chain of Craters Road to the **Hilina Pali Overlook**, which offers sweeping views of the south coast of the island, all the way down to South Point. Along Hilina Pali Road, too, is the **Kipuka Nene Campground**, roughly 5 miles from the Chain of Craters Road, which has some camping and picnicking possibilities, and where you can often see some *nene*, Hawaii's native birds. There is also a trail here, the Halape Trail, which heads out from the campground, offering a somewhat difficult, 7.2-mile hike over dry, arid terrain, eventually descending some 3,000 feet to the ocean.

▶ Another worthwhile trail is the **Napau Trail**, which can be accessed from a short spur road that goes off the Chain of Craters Road, approximately 4½ miles south of the Crater Rim Road intersection. The Napau Trail is a strenuous, 7-mile hike that leads to the Napau Crater, passing by, a mile or so from the trailhead, an
▶ overlook at **Pu'u Huluhulu**—a cinder cone located near the Mauna Ulu volcano, which, in turn, is located along Kilauea's east rift zone. Interestingly, Mauna Ulu, which means "growing mountain," erupted from 1969 to 1974, covering an extensive area here, all the way down to the ocean, with fresh lava flows.

Also along the Chain of Craters Road, some 10 miles south of
▶ Crater Rim Road, at mile marker 10, is **Ke Ala Komo**, a lookout at an elevation of around 2,000 feet, with views of the island's southern coastline. There are some picnic tables and a pavilion at the lookout.

Farther still, just before reaching mile marker 14 on the Chain of Craters Road, there is a turnout at Alanui Kahiko, from where, looking *makai* (toward the ocean), you can see traces of the old Chain of Craters Road. Between 1969 and 1974, lava from Mauna Ulu, the shield volcano along Kilauea's east rift zone, buried nearly 12 miles of this road, at places some 300 feet deep.

Some 2 miles farther, along the Chain of Craters Road, is another
▶ trailhead, from where an easy, 1-mile trail leads to the **Pu'u Loa Petroglyphs**. Here, in a large field of *pahoehoe* (smooth lava), you can see more than 15,000 petroglyphs. Several of the petroglyphs are simply holes in the lava, surrounded by circles; it was once believed, that if the umbilical cord of a newborn was placed in any of these holes and covered with a rock, the entire family would be blessed with long life, power and wealth. There is also a boardwalk here, surrounding a particularly rich concentration of petroglyphs.

Another 2½ miles south of the Pu'u Loa Petroglyphs, along the Chain of Craters Road, is yet another turnout, from where you can see, along the shoreline directly below, a sea arch known as the
▶ **Holei Sea Arch**.

Finally, at mile marker 21, at Lae'apuki, the Chain of Craters
▶ Road ends. **Lae'apuki** is of course the most recent, and current, lava flow site, where lava from an early 1993 flow has completely covered the area. Park rangers are usually on hand to direct visitors to a safe point to view the nearest eruption site.

Of interest, too, offshore from Lae'apuki, 20 miles or so to the
▶ southeast, is the **Loihi Seamount**, an active submarine volcano, and Hawaii's newest island in the making. The Loihi Seamount is approximately 3,000 feet below the ocean surface, with regular eruptions now occurring, and is expected to surface in roughly 2,000 years.

Accommodations | Volcano, Hawaii Volcanoes Park

Lodges

Kilauea Lodge. *$140-$185*. P.O. Box 116, Old Volcano Rd., Volcano Village (at the Hawaii Volcanoes National Park), HI 96785; (808) 967-7366/*www.kilauealodge.com*. Country inn with 12 units, built in 1938; also two cottages, one and two bedrooms. Fireplaces, library, gardens, hot tub. Restaurant on premises. Full breakfast. Handicapped facilities.

Volcano House. *$95-$225*. P.O. Box 53, Crater Rim Dr., Hawaii Volcanoes National Park, HI 96718; (808) 967-7321/*www.volcanohousehotel.com*. Historic, 42-room country lodge, located on the rim of the Kilauea Crater. Features koa wood furniture, and a fireplace where the fire has been burning since 1866. Also restaurant and cocktail lounge, and shop on premises. Daily maid service. Handicapped facilities.

Bed and Breakfast

Carson's Volcano Cottage. $75-$125. P.O. Box 503, Volcano, HI 96785; (808) 967-7683/(800) 845-5282/*www.carsoncottage.com*. Cottage with 3 guest rooms, in secluded, romantic setting, near the Hawaii Volcanoes National Park. Also 4 additional cottages, including 2 with woodstoves and 1 with hot tub. Outdoor Jacuzzi and pavilion, surrounded by tree ferns, adjacent to main house. Full breakfast. Daily maid service.

The Inn at Volcano. $75-$175. P.O. Box 998, Volcano, HI 96785; (808) 967-7786/*www.volcano-hawaii.com*. Located in Volcano Village, near the Kilauea Crater. Offers 3 individually-decorated rooms, a Treehouse Suite, and 3 guest cottages. Gourmet breakfast, served in art deco dining room; also complimentary afternoon tea. Daily maid service.

The Country Goose. $75. P.O. Box 597, Volcano, HI 96785; (808) 967-7759/(800) 238-7101/*www.countrygoose.com*. Located 2 miles from Hawaii Volcanoes National Park. 2 rooms with TV and VCR. Gourmet breakfast. Daily maid service. Handicapped facilities.

My Island Bed & Breakfast. $60-$100. Old Volcano-Wright Rd., Volcano, HI 96785; (808) 967-7216*www.myislandinnhawaii.com*. Historic, former missionary summer home, built in 1886, and situated on Kilauea Volcano, on a spacious, 5-acre garden estate. Offers 5 guest rooms, and also a separate house which sleeps 8. Full breakfast.

HAWAII VOLCANOES NATIONAL PARK

Volcano Cedar Cottage. *$75-$85*. 113799 7th St., Volcano; (808) 985-9020/*www.volcanocc.com*. Offers two cozy rooms with private baths, and a cottage. Also great room on premises.

Volcano Country Cottages. *$95-$120*. P.O. Box 545, Volcano, HI 96785; (808) 967-7960/(888) 446-3910/*www.volcanocottages. com*. Nestled amid 100-year-old cedar trees. Offers two 1-bedroom cottages and a 2-bedroom house. Breakfast features eggs, baked goods, cereal, local fruit, hot cocoa, juice, tea and locally-grown coffee.

Volcano Inn. *$105-$140*. P.O. Box 490, Volcano, HI 96785; (808) 967-7293/*www.volcanoinn.com*. Offers six rooms and a cottage, all with private baths, TV, VCR and refrigerators. Self-serve, island-style, all-you-can-eat breakfast, with pastries and muffins, whole grain bread, granola, fresh fruit, juices, tea, hot cocoa and Kona coffee.

Volcano Lava Lodge. *$65-$165*. P.O. Box 28, Volcano, HI 96785; (808) 967-7591/967-8662/(800) 733-3839/*www.hawaii-vol-cano.net*. 3-acre estate in Volcano Village, with pine and ohia trees. Offers one-bedroom cottages with TV, VCR, kitchen, and private bath with full-size bath tub. Continental breakfast.

Dining | Volcano, Hawaii Volcanoes National Park

[Restaurant prices—based on full course diner, excluding drinks, tax and tips—are categorized as follows: *Deluxe*, over $30; *Expensive*, $20-$30; *Moderate*, $10-$20; *Inexpensive*, under $10.]

Ka Ohelo Dining Room. *Moderate*. At the Volcano House on Crater Rim Rd. (off Hwy. 11), Hawaii Volcanoes National Park; (808) 967-7321/*www.volcanohousehotel.com*. Situated on the rim of Kilauea Caldera, with spectacular views of the caldera. Casual atmosphere; koa wood furniture. Offers a blend of Continental, American and Pacific Rim cuisines. Menu features fresh island fish, chicken, roast prime rib, New York steak, filet mignon, Cornish game hen, and seafood pasta dishes. Cocktails. Open for breakfast, lunch and dinner daily. Reservations suggested.

Kilauea Lodge Restaurant. *Expensive-Deluxe*. Old Volcano Rd., Volcano; (808) 967-7366. Housed in an old mountain lodge built in 1938, with hardwood floors, koa furniture and a stone fireplace. Continental cuisine, featuring fish, fowl and beef. Entrées include Arctic Lobster, Pepper Steak, Lamb Provençal, Antelope Filet, Osso Buco, Eggplant Supreme, meatloaf, prime rib and medallions of venison. Cocktails. Open for dinner. Reservations recommended

KAU | 7

The Kau district lies largely to the south of the Kona District, or west and southwest of the Hawaii Volcanoes National Park, below the southwest rift zone of Mauna Loa, the 13,679-foot volcano. It is one of the most sparsely populated parts of the island, and also the largest district of the island, encompassing some 800 square miles. It comprises, for the most part, barren, desert wasteland and lava flows. It also boasts, at its southern end, the southernmost point in the U.S., as well as the southernmost town in the country. To add to that, Kau has some good beach parks and the only green-sand beach in Hawaii.

South Point | *South Point Overlook, Heiau O Kalalea, Mahana Beach* | 10 | *See Map 10 fon Page 84*

The first place of interest in the Kau district, when journeying south from Kailua-Kona on Highway 11, is the **Manuka State Wayside Park**. It is located some 40 miles south of Kailua-Kona, with its entrance just off the highway, at mile marker 81. The park is really quite splendid, comprising approximately 8 acres, and boasting an arboretum with 48 species of native Hawaiian plants and more than 130 species of other exotic plants and flowers, mostly planted in the 1930s. A short, 2-mile loop trail leads through the arboretum for self-guided tours. Interestingly, Manuka Park itself is part of the larger, 25,550-acre Manuka Natural Area Reserve.

Some 6 miles southeast from Manuka State Wayside Park on the highway (11), at mile marker 75, is the **South Point Overlook**, situated on the 1907 lava flow from Mauna Loa. The overlook offers superb views of the Kau region, including, at the southern tip of the island, South Point.

From the South Point Overlook, it is another 5 miles or so south-eastward to the intersection of South Point Road, which dashes off directly south from the highway (11), some 12 miles, to South Point, passing by, approximately 7 miles before reaching South Point, the **Kamoa Wind Farm**, where you can see 37 Mitsubishi wind and turbine generators, each 60 feet high, generating electricity for the local community.

South Point, which is also known as Ka Lae, meaning, simply, "the point," is the southernmost point in the U.S. It is also notable as the first landing site of the original Polynesians, who arrived in Hawaii between 500 AD and 700 AD, journeying across the open ocean from the South Pacific. At South Point, too, adjacent to a light station, is the **Heiau O Kalalea**, an ancient fishing temple, 60 feet long and 40 feet wide, believed to have been built by Hawaii's

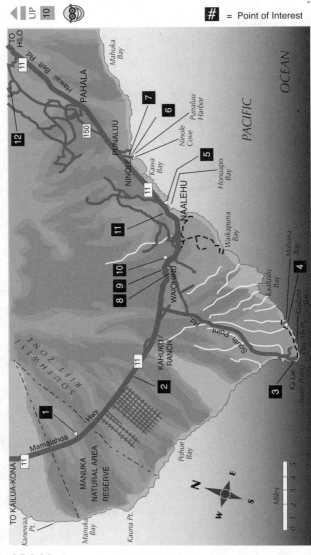

UP 10

= Point of Interest

KAU

1. Manuka State Wayside Park
2. Lookout
3. Ka Lae County Park
4. Mahana Beach (Green Sand Beach)
5. Whittington Beach
6. Punaluu Black Sand Beach
7. SeaMountain Resort
8. Kauahaao Church
9. Mark Twain Monkeypod Tree
10. Waiohinu County Park
11. Lookout
12. Wood Valley Temple

mysterious little people, the *menehune*. Near the *heiau*, you can still see several canoe mooring holes in the boulders, believed to have been dug out by hand by ancient Hawaiians. Also of interest, a quarter mile to the east of the point, is the ancient **Pu'u Ali'i Burial Site**, consisting of a small mound, some 50 feet inland from the shoreline, that was once used as a burial site for Hawaiian royalty.

At any rate, South Point is now frequented mostly by fishermen, who have built here, near the South Point parking area, wooden platforms with pulleys to haul fish up, some 50 feet, from fishing boats below. This is also one of the best places in the islands to gaze upon the ocean, as it is surrounded on three sides by water. During the winter and spring months, you can also see whales frolicking in the water just offshore from here.

Another place of interest in the South Point area is **Mahana Beach**, also known as "Green Sands Beach" for its green sand. It can be reached by following South Point Road north—or directly inland—a mile or so from South Point, then off on a small road that dashes eastward to the coast at Kaulana Bay, where there is also a boat ramp. From Kaulana Bay it is another 2½ miles northeastward along the coast—along a wild sort of trail that is accessible only on foot or in a four-wheel-drive vehicle—to the beach. The beach itself is situated in a cove that was formed by a littoral cone, Pu'u o Mahana, which, in turn, was formed as a result of the molten lava (from the Mauna Loa flow) cooling rapidly and hardening as it entered the ocean. Mahana Beach is the only green-sand beach in Hawaii, with the green sand derived from eroded olivines—small, dark green volcanic crystals—from the cone, Pu'u o Mahana. There are no facilities at the beach, and swimming, too, is not encouraged, except in calm weather, when the ocean conditions are favorable.

Waiohinu, Na'alehu and Punalu'u

From Mahana Beach, let us return to Kaulana Bay and South Point Road, and proceed north on South Point Road to Highway 11, our main route of travel. Eastward on Highway 11, some 5 miles from the South Point Road and Highway 11 intersection, lies Waiohinu, a small, roadside village with one or two shops, a hotel, and a couple of points of visitor interest. Here, just off the highway, on the *makai* (ocean) side, stands the old **Kauaha'ao Church**, built in 1841. Also, 200 yards or so east of the Shirakawa Hotel, on the *mauka* (inland) side of the highway, you can search out the **site of the Mark Twain Monkeypod Tree**, which was originally planted here in 1866 by celebrated humorist Mark Twain, during his visit to the Big Island, but was subsequently uprooted in a storm in the 1950s. A few new shoots can now be seen where the tree once stood.

Eastward from Waiohinu, another 2 miles, and we are at **Na'alehu**, the southernmost town in the United States. Na'alehu, which literally means "volcanic ashes," has a few shops, a movie theater, a school, churches, and a post office, but little else to interest the visitor.

Just to the northeast of Na'alehu, approximately 2 miles—a half mile east of mile marker 62—is a lookout, from where you can see, looking eastward, Honuapo Bay and Whittington Beach. The beaches are located more or less adjacent to one another, a mile or so from the lookout, just south of the little village of Honuapo, and can be reached by way of a small access road off the highway (11). Interestingly, a wharf was built at **Honuapo Bay** in the late 1800s, for the transportation of passengers and cargo, including sugarcane from nearby plantations, but was destroyed some years later, in 1946, by a *tsunami* (tidal wave), with only some ruins of the wharf visible here now. As for the **Whittington Beach Park**, there is no sandy beach here, only a grassy area with picnic tables, restrooms, showers, and limited camping possibilities.

Farther still, 4 miles or so northeastward along the highway (11), approximately 7 miles northeast of Na'alehu, is the **SeaMountain Resort and Golf Course**, situated on the *makai* (ocean) side of the highway, in the Punalu'u-Ninole area. The port town of Punalu'u once stood here, in the late 1800s, at the center of surrounding sugar plantations, only to be displaced in later years by the growing commercial center of Hilo and, finally, to be destroyed by the 1946 *tsunami*.

At Punalu'u, too, three quarters of a mile east of the highway, at mile marker 55, Punalu'u Road dashes off toward the coast, approximately a mile, to the **Punalu'u Black Sand Beach**. This is one of the island's best known black-sand beaches, bordered along its northeastern end by a row of palm trees. The beach offers good swimming and snorkeling possibilities, as well as picnic tables, showers and restrooms. It is also notable as a nesting site for Hawksbill turtles. Additionally, there is a large *heiau* at the beach, the **Kane'ele'ele Heiau**, some 250 feet long and 150 feet wide, reached by way of a short walk northeastward from the beach.

Another point of interest, quite close to Punalu'u Beach, is the **Henry Opukaha'ia Memorial**, located at the Hokuloa Church that stands on a hillside just to the northwest of Punalu'u Beach. The small, open-air church, with its single stone wall and a jutting, steepled roof, was built in 1957 and dedicated to Henry Opukaha'ia, who sailed from Hawaii to New England in 1809, at the age of 17, and became the first Hawaiian to convert to Christianity. In 1818, at the age of 26, as he was preparing to return to the islands, Opukaha'ia died of typhus fever; but he had already kindled a deep curiosity of Hawaii among New England missionaries, and the following year, on October 23, 1819, the first missionaries departed for the islands from the Boston Harbor, on board the brig *Thaddeus*.

Try to also visit nearby **Ninole Cove**, located just to the south of Punalu'u Beach, and reached by way of a small road that heads southwestward, directly across from the SeaMountain Golf Course clubhouse, a quarter mile or so, to the cove. There is a small black-sand beach nestled along the western edge the cove, and a *heiau*, the Ka'ie'ie Heiau, 100 feet square and with several smaller plat-forms inside it, located directly above the cove, at its southwestern end. The beach is frequented primarily by fishermen. There are no facilities at the beach.

Pahala | Wood Valley Temple and Retreat Center

Finally, some 12 miles from Punalu'u, there is Pahala, a small, sugar plantation town, which has little to interest the visitor, save for the **Wood Valley Temple and Retreat Center**. The temple can be reached by way of Kamani Street off the highway (11), *mauka* (inland) to Pikake Street, then right, or northeastward, on the paved cane road, some 4 miles to a "Y" intersection, from where the left fork leads a short distance to the temple. The Wood Valley Temple is a classic Buddhist temple, situated at an elevation of around 2,000 feet, nestled amid eucalyptus trees. It was originally built in the early 1900s by Japanese immigrants working in the nearby sugar plantations, and formally dedicated several years later, in October, 1980, by the Dalai Lama. The temple and retreat center now offer seminars and retreats in the Tibetan tradition.

Beyond Pahala, approximately 24 miles northeastward on High-way 11 lies the Hawaii Volcanoes National Park. Alternatively, you can journey southwest and west on the highway (11) from Pahala, some 35 miles, to return to the Kona district.

Accommodations | Pahala, Na'alehu

Colony I at Sea Mountain. *$145-$180.* P.O. Box 70, Pahala, HI 96777; (808) 928-6200/(800) 444-6633/*www.viresorts.com*. 76-unit resort, situated near the black-sand beach at Punalu'u. Rooms with TV, phones, and kitchen facilities. Also swimming pool, tennis courts, golf course, and restaurant on premises.

Shirakawa Motel. *$45-$65.* Hwy. 11, Na'alehu; (808) 929-7462/ *www.shirakawamotel.com*. 13-unit hotel, located near the Mark Twain monkeypod tree. Some rooms have kitchen facilities. Daily maid service.

Bed and Breakfast

Bougainvillea Bed & Breakfast. *$75-$85*. P.O. Box 6045, Oceanview, HI 96737; (808) 929-7089/(800) 688-1763/*www.hi-inns.com/bouga*. Plantation-style home located on 3 secluded acres near South Point. 4 guest rooms, with TV and VCR, and phones. All rooms have private entrances and private baths. Generous breakfast. Also swimming pool and hot tub. Pavilion.

Macadamia Meadows Farm Bed and Breakfast. *$69-$129*. P.O. Box 756, Na'alehu, HI 96772; (808) 929-8097/(888) 929-8118/*www.macadamiameadows.com*. Five individually-decorated rooms, most with private baths. Cable TV, microwave, refrigerator. Breakfast includes fresh fruit, macadamia nuts and Kona coffee.

SADDLE ROAD | 8

Saddle Road—or Highway 220—traverses the center of the island. It journeys some 53 miles westward from the outskirts of Hilo to intersect with the Hawaii Belt Road (Highway 190), at a point approximately 6 miles south of Waimea, passing between Hawaii's two tallest volcanoes, Mauna Kea and Mauna Loa, with elevations of 13,796 feet and 13,679 feet, respectively. Saddle Road itself reaches an elevation of around 6,500 feet near the base of Mauna Kea, and is remote, narrow in places, and frequently overhung by low clouds and fog, making driving difficult at times, with poor visibility. In fact, rental car companies on the island prohibit the use of their vehicles on Saddle Road.

The Saddle Road Area | **1** See Map 1 on Page 14

If you are journeying from Hilo, follow Kaumana Drive westward, which soon becomes Saddle Road, and some 28 miles later, at mile marker 28, Summit Road heads off north from Saddle Road, another 14½ miles or so, to the summit of Mauna Kea, the chief attraction here. But first, before reaching the summit, approximately 6 miles from the Saddle Road intersection, on Summit Road, is the **Mauna Kea Visitor Center**—which is in fact part of the **Onizuka Center for International Astronomy**—situated at an elevation of around 9,300 feet. At the center, you can see a variety of exhibits and displays centered around the natural history of the cosmos, as well as astronomical facilities. The center also offers informative video presentations, and star-gazing programs on Friday and Saturday nights, viewing through an 11-inch Celestron telescope. On weekends, there are guided tours to the summit, which include a visit to one of the four University of Hawaii telescopes. The center is open on Fridays, Saturdays and Sundays.

From the Mauna Kea visitor center, it is another 8½ miles to the Mauna Kea summit. However, this final ascent is on an unpaved section of road that is also rather steep, quite unsuitable for a conventional vehicle, and a four-wheel-drive vehicle is strongly recommended. The **Mauna Kea summit** is the highest point in Hawaii, with an elevation of 13,796 feet. This is also the tallest volcano in Hawaii—which has been dormant for more than 4,000 years—and when measured from its base some 18,000 feet below the surface of the ocean, it is also the tallest mountain in the world. The name, Mauna Kea, is Hawaiian for "white mountain," derived from its frequently snow-covered peak, where winds can gust at nearly 70 miles per hour, and temperatures can just as easily drop to around 20°F.

On the summit is the **Mauna Kea Observatory Complex**, an international astronomical observatory complex with no fewer than 10 different observatories and 13 of the world's most powerful telescopes located there, trained on the stars and galaxies. In fact, this is one of the best places in the world to view the universe, situated above 40% of the Earth's atmosphere, in a low population density area, thus minimizing surface light and enhancing viewing. The first observatory, that of the University of Hawaii, was established here in 1968, with a 0.6-meter (24-inch) optical telescope. It was followed, in 1979, by the NASA Infrared Telescope Facility, featuring a 3-meter (144-inch) infrared telescope. Since then, other facilities have sprung up here, notable among them the W.M. Keck Observatory, which boasts the world's largest mirrored telescope—a 10-meter (394-inch) telescope, with 36 computer-controlled, mirrored segments, built at a cost of $70 million. The Keck Telescope has viewed a galaxy so distant, that light reaching the Earth left there more than 12 billion years ago!

The Mauna Kea summit and surrounding area are part of the larger, 3,894-acre **Mauna Kea Ice Age Natural Reserve**, which once was covered with snow, with evidence of Pleistocene glaciation, but which now is largely barren, scrub land, made up of lava deserts and cinder cones. Within the reserve are an aeolian desert, an alpine lake—Lake Waiau—several archeological sites, and an adze quarry, Keanakakoi. This last, the adze quarry—or Keanakakoi Crater—is actually located some 5 miles north of the Mauna Kea visitor center, 3½ miles below the summit, on Summit Road, at an elevation of approximately 12,000. Keanakakoi, in Hawaiian, means "adze-making cave," and it was here, in ancient times, that Hawaiians would come, for several months at a time, to make their stone tools.

▶   Closer to the summit is **Lake Waiau**, at an elevation of 13.020 feet, with the distinction of being the highest perennial lake on earth. The lake itself is approximately 300 feet long, 150 feet wide and 8 feet deep, boasting some 1.28 acres of water. Interestingly, according to ancient Hawaiian belief, a new-born baby whose umbilical cord—or *piko*—is thrown into this lake, is blessed with a long life.

▶   Close at hand, too, is **Pu'u Poliahu**, a 13,631-foot, snow-capped peak, believed to be the home of Poliahu, the Hawaiian goddess of snow. The peak is located just below the Mauna Kea summit.

Mauna Kea, we must also point out, offers snow skiing possibilities for dedicated skiers, with three different access points along Summit Road, above the visitor center. However, there are no ski lifts, trams or rope tows here, and the runs must be accessed in a four-wheel-drive vehicle, by driving to the top of these. Alternatively, you can join an organized ski tour to Mauna Kea; for information and reservations, contact Ski Guides Hawaii, at (808) 885-4188.

From Mauna Kea, we suggest you return to Saddle Road (Highway 220) via Summit Road and proceed west, another 7 miles or so
▶ from the Summit Road intersection, to the **Mauna Kea State Park**—or Pohakuloa Area—passing by, a couple of miles before reaching the park, two distinctly different lava flows from Mauna Loa, an *a'a* (rough) lava flow and a *pahoehoe* (smooth) lava flow, and also a young ohia forest, all to the south of Saddle Road. The Mauna Kea State Park itself is situated at an elevation of 6,500 feet, along the slopes of Mauna Kea, and is characteristically populated with pine and eucalyptus trees. The park also offers cabins for overnight accommodations, as well as picnic tables and restroom facilities.

▶   South of Saddle Road, too, looms the 13,679-foot **Mauna Loa** volcano, the second tallest volcano in Hawaii. Mauna Loa is actually a dome-shaped, shield volcano, with the world's largest mountain mass. Mauna Loa, which in Hawaiian means "long mountain," is still active. Its last eruptions occurred in 1942 along its northeast rift zone, when lava flows came within 12 miles of Hilo. So far, the volcano has erupted more than 3.5 billion cubic yards of lava.

Westward on Saddle Road, 1 mile and 2 miles from the Mauna Kea State Park, respectively, are the Pohakuloa Military Camp and Bradshaw Army Air Field; and some 10 miles farther lies Waiki'i Ranch, itself made up of several individual ranch estates, with rolling pasture lands, bordered by pine and eucalyptus trees, and dotted with cattle. From here it is another 6½ miles or so to the intersection of the Hawaii Belt Road (Highway 190), which leads westward to Kailua-Kona (34 miles), and north to Waimea (6 miles).

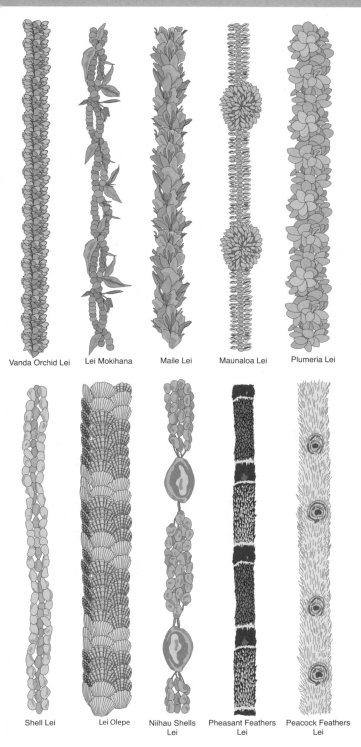

Vanda Orchid Lei

Lei Mokihana

Maile Lei

Maunaloa Lei

Plumeria Lei

Shell Lei

Lei Olepe

Niihau Shells
Lei

Pheasant Feathers
Lei

Peacock Feathers
Lei

HAWAIIAN FLOWERS

Hibiscus

Anthurium

Bird of Paradise

Torch Ginger

White Ginger

Plumeria

Passion Flower

Lobster Claw

Miss Joaquin Orchids

Silversword

HAWAIIAN FLOWERS

HAWAIIAN REEF FISH

Moorish Idol

Hawaiian Squirrelfish

Redlip Parrotfish

Hawaiian Turkeyfish

Achilles Tang

Yellowstripe Goatfish

Fourspot Butterflyfish

Bluestripe Butterflyfish

Lei Triggerfish

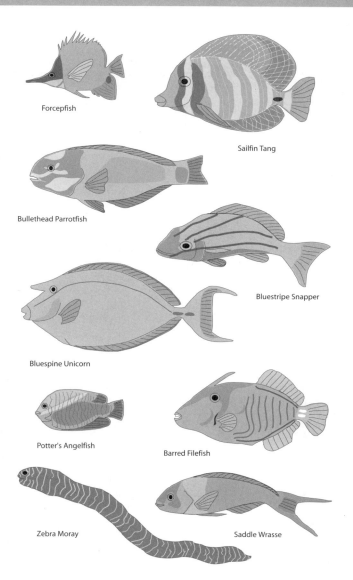

Forcepfish

Sailfin Tang

Bullethead Parrotfish

Bluestripe Snapper

Bluespine Unicorn

Potter's Angelfish

Barred Filefish

Zebra Moray

Saddle Wrasse

HAWAIIAN REEF FISH

HAWAIIAN GAME FISH

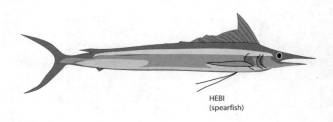

HEBI
(spearfish)

OPAH
(moonfish)

AHI
(yellowfin tuna)

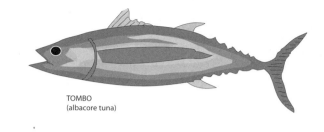

TOMBO
(albacore tuna)

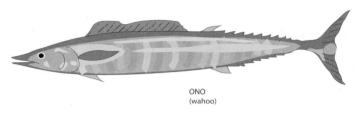

ONO
(wahoo)

MAHI MAHI
(dolphin or dorado)

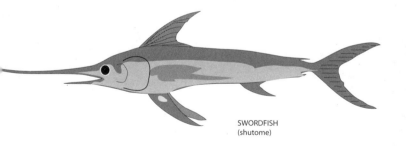

SWORDFISH
(shutome)

THINGS TO SEE AND DO

Places to See | Points of Interest at a Glance

Kailua-Kona | | See Map 2 on Page 17

4   **Ahu'ena Heiau.** Situated on the grounds of King Kamehameha's Kona Beach Resort—or the King Kamehameha Hotel—off Ali'i Dr., near Palani Rd., Kailua-Kona. Ancient heiau (shrine), restored in 1812 by King Kamehameha I. Comprises two main structures: *Hale Mana*, or "House of Spiritual Power," which consists of a thatched hut that in the early 1800s served as both a place of worship and a meeting house; and *Hale Pohaku*, a stone house, once used as a mortuary, and where Kamehameha I's body was prepared for burial upon his death.

6   **Hulihe'e Palace.** 75-5718 Ali'i Dr., Kailua-Kona; (808) 329-1877/329-9555/*www.huliheepalace.org*. Two-storied Victorian-style home, situated on the ocean side of the street, overlooking Kailua Bay. It was originally built in 1838 by Big Island governor John Adams Kuakini, and served as a vacation home for monarchs until 1916. It now houses a museum, with a good collection of Royal Hawaiian koa furniture and other ancient Hawaiian artifacts. Informative tours offered daily, every hour. The museum is open Mon.-Fri. 9am-4pm, Sat.-Sun. 10am-4pm. Admission fee: $6.00 adults, $1.00 children (under 18).

    Kahalu'u Bay. Located at the foot of Keauhou Beach Hotel and Kuemanu Heiau, a mile south of White Sands Beach in Kailua-Kona, and accessed from Ali'i Dr. Features a palm-fringed, gray-sand snorkeling-cum-swimming beach, Kahalu'u Beach, as well as an ancient, 3,900-foot-long breakwater, *Pu O Ka Menehune*, or "menehune breakwater," believed to have been built by Hawaii's legendary little people, the "menehune."

2   **Kailua Pier.** Located off Ali'i Dr., near the corner Palani Rd., at the north end of Kailua-Kona. Old, historic pier, built in 1915 at the site of the first landing of American missionaries in Hawaii, on April 4, 1820. The pier is now a hub of activity, centered around water sports and recreation, from where several chartered sportfishing trips and boat excursions set out. It is now also the site of the annual Hawaiian International Billfish Tournament and the Ironman Triathlon World Championship (which begins and ends here).

    Keauhou Beach Hotel Grounds. 78-6740 Ali'i Dr., Kailua-Kona; (808) 322-3441. There are several points of historical interest on the hotel's grounds, including ancient house sites and heiaus, situated along the southern end of Kahalu'u Bay. Among these are the sites of the historic *Hapaiali'i Heiau* and *Ke'eku Heiau*, the latter formerly a place for human sacrifices. Another, the *Kapuanoni Heiau*, the site of which is located adjacent to the hotel swimming pool, was once a place of worship for ordinary Hawaiians as well as a fishing temple. Also near the hotel pool is the site of the former Big Island governor John Kuakini's summer home, *Halau O Kuakini*; and adjacent to that, the 150-foot-long and 75-foot-wide *King's Pond*, which was once reserved for the recreation of Hawaiian nobility. On the grounds, too, is the historic, New England-style wood-frame *beach house* of King Kalakaua, dating from the late 1800s. The hotel has complimentary maps of its grounds for self-guided tours.

Keauhou Bay. Situated just south of Kahalu'u Bay and Keauhou Beach Hotel, reached by way of Ali'i Dr. Keauhou Bay is notable as the birthplace of Kauikeaouli (Kamehameha III), born to King Kamehameha I and Queen Keopuolani. A bronze plaque near the head of the bay marks the historic site.

Keauhou Holua Slide National Historical Landmark. At the Kona Country Club Golf Course in Kailua-Kona, near He'eia Bay, accessed from Ali'i Dr. The "holua," or sled run, which runs from Kaneaka Hill to He'eia Bay, was built here in the early 1800s, commissioned by Kamehameha I. It was once used by Hawaiian chiefs to race their 12- to 16-foot-long hardwood sleds. The slide is now largely covered by the golf course.

Kuemanu Heiau. Located off Ali'i Dr., a mile south of White Sands Beach Park, in Kailua-Kona. Comprises a large stone platform, approximately 100 feet long and 50 feet wide. The ancient heiau was once used by Hawaiian chiefs to pray for good surf.

Mokuaikaua Church. Located on Ali'i Dr., across from Hulihe'e Palace, in Kailua-Kona; (808) 329-1589/329-0655. Steepled, 112-foot-high church, with the distinction of being the tallest structure in Kailua-Kona. This is also the oldest Christian church in the islands, originally dedicated in 1825 by Queen Ka'ahumanu, and rebuilt in 1837, from coral from the nearby ocean. Now fully restored, it features antique ohia wood beams inside, and koa wood pews and pulpits. Also houses an exhibit room with a scale model of the historic brig *Thaddeus*, which brought the first missionaries to Hawaii. Call the church for visiting hours.

St. Peter's Church. Off Ali'i Dr. (located adjacent to Kuemanu Heiau), a mile south of White Sands Beach, in Kailua-Kona. Picturesque little blue-and-white church, popularly known as "The Little Blue Church by the Sea," overlooking Kahalu'u Bay. The church was originally built in 1880.

South Kona | | See Map 3 on Page 23

Daifukuji Buddhist Temple. Situated on Mamalahoa Hwy. (11) in Honalo, just south of mile marker 114. Large, ornate temple with two altars.

Kealakekua Bay. Situated just off Napo'opo'o Rd. (Hwy. 160), 4½ miles west of Hwy. 11; accessed by way of a small road that goes north a little way, off Hwy. 160. Sweeping, mile-wide bay, encompassing some 315 acres, now preserved as the *Kealakekua Bay Marine Life Conservation District*. The bay is quite popular with scuba divers and snorkelers, offering excellent opportunities for viewing a variety of tropical fish as well as Spinner Dolphins. There is also a beach here, *Napo'opo'o Beach*, with good swimming and snorkeling. Directly above the bay is the historic *Hikiau Heiau*, a 200-foot-long and 100-foot-wide heiau, where in 1779 Captain Cook was revered as the god Lono. Also at the north end of the bay is the *Captain Cook Monument*, a 27-foot obelisk, erected in 1874 at the site of Captain Cook's death on February 14, 1779. The monument is best viewed from the beach.

Kona Historical Society Museum. Located on Hwy. 11, ½ mile south of mile marker 112, or ¼ mile south of Kealakekua; (808) 323-3222/323-2005/*www.hawaiimuseums.org/mc/ishawaii_kona-hist.htm*. Preserved and operated by the Kona Historical Society, the museum is housed in the historic, stone-built *Greenwell Store*, dating from 1875. Displays are of historical artifacts and memorabilia, including old maps and photographs, centered around the history of the Kona district. Museum hours: Mon.-Fri., 9am-3pm. Admission: $2.00 per person.

Mauna Loa Royal Kona Coffee Mill & Museum. 83-5427 Mamalahoa Hwy. (11), Captain Cook (located approximately 2 miles south of downtown Captain Cook); (808) 328-2511/*www.hawaiicoffeeco.com*. Small museum-cum-gift shop. Features artifacts and photographs from the early 1900s, illustrating the coffee growing and coffee picking processes; also short video focusing on coffee picking in the area. Visitors can even sample the famous Kona coffee here. Open daily, 8am-5pm.

Pu'uhonua O Honaunau National Historical Park (City of Refuge). Off Hwy. 160, 3½ miles west of Hwy. 11, in Honaunau: (808) 328-2288/328-2326/*www.nps.gov/puho*. 180-acre preserve, centered around the sacred Pu'uhonua O Honaunau, or "Place of Refuge," where violators of the ancient Hawaiian "kapu" system (a strict social order) once sought refuge. This is one of the best-preserved such relics of ancient Hawaii in the islands, which has in it three heiaus (shrines), several *tikis* (carved, wooden idols), petroglyphs, thatched Hawaiian huts, and the *Great Wall*—a massive lava-rock wall, 1,000 feet long, 17 feet wide and 10 feet high, that encloses a peninsular coastal tract, the "pu'uhonua" compound, originally built in the mid-1500s. The three heiaus here are an *old, unnamed heiau*, the large *Ale'ale'a Heiau*, and the *Hale O Keawe Heiau*, the most sacred of all, which was built around 1650 and which has in it the remains of some 20 Hawaiian chiefs. Swimming, sunbathing and picnicking are discouraged here, due to the sanctity of the site. The park is open daily, 6am-8pm; visitors center is open 8am-5.30pm. Also, orientation talks are given every half hour, 10am-3.30pm. Park entrance fee: $5.00.

St. Benedict's Painted Church. Situated near Honaunau (7 miles south of Captain Cook); reached by way of Hwy. 160 west from the Hwy. 11 intersection a short distance, to a point just past mile marker 1, then north on a small road another ¼ mile to the church. This is one of the oldest Catholic churches on the island, built in 1902 by Belgian priest John Berchman Velghe. The interior of the church features biblical scenes, such as 'The Handwriting on the Wall," "Cain & Abel" and "Hell," all painted by Velghe. There is also a cemetery at the front of the church, with commanding views of the coastline, from the Pu'uhonua O Honaunau National Historic Park to Kealakekua Bay.

Uchida Coffee Farm. Located on Hwy. 11, across from mile south of mile marker 110, or 1½ miles south of Kealakekua; (808) 323-3222/323-2005/*www.hawaiimuseums.org/mc/ishawaii_kona-hist.htm*. Historic, 6-acre Japanese family ranch, now preserved and operated by the Kona Historical Society. Comprises one of the most extensive collections of material centered around coffee farming in Hawaii, with displays centered around the history of the coffee farm and the origins of Kona coffee. The property includes the original farmhouse, a Japanese bathhouse, outbuildings, and coffee-processing mill, most of them dating from the early 1900s. Tours are offered by reservation only. Tour cost: $15.00 per person.

North Kona | | 4   See Map 4 on Page 29

Astronaut Ellison S. Onizuka Space Center. Located at the Keahole Airport, off Queen Ka'ahumanu Hwy. (19), roughly 7 miles north of Kailua-Kona; (808) 329-3441/*www.hawaiimuseums.org/mc/ishawaii_astronaut.htm* or *www.onizukaspacecenter.org*. Features a variety of displays, including a moon rock, and educational films and participatory and audio-visual exhibits centered around NASA'S manned space flight program. Also featured are computer exhibits. The center is named for Hawaii's first astronaut, Ellison S. Onizuka, who was born in Kona and who died in the 1988 Challenger space shuttle disaster. The center is open daily, 8.30am-4.30pm; admission fee: $3.00 adults, $1.00 children (under 18).

Kaloko-Honokohau National Historical Park. Park entrance located off Queen Ka'ahumanu Hwy. (19), ½ mile north of mile marker 97, or 3½ miles north of Kailua-Kona; (808) 329-6881/*www.nps.gov/kaho*. The park is situated along Honokohau Bay and encompasses approximately 1,200 acres, taking in the white-sand *Honokohau Beach* and more than 200 historical sites, including shelters, heiaus, petroglyphs and ancient burial sites. There are also two old fishponds here—the 11-acre *Kaloko Fishpond*, located just to the north of the park's parking lot, and the 20-acre 'Aimakapa *Fishpond*, located a mile south of the Kaloko Fishpond—and the 1.7-acre *'Ai'opio Fish Trap*, located at the north end of Honokohau Harbor (just south of the Kaloko and 'Aimakapa fishponds). Also in the park are the *Queen's Bath*, a 20-foot-wide, spring-fed natural pool, where Queen Ka'ahumanu once bathed, located ¼ mile southeast of the Kaloko Fishpond; and a section of the historic *Mamalahoa Trail* (or "King's Highway"), built between 1822 and 1855, which runs parallel to the coastline, between the Kaloko Fishpond and Honokohau Harbor. The park is open 8.30am-4pm daily.

12 **Kona Village Resort.** Situated 13 miles north of Kailua-Kona; accessed from Queen Ka'ahumanu Hwy. (19) and a side road that goes off the highway, ¼ mile south of mile marker 87, and leads another 2½ miles to the resort; (808) 325-5555/*www.konavillage.com*. Unique, 82-acre beachfront resort, featuring 125 luxury thatched *hales* (huts) representing Tahitian, Hawaiian, Fijian, Marquesan, Samoan and other South Pacific architectural styles, set amid landscaped tropical gardens. The resort was developed in 1965.

Lava Tube. Located on the inland side of Queen Ka'ahumanu Hwy. (19), 250 yards north of mile marker 92, or 7½ miles north of Kailua-Kona. Large lava tube, approximately 50 feet in diameter. The lava tube is easily accessible from the highway.

Scenic Overlook. On the *makai* (ocean) side of Queen Ka'ahumanu Hwy. (19), at mile marker 82. Offers sweeping views of Kiholo Bay.

South Kohala | | 5 | See Map 5 on Page 39

Anchialine Pond Preservation Area. Located in the Waikoloa Beach Resort area, and reached by following Waikoloa Beach Dr. northwest, ½ mile past the Royal Waikoloan, to an unmarked, two-lane paved road that leads approximately 200 yards seaward to a parking lot, from where a well-marked, paved pathway heads off to the shoreline and the ponds. The ponds are essentially brackish-water pools in the lava flow, filled with tiny red shrimp (opae'ula) and clear glass shrimp (opae'huna). The park area has no facilities.

3 **Historical Park.** Situated in the Mauna Lani Beach Resort area, just off Mauna Lani Dr., 1¼ miles west of Queen Ka'ahumanu Hwy. (19). The Historical Park is a 27-acre preserve, which has in it five ancient fishponds—including the 5-acre *Kalahuipua 'a Fishpond*, where mullet and milkfish are still being raised—as well as shelter caves, petroglyphs, burial sites and other archaeological sites. The park also has in it the historic *Keawanui Landing*, once used by Kamehameha I, where a thatched canoe shed and an outrigger canoe can now be seen. There is a well-marked, paved trail here, the *Kalahuipua'a Trail*, that heads out from the park's parking lot and loops through the park, past all the points of interest.

Hokuloa Church. Located on Puako Rd., 1¼ miles west of Queen Ka'ahumanu Hwy. (19), at Puako. Small, white stucco church, built by early-day missionary Reverend Lorenzo Lyons, dedicated in March, 1859.

Petroglyphs. Located near the Waikoloa Beach Resort; reached by way of Waikoloa Beach Dr., ¾ mile from the Waikoloa Resort entrance, to the head of a well-marked, paved pathway (part of the ancient King's Trail) that leads another 1/3 mile northward to the petroglyphs. This is one of the most accessible and largest concentrations of petroglyphs on the island, covering approximately 2 acres of "pahoehoe" (smooth lava) flow, believed to date from the 15th century. There are several thousand petroglyph figures here, depicting mainly humans and animals, with some evidence of the western alphabet as well. There are also several cave and rock shelters and a few ancient house sites located along the trail.

8

Puako Petroglyphs. Located near the Mauna Lani Resort; reached by way of Mauna Lani Dr. west from Queen Ka'ahumanu Hwy. (19), roughly a mile, to North Kaniku Dr., then north another ½ mile on North Kaniku Dr. to the end of the road, where there is a parking lot; from the parking lot, a ¾-mile trail leads directly north to the petroglyphs. There are approximately 3,000 petroglyphs here, carved into a field of "pahoehoe" (smooth lava). These are among the oldest and largest concentrations of petroglyphs on the island.

Pu'ukohola Heiau National Historical Site. Situated just southwest of Kawaihae, with the park entrance located off Hwy. 270, ¼ mile west of the junction of Hwys. 270 and 19. 77-acre park, established in 1972, centered around the historic *Pu'ukohola Heiau*, which is 224 feet long and 100 feet wide, built in 1791 by Kamehameha I, atop Pu'ukohola, or "Hill of the Whale." The heiau (shrine) is important in that it marked the beginning of the ascendancy of Kamehameha, culminating in his conquest of all the Hawaiian islands in 1810. Two other heiaus of note here are the ancient *Mailekini Heiau*, located below—and a little to the west of—the *Pu'ukohola Heiau*; and the *Haleokapuni Heiau*, a 100 feet or so offshore from Pu'ukohola, and now submerged in the ocean.

North Kohala | | See Map 6 on Page 45

Ironwood Avenue. Hwy. 250 (Kohala Mountain Rd.), south of Hawi, between mile markers 14 and 9. Scenic, 5-mile section of highway, lined with ironwood trees, passing through the Kohala district's upcountry pasture lands.

17

Kamehameha Rock. Off Hwy. 270, ½ mile east of mile marker 25 (just east of Kapa'au). Historic rock, 3 feet wide and 1½ feet high, which Kamehameha I is believed to have carried from the

10

nearby beach to its present location in a brash display of his extraordinary strength.

8 **Kamehameha Statue.** Located off Hwy. 270, in Kapa'au (approximately 2 miles east of Hawi), directly in front of the Kapa'au Courthouse. 9-ton bronze statue, cast in 1880 in Florence, Italy. The statue was once lost at sea in the south Atlantic, but recovered a few years later and subsequently transported and erected here in 1884. A duplicate of this statue stands in front of the Judiciary Building on King Street in Honolulu.

6 **King Kamehameha I Birthplace State Memorial.** Located northeast of Hawi, or 1½ miles west of Upolu Point (¼ mile west of Mo'okini Heiau); reached by way of Hwy. 270 to mile marker 20, then 2 miles north on a secondary road to Upolu Point, and 1½ miles west from Upolu Point on a small dirt road to the memorial. This is the birth site of King Kamehameha I (Kamehameha the Great), who was born here around 1755. The birthstones are located at the center of a 240-square-foot compound, enclosed by a 4½-foot-high rock wall. There is an entrance on the south side of the memorial.

3 **Koaie Cove Marine Conservation District.** At Mahukona (13 miles north of Kawaihae, just offshore from Lapakahi State Historical Park), accessed from Hwy. 270 at mile marker 14. 262-acre marine preserve, created in 1979. Features a variety of marine life.

Lapakahi State Historical Park. Located just south of Mahukona (13 miles north of Kawaihae), with the park entrance off Hwy. 270, at mile marker 14. A 265-acre historical park, strung along the Kawaihae Coast, at the site of an ancient fishing village dating from the 1300s. An easy 1½-mile trail loops through the park, with several points of interest along it, including a recreated, old working Hawaiian village, a few ancient house sites, canoe sheds, animal pens, salt pans, and fishing shrines. The park is also a good place to view breaching whales just offshore, during the winter and spring months.

7 **Mo'okini Heiau National Historic Site.** Located northeast of Hawi, 1½ miles west of Upolu Point; reached by way of Hwy. 270 to mile marker 20, then 2 miles north on a secondary road to Upolu Point, and 1½ miles west from Upolu Point on a small dirt road to the heiau. This is one of the most famous heiaus on the Big Island, originally built in 480 AD and rebuilt in the 12th century with boulders taken from Pololu, 12 miles distant. The heiau is 280 feet long, 140 feet wide and 25 feet high. It was designated a national historic site in 1963.

11 **Pololu Valley Lookout.** Located at the end of Hwy. 270, at mile marker 28.93, 8 miles east of Hawi (6 miles east of Kapa'au). The lookout offers spectacular views of the mile long and ½ mile wide Pololu Valley, and, looking south, of the coastline and a series of offshore islets preserved as bird sanctuaries. There is also a 4-mile

HAWAII | Points of Interest

trail that sets out from here, descending into the valley, eventually leading to a black-sand beach at the mouth of the valley; swimming at the beach is not advised due to the adverse ocean conditions.

Scenic Overlook. Off Hwy. 250, at mile marker 8, south of Hawi. Offers views of the Kohala and North Kona coastlines.

Upolu Point. At the north end of the island, northeast of Hawi; reached by way of a secondary road that goes off Hwy. 270 at mile marker 20, some 2 miles directly north. Upolu Point is the northern-most point on the island of Hawaii.

Waimea (Kamuela) | | **6** See Map 6 on Page 45

Imiola Congregational Church. Located on Church Row, off Hwy. 19, ¼ mile east of Waimea. Historic, New England-style wood-frame church, originally built in 1832 by early-day mission-ary Reverend Lorenzo Lyons, and rebuilt in 1857. Features a koa wood interior and a courtyard surrounded by a rock wall where Reverend Lyons is buried.

Kamuela Museum. Located on Hwy. 19, just west of the inter-section of Hwy. 250, in Waimea; (808) 885-4724/*www.hawaii-museums.org/mc/ishawaii_kamuela.htm*. Features an extensive collection of Hawaiian artifacts, amassed over a period of some 65 years. Displays include traditional poi pounders, tapa beaters, ancient war clubs, ceremonial salt pans, and old Hawaiian mooring rocks and fish-hooks. Also on display are several rare exhibits, such as dinosaur bones from the Jurassic era, tables inlaid with abalone, an ivory carving of a Chinese temple, rare Chinese vases, King Kalakaua's ivory domino set, and an original Royal Hawaiian koa table from the Iolani Palace in Honolulu. The museum opened in 1968. Museum hours: 8am-5pm daily; admission fee: $5.00 adults, $2.00 children (under 12).

Parker Ranch Historical Homes. On Hwy. 190, ½ mile west of the junction of Hwys. 190 and 19, Waimea (Kamuela); (808) 885-5433/*www.parkerranch.com/historichomes.html*. Features two historic homes: *Mana Hale* and *Pu'uopelu*. *Mana Hale* is a New England-style home, with original koa wood floors, ceilings and walls, dating from the 1850s. Among the displays here are a family tree and photographs of the Parker family, as well as a scale model of the original residence. The other home, *Pu'uopelu*, situated adjacent to Mana Hale, is an-elegant 8,000-square-foot home with a 55-foot-long and 35-foot-wide living room, featuring 16-foot-high ceilings, originally built in 1862. Pu'uopelu was once the residence of Samuel Parker, founder of the town of Waimea, and then of Richard Smart, owner of Parker Ranch until his death recently. Pu 'uopelu now houses Mr. Smart's personal art collection, including works of impressionists Monet and Renoir, as well as 18th-century

Venetian paintings, rare art objects from the Ming Dynasty, and French and Italian antique furniture pieces. There are also a rose garden and small lake at Pu'uopelu. The homes are open to the public Mon.-Sat. 10am-5pm (last tour departs at 4.00pm). Admission fee: $8.50 adults, $5.50 children.

12 **Parker Ranch Visitor Center.** Located at the Parker Ranch Shopping Center, at the junction of Hwys. 19 and 190, in Waimea (Kamuela); (808) 885-7655/*www.parkerranch.com/visitorcenter.html*. Offers a short video presentation, giving an overview of the history of the Parker Ranch and Waimea. Also has two small museum rooms, one with displays centered around the history of the Parker family, including several artifacts from the Parker Ranch, such as old saddles, tack, and photographs; and the other dedicated to champion Hawaiian surfer and swimmer, Duke Kahanamoku, gold medalist in the 100-meter freestyle at the 1912 Olympics. The center is open daily, 9am-5pm (last tour departs at 4pm). Admission fee: $6.50 adults, $4.50 children.

Hilo | | | *See Map 7*
                                                      fon Page 58

Banyan Drive. On the ocean side of Kamehameha Ave. in Hilo; accessed from either Lihiwai St. or Kanoelehua Ave. (Hwy. 11). Scenic 1-mile drive, lined with over 50 banyan trees, each bearing the name of its planter, among them such well-known figures as Amelia Earhart, Cecil B. DeMille, Richard Nixon, Babe Ruth, King George V and Franklin Delano Roosevelt.

2 **Kalakaua Park.** Situated between Waianuenue Ave. and Kalakaua, Kino'ole and Keawe Sts., in downtown Hilo. Large grassy park, dedicated to King Kalakaua, the "Merrie Monarch," with a statue of the king located in the park. Also in the park are an old, spreading banyan tree, a veterans' memorial, a small reflecting pool, and a sun-dial dating from 1877.

Kaumana Caves. Located off Kaumana Dr.-Saddle Rd. (Hwy. 220), approximately 5 miles west of downtown Hilo. There are two caves here, one roughly 100 feet deep and the other more than 600 feet, both created from lava tubes during the 1881 Mauna Loa lava flow. Stairs lead down into the caves in the darkness, and flashlights are necessary. Picnic tables and restroom facilities on premises.

13 **Liliuokalani Gardens.** Cnr. Banyan Dr. and Lihiwai St., Hilo. Largest Yedo-type gardens outside Japan, encompassing some 30 acres, named for Hawaii's Queen Liliuokalani. The gardens feature pagodas, ornamental stone structures, waterways, and ponds. Also superb views of Hilo Bay and Coconut Island.

5 **Lyman Museum & Mission House.** 276 Haili St., Hilo; (808) 935-5021/*www.lymanmuseum.org*. The Mission House is a New England-style, thatched former home of early-day missionaries Da-

HAWAII | Points of Interest

vid and Sarah Lyman, originally built in 1819. It features ohia wood beams and original ohia and koa wood floors and furniture. Also, adjacent to the Mission House is the Lyman Museum, with displays and exhibits centered around the history and geology of the Big Island. On the ground floor of the museum is the *Island Heritage Gallery*, devoted to the cultural aspect of Hawaii, with a large, ethnic origins map and displays featuring old Hawaiian tools, fish-hooks, bowls, jewelry, leis, and exhibits illustrating the art of producing "tapa" fiber, as well as ancient Hawaiian games. On the upper floor of the museum are the *Earth Heritage Gallery*, with educational exhibits centered around Hawaii's geology, including an extensive collection of labeled minerals and seashells; and the *Chinese Art Gallery*, which showcases Chinese art, including rare treasures from the Ching Dynasty and pottery dating from 2 BC. Open Mon.-Sat. 9.30am-4.30pm; guided tours of the Mission House at 10am, 11am, 1pm, 2pm and 3pm. Admission fee (including guided tour): $10.00 adults, $8.00 seniors, $3.00 children.

Maui's Canoe. Located near the mouth of the Wailuku River in Hilo. The "canoe" is actually a large rock, shaped a little like a canoe. Legend endures that demigod Maui, answering a call for help from his mother who had become trapped in her home under Rainbow Falls—1½ miles upstream—arrived from the island of Maui in his canoe and landed here, at the mouth of the Wailuku River, where his canoe has remained since. The rock is best viewed from the Pu'ueo Street Bridge, looking inland, or upriver.

1

Mauna Loa Macadamia Nut Visitor Center. On Macadamia Rd., which goes off Hwy. 11, 5½ miles south of Hilo; (808) 966-8618/(888) 628-6256/*www.maunaloa.com*. Features a macadamia nut orchard with more than a million macadamia nut trees, as well as a processing plant and visitor center. At the plant, visitors can view the entire process of roasting and packaging the nuts, and even sample the end product. Also at the visitor center, video films on growing, harvesting and processing macadamia nuts are shown. Gift shop and snack bar on premises. Open daily, 8.30am-5.30pm. Free admission.

Naha and Pinao Stones. Located on Waianuenue Ave., in front of the Hawaii Public Library Building in Hilo. Features two ancient stones, one horizontally placed, the other upright. The upright stone, Pinao, is the smaller of the two, approximately 4 feet high and 1½ feet wide, believed to be an entrance pillar from the *Pinao Heiau*. The larger, horizontal stone, *Naha*, is 12 feet long and 1½ feet high, and weighs nearly 3½ tons; it was once claimed that anyone who could move this stone would become king of all Hawaii, and Kamehameha I is believed to have done just that as a boy.

3

Nani Mau Gardens. 421 Makalika St. (off Hwy. 11, just southeast of mile marker 3); (808) 959-3500/*www.nanimau.com*. This is one of the largest gardens of its kind in Hilo, with over 20

18

acres of sculpted floral displays of labeled orchids, anthuriums and gardenias, as well as a macadamia nut orchard. Guided tours of the gardens are offered on board trams. Restaurant at the gardens serves buffet-style lunch. Also gift shop on premises. Open daily, 9am-4.30pm. Admission fee: $10.00 adults, $5.00 children (4-10 years); tram tours (includes admission): $15.00 adults, $8.00 children.

19 **Panaewa Rainforest Zoo.** Located off Mamaki St. (which goes off Hwy. 11, ¼ mile south of mile marker 4), about a mile inland from Hwy. 11; (808) 959-7224/*www.hilozoo.com*. This is the only tropical rainforest zoo in the U.S., which originally opened to the public in 1978. The property comprises roughly 40 acres, with some 12 acres currently used for the zoo. There are over 50 species of animals and birds here, including African pygmy hippopotamuses, monkeys, tigers, and a variety of exotic birds. The area receives more than 125 inches of rain annually. Petting zoo and gift shop on premises. The zoo is open 9am-4pm daily; free admission.

12 **Suisan Fish Auction.** Located near the intersection of Lihiwai St. and Banyan Dr. (adjacent to the Liliuokalani Gardens), in Hilo. This is one of the best known public auctions of fresh fish in Hawaii. Offers an authentic cultural experience for visitors. Every morning the day's catch—including mahi mahi. opah, ahi, hebi, ono, tuna and swordfish—is publicly displayed and auctioned to local restaurants and wholesalers amid a smattering of pidgin English and other local dialects. Auction hours: 7am-9am, Mon.-Sat.; fish market hours: 8am-3.45pm, Mon.-Sat.

Wailuku River State Park. Situated approximately 1½ miles west of Hilo, reached on Waianuenue Ave. 16-acre park, lying along the east-west Wailuku River. At the east end of the park are the *Rainbow Falls*—an 80-foot-high waterfall, plunging into a pool roughly 100 feet wide, named for the rainbows that form here at certain times in the morning—accessed from a parking lot located alongside a small access road that goes off Waianuenue Ave. At the west end of the park are the *Boiling Pots* and *Pe'epe'e Falls*, reached on Waianuenue Ave. and Pe'epe'e Falls St. The rumbling "boiling pots" here are in fact depressions in the streambed, formed as a result of irregular formation of hot lava. There is also a large grassy area here, ideal for picnicking. Restrooms are available at both the Rainbow Falls and Pe'epe'e Falls.

11 **Wailoa River State Park.** Located along the southern edge of Hilo Bay, off Bayfront Hwy. (19). Large, 150-acre grassy park, developed as a tsunami (tidal wave) buffer zone following the Shinmachi Tsunami of May 23, 1960, in which 35-foot-high waves wreaked havoc on Hilo, killing 61 people, destroying 288 structures, and causing nearly $50 million in damage. Also at the park are the 27-acre *Waiakea Pond* and the *Wailoa Center*, the latter serving as both a visitor center and an art center, with information on tsunamis and displays of photographs of Hilo during and after the tsunami devastation, as well as periodic art exhibits. There are also two memorials in the park close to the Wailoa Center: the *Shinmachi Tsunami Memorial* and the *Hawaii County Vietnam Memorial*. The center is open 8am-4.30pm, Mon., Tues., Thurs., Fri.; 12pm-8.30pm Wed.; and 9am-3pm Sat.

Hamakua Coast | | 8   See Map 8 on Page 69

Akaka Falls State Park. Situated at the end of Hwy. 220 (which goes off Hwy. 19, some 10½ miles north of Hilo), 3¾ miles directly inland from the Hwy. 19 intersection. 66-acre park, at 1,200-foot elevation. Features a short, paved loop trail that passes by lush vegetation, including torch ginger and philodendrons and groves of bamboo, and leads to the picturesque, 100-foot *Kahuna Falls* [4] and 420-foot *Akaka Falls*. Park facilities include picnic tables and restrooms.

Hawaii Tropical Botanical Garden. Situated along the Pepe'ekeo [3] Scenic Drive (off Hwy. 19), at Onomea Bay (8½ miles north of Hilo); (808) 964-5233/*www.htbg.com* or *www.hawaiigarden.com*. 40-acre garden with over 2,000 species of plants indigenous to rainforests. The garden was originally established in 1984 and now draws an estimated 30,000 visitors annually. Open daily 9am-4pm. Admission fee: $15.00 adults, $5.00 children (6-16 years).

Kalopa State Park. Situated approximately 37 miles north of [8] Hilo; reached by way of Hwy. 19 north to Kalopa Rd.—which goes off Hwy. 19, a half mile past mile marker 39—then inland on Kalopa Rd. another ¾ mile to Kalanai Rd., which leads, 2¼ miles farther, to the park. The park is situated at an elevation of around 2,000 feet, and takes in some 100 acres of virgin Hawaiian rainforest. There are several self-guided nature trails winding through the park, including the popular, ¾-mile Native Forest Nature Trail which loops through the park. Trail guides-cum-maps are available at the trailheads.

Pepe'ekeo Scenic Drive. Off Hwy. 19, approximately 5 miles north of Hilo. 4-mile scenic drive, featuring lush, tropical foliage, and narrow, single-lane bridges.

Waipio Overlook. Located at the end of Hwy. 240, approxi- [11] mately 9½ miles northwest of Honoka'a and the Hwy. 19 intersection. Offers views of Waipio Valley, as well as the switchback trail that leads to the nearby Waimanu Valley, visible as a giant "Z" on the north valley wall of Waipio Valley.

Waipio Valley. Situated at the north end of Hamakua Coast, approximately 48 miles north of Hilo; reached by way of Hwy. 240—which goes north off Hwy. 19—some 19½ miles to the end (to the Waipio Overlook), then another ¾ mile down a steep, narrow road into the valley. The valley is one of the most famous and most beautiful in Hawaii, 3 miles deep and a mile wide, surrounded by steep cliffs overlooking the ocean. At the southern end of the valley are the 1,200-foot *Hi'ilawe Falls*, the highest waterfalls in Hawaii; and on the east side of the valley, directly beneath the Waipio Valley Lookout, are the 620-foot *Kaluahine Falls*. There is also a mile-long black-sand beach here, the Waipio Beach, the longest black-sand beach in Hawaii. Swimming is not encouraged at the beach due to adverse ocean conditions.

Puna |

Lava Tree State Monument. Situated some 2 miles southeast of Pahoa (which lies 17 miles south of Hilo, at the junction of Hwys. 130 and 132), on Hwy. 132. 40-acre park, filled with lava tree molds (vertical columns of black lava, rising in place of trees). This was once an ohia forest, which in 1790 was engulfed by lava that hardened into the vertical columns and shapes now seen here—the "lava trees." The park offers a short, ¾-mile loop trail, and also some shelters and restroom facilities.

Star of the Sea "Painted" Church. Located on Hwy. 130 at mile marker 20, roughly 8½ miles south of Pahoa (or 1 mile from Kaimu). The church dates from 1929 and features stained glass windows and murals on its interior walls.

Hawaii Volcanoes National Park |

Chain of Craters Road. 21-mile-long southeast-northwest road; goes off Crater Rim Rd., some 3 miles southeast of the park entrance. The Chain of Craters Rd. passes by a series of craters that can easily be viewed from the road, and traverses several lava flows, ending roughly 21 miles to the southeast, at the current eruption site, where lava is presently flowing into the ocean. Sections of this road continue to be devoured by lava, with new sections being paved as the situation allows.

Crater Rim Road. 11-mile drive that goes off Hwy. 11 and circles the Kilauea Caldera, offering several interesting sights and views en route.

Current Lava Flow Site (Lae'apuki). At the end of the Chain of Craters Rd., at mile marker 21 (or 21 miles southeast of the intersection of the Chain of Craters Rd. and Crater Rim Rd.). This is the most recent lava flow site, also known as Lae'apuki, where lava from an early 1993 flow has completely covered the area. Park rangers are usually on hand to direct visitors to a safe point to view the nearest eruption site.

Kilauea Caldera. Situated directly below the Kilauea Visitor

Center and Volcano House, and accessed from Crater Rim Rd. and a series of foot trails. The Kilauea mountain, which rises approximately 20,000 feet from the ocean floor, is the youngest volcano in Hawaii, and also the most active volcano in the world. It has been erupting continuously since early 1983, mainly along its south and east rift zones, averaging roughly 300,000 cubic meters of lava per day, covering some 30 square miles and adding more than 350 acres of new land mass to the island. The Kilauea "caldera"—which is essentially a crater that measures more than a mile in diameter, formed as a result of the collapse of a summit when the magma drains out from below—is 2½ miles long and 2 miles wide, encompassing roughly 2,600 acres. Its primary vent, *Halemaumau Crater*, is located within the caldera, near the southern edge.

Kilauea Visitor Center. Situated at the entrance to the Hawaii Volcanoes National Park, off Crater Rim Rd. which goes off Hwy. 11; (808) 985-6000/*www.nps.gov/havo*. Offers information on eruption sites, hiking trails and campsites, and issues hiking and camping permits. Also features a natural history museum, with films on volcanic eruptions, as well as educational lectures given by park rangers. Open daily, 7.45am-5pm.

Kipuka Puaulu. Off Mauna Loa Rd. (which goes off Hwy. 11), 1½ miles northwest of Hwy. 11. This is a 100-acre forest preserve and bird sanctuary, also known as Bird Park. Features native Hawaiian birds, including elepaio and apapane, as well as other such birds as the house finch, hill robin and Japanese white eyes. The park is also abundant in native Hawaiian plants, and has a 1.2-mile loop trail that leads through forested areas and open meadows and passes by a lava tube and a giant koa tree.

Lava Tree Molds. Located at the end of a short, ½-mile road that goes east off Mauna Loa Rd., just north of the intersection of Mauna Loa Rd. and Hwy. 11. The tree molds are essentially holes in the ground, created as a result of the burning out of tree trunks by lava, leaving behind molds where the trees once stood.

Halemaumau Overlook. Off Crater Rim Rd., approximately 6½ miles from the Kilauea Visitor Center when traveling southward, counter-clockwise, around the Kilauea Caldera. Offers commanding views of the Halemaumau Crater. Also, a short, 0.15-mile walk leads from the lookout to the rim of the crater for a close-up view. The Halemaumau Crater, which is situated near the southern end of the Kilauea Caldera, is nearly 3,000 feet in diameter and 1,300 feet deep; it is also Kilauea's primary vent.

Holei Sea Arch. Located some 18½ miles southeast from the intersection of Crater Rim Rd. and the Chain of Craters Rd. (2½ miles east of the Pu'u Loa Petroglyphs), just offshore. There is a turnout along the Chain of Craters Rd., along the low shoreline cliffs, from where the sea arch can be seen.

Kilauea Iki Crater and Overlook. Situated alongside Crater Rim

Rd., 2 miles northeast of the intersection of the Chain of Craters Rd. Kilauea Iki, which means "little Kilauea," is memorable for its spectacular 1959 eruption, when a series of lava fountains, including one that reached a height of approximately 1,900 feet, could be seen along a 1,200-foot-long stretch. There is an overlook here, with sweeping views of the crater, and a trail, the Kilauea Iki Trail, which begins near the north end of the parking lot at the nearby Thurston Lava Tube, descends some 400 feet into the crater.

Mauna Loa Road. 11-mile-long northwest-southeast road; goes off Hwy. 11, approximately ¼ mile east of mile marker 31 (1½ miles or so east of Volcano House and the Kilauea Visitor Center). The road leads 11 miles northwestward from the highway to end at the *Mauna Loa Lookout* and *Mauna Loa Trailhead*, both situated at an elevation of 6,626 feet, from where a trail dashes off to the 13,679-foot Mauna Loa Summit.

Mauna Loa Road Lookout. Located at the end of Mauna Loa Rd. (which goes off Hwy. 11), some 11 miles northwest of Hwy. 11. Offers superb views of the Hawaii Volcanoes National Park, including the Kilauea Caldera and Volcano Village.

Mauna Ulu. Situated along Kilauea's East Rift Zone; reached by way of Chain of Craters Rd., some 4½ miles south of the intersection of Crater Rim Rd., then off on a short spur road eastward to the Napau Trailhead, from where the 7-mile Napau Trail heads out to the Napau Crater, passing by, a mile from the trailhead, a lookout overlooking the Pu'u Huluhulu cinder cone and the adjacent Mauna Ulu shield volcano. Mauna Ulu, which in Hawaiian, means "growing mountain," erupted continuously between 1969 and 1974, covering much of the area from here down to ocean with lava flows.

Pu'u Loa Petroglyphs. Located approximately 16 miles south of the intersection of Crater Rim Rd. and the Chain of Craters Rd., and reached by way of Chain of Craters Rd. to the Pu'u Loa Petroglyphs Trailhead, from where an easy, 1-mile trail leads directly to the petroglyphs. There are more than 15,000 petroglyphs here, in a large field of pahoehoe (smooth lava). There is also a boardwalk here, surrounding a particularly rich concentration of petroglyphs.

Steam Vents. Located along a bluff on the south side of Crater Rim Rd., ½ mile west of the Sulphur Banks. Comprises a series of steam vents that are essentially cracks in the ground where rainwater is trapped and heated by embedded rocks, which, in turn, are heated by the magma below, thus releasing steam. A short, 150-yard walk leads from the vents to the *Steaming Bluff*, situated along the rim of the crater, which also offers good, all-round views of the Kilauea Crater, Halemaumau and Volcano House.

Sulphur Banks. On the north side of Crater Rim Rd., approximately 1/3 mile west of the Kilauea Visitor Center. Consists of steaming banks, where, amid yellow and orange mounds of dirt and rocks, sulphur gases from Kilauea, containing small amounts of carbon dioxide and hydrogen sulfide, rise with the water vapor and steam released from the hot magma below, and escape through cracks in the earth.

Thomas A. Jaggar Museum. Situated off Crater Rim Rd., on Uwekahuna Bluff, adjacent to the Hawaii Volcano Observatory, some 3¼ miles southwest of Volcano House and the Kilauea Visitor Center; (808) 985-6000/*www.nps.gov/havo* or *www.hvo.wr.usgs. gov*. Features several informative exhibits centered around the geology of the earth, eruption history, and the present seismic activity in the area; displays include samples of different types of lava found in the Hawaii Volcanoes park, such as "a'a," rough lava; "pahoehoe," smooth lava; "Pele's Tears," tiny, smooth, volcanic rocks; "Pele's Hair," tiny, glass-like volcanic strands; "cinder," fragments of pumice thrown out in volcanic fountains; and volcanic bombs. The museum also offers superb, unobstructed views of the Kilauea Caldera. The museum is named for Dr. Thomas A. Jaggar, founder of the Hawaii Volcano Observatory. Museum hours: 8.30am-5pm. Free admission.

Thurston Lava Tube. Located along Crater Rim Rd., 1½ miles east of the intersection of the Chain of Craters Rd. A short, 0.3-mile loop trail sets out from the parking lot situated just off Crater Rim Rd., passing through a lush, fern forest, and leads to the Thurston Lava Tube—a 450-foot-long tunnel, nearly 20 feet high places, formed as a result of the outer part of the lava flow cooling and the inner portion continuing to flow, eventually draining to create a hollow tube.

Volcano Art Center. Located adjacent to the Kilauea Visitor Center, off Crater Rim Rd.; (808) 967-7565/967-8222/*www.volcanoartcenter.org*. Housed in the original Volcano House that was built in 1877 and relocated here in 1941, and which hosted several novelists, scientists, adventurers and even heads of state during the 19th century, including Mark Twain, Theodore Roosevelt, and the last Hawaiian monarch, Queen Lili'uokalani. It now houses an art center, exhibiting works of nearly 300 local artists, photographers and crafts people, and features workshops for painting, pottery and music. Open 9am-5pm daily. No admission fee.

Kau | | *See Map 10 fon Page 84*

Henry Opukaha'ia Memorial. Also near Punalu'u Beach, reached by way of Punalu'u Rd., which goes off Hwy. 11, some 8 miles east of Na'alehu (or 68 miles southeast of Kailua-Kona). The memorial is located at the small, open-air Hokuloa Church, on a hillside just to the northwest of the beach. The church consists of a single stone wall and jutting roof with a steeple, built in 1957 as a memorial to Henry Opukaha'ia, who, in 1809, at the age of 17, became the first Hawaiian to convert to Christianity.

Ka Lae - South Point Park. Located on the southern tip of the island of Hawaii; reached by way of Hwy. 11 some 51 miles south from Kailua-Kona to the intersection of South Point Rd., then another 12 miles directly south on South Point Rd. to Ka Lae. This is the southernmost point in the U.S., where the first Polynesians to arrive in Hawaii landed, between 500 AD and 700 AD. At South Point there is a light station and an ancient fishing temple, *Heiau O Kalalea*, that is 60 feet long and 40 feet wide and is believed to have been built by Hawaii's mysterious little people, the "menehune." Also, ¼ mile east of the point is the ancient *Pu'u Ali'i Burial Site*, once used as a burial site for Hawaiian royalty. South Point also offers unparalleled, all-round views of the open ocean, and some whale-watching opportunities in the winter and spring months.

Kane'ele'ele Heiau. Located at Punalu'u, some 8 miles east of Na'alehu (or 68 miles southeast of Kailua-Kona); accessed by way of Punalu'u Beach, which can be reached on Punalu'u Rd. (which goes off Hwy. 11). From the beach, a short walk northeastward leads to the heiau. The heiau is 250 feet long and 150 feet wide.

1 **Manuka State Wayside Park.** Off Hwy. 11, approximately 40 miles south of Kailua-Kona. 8-acre park, contained within the larger, 25,550-acre Manuka Natural Area Reserve. Features an arboretum with 48 species of native Hawaiian plants and more than 130 species of other exotic plants and flowers, mostly planted in the 1930s. A small, 2-mile loop trail leads through the arboretum for self-guided tours.

12 **Wood Valley Temple and Retreat Center.** P.O. Box 250, Pahala; (808) 928-8539/*www.nechung.org*. The temple and retreat are located at Pahala, some 4½ miles east of Punalu'u (or 72 miles southeast of Kailua-Kona), reached by way of Hwy. 11 to Kamani St. in Pahala, then inland on Kamani St. to Pikake St. (a paved cane road) which heads northeast some 4 miles to a fork in the road, from where the left fork leads another ¼ mile to the temple. The temple is a classic Buddhist temple, situated at an elevation of around 2,000 feet. It was originally built in the early 1900s by Japanese immigrants, and formally dedicated by the Dalai Lama in 1980. The temple offers seminars and retreats in the Tibetan tradition.

Mauna Kea — Saddle Road

Mauna Kea Ice Age Natural Reserve. Situated on Mauna Kea, at the end of Summit Rd. (which goes off Saddle Rd.—Hwy. 220), roughly 8 miles north of the Visitor Center. The reserve comprises some 3,894 acres, and takes in the 13,796-foot *Mauna Kea summit* and the surrounding, largely barren, scrub land, made up of lava deserts and cinder cones. Within the reserve are an aeolian desert and *Lake Waiau*—an alpine lake that is 300 feet long, 150 feet wide and 8 feet deep, covering 1.28 acres and situated at an elevation of 13,020 feet, with the distinction of being the third highest lake in the U.S. Also in the reserve are several archaeological sites and an adze quarry, the *Keanakakoi Crater*, located some 3½ miles below the summit (or 5 miles north of the Mauna Kea Visitor Center) at an elevation of around 12,000 feet. The quarry was used by ancient Hawaiians to make stone tools.

Mauna Kea Observatory Complex. Located on the summit of Mauna Kea, at an elevation of 13,796 feet, at the end of Summit Rd.—14½ miles from the Saddle Rd. (Hwy. 220) intersection. This is an international astronomical observatory complex, with 10 different observatories with 13 of the world's most powerful telescopes. Among the facilities here are the *University of Hawaii Observatory*, the oldest in the complex, built in 1968, with a 0.6-meter (24-inch) optical telescope; the *NASA Infrared Telescope Facility*, built in 1979 and featuring a 3-meter (144-inch) infrared telescope; and the *W.M. Keck Observatory*, which boasts the world's largest mirrored telescope: a 10-meter (394-inch) telescope with 36 computer-controlled, mirrored segments, built at a cost of $70 million. There are no public facilities at the complex.

Mauna Kea State Park - Pohakuloa Area. Situated off Hwy. 220, at mile marker 35 (35 miles west of Hilo; or, when journeying from Waimea, 18 miles east of the intersection of Hwys. 220 and 190). The park is situated at an elevation of 6,500 feet, along the slopes of Mauna Kea, the 13,796-foot volcano, and is unique in that it has both pine trees as well as eucalyptus trees growing there. The park has rental cabins with heating and kitchens and bathrooms, and also picnic tables and restroom facilities. Cabin rental: $14.00 per couple per night. For reservations, call the Division of State Parks in Hilo, at (808)) 974-6200/933-0416.

Onizuka Center for International Astronomy (Visitor Center). Located on Summit Rd. (which goes off Hwy. 220, Saddle Rd., at mile marker 28), some 6 miles north of the Saddle Rd. (Hwy. 220) intersection, at an elevation of 9,300 feet; (808) 961-2180/974-4205/*www.ifa.hawaii.edu/info/vis*. Houses multi-media exhibits and displays, centered around the astronomical facilities and the natural history of the cosmos. Also informative video films. 2-hour tours to the summit are offered on Saturdays and Sundays, 1pm-5pm, which include a visit to one of the University of Hawaii's telescopes; also star-gazing programs every night, 6pm-10pm, with viewing through six different telescopes, including an 11-inch Celestron telescope. The center is open daily 9am-10pm. For current road conditions, call (808) 935-6268.

HAWAIIAN SEASHELLS

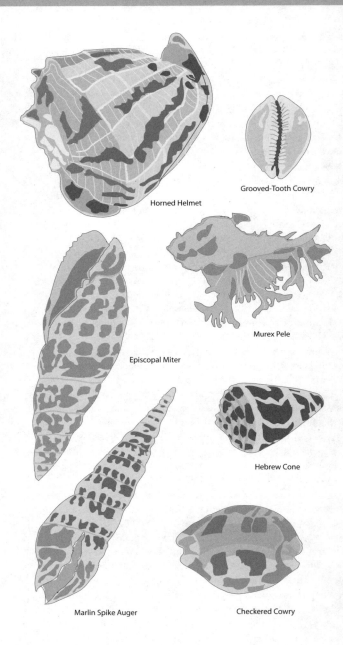

Horned Helmet

Grooved-Tooth Cowry

Murex Pele

Episcopal Miter

Hebrew Cone

Marlin Spike Auger

Checkered Cowry

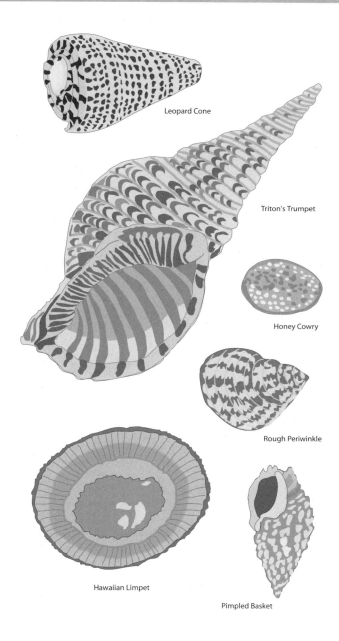

Leopard Cone

Triton's Trumpet

Honey Cowry

Rough Periwinkle

Hawaiian Limpet

Pimpled Basket

HAWAIIAN SEASHELLS

Places to Go | Beaches

The Big Island of Hawaii has some of the loveliest beaches in the Pacific, both white-sand and black-sand beaches, mainly along the island's Kona and Kohala coasts and along its south shore in the Kau and Puna districts. All beaches are public beaches, and nude bathing at public beaches is prohibited under Hawaiian state law (even though a few of them continue to be unofficial nudist beaches). Visitors to Hawaii's beaches should also be forewarned that coastal waters are subject to strong undercurrents or rip tides, especially during winter and spring, and caution is strongly advised.

[Symbols: = Swimming | = Lifeguard | = Restrooms]

Kailua-Kona |

Hale Halawai Beach Park. Situated in Kailua-Kona, just to the southwest of Ali'i Dr. and Hualalai Rd. Small, rocky beach, not especially suited to swimming. Park facilities include a covered pavilion and restrooms.

 He'eia Bay. Located approximately ¾ mile south of Kahalu'u Bay; accessed from Manukai St., which goes off Ali'i Dr. and Kamehameha III Rd. He'eia Bay adjoins to the north of Keauhou Bay, and has a boulder-lined, sheltered beach with good swimming and snorkeling possibilities, and also some surfing. However, there are no facilities here.

Holualoa Bay. Off Ali'i Dr., near mile marker 3. This is one of the best and most popular surfing spots on the Kona Coast. Features two notable surfbreaks: "Banyan's," which is directly opposite a large banyan tree located on the ocean side of Ali'i Drive; and "Lyman's," which can be found along the southern part of Holualoa Bay, off Kamoa Point, not far from the former Lyman home. The beach park has a rocky shoreline. No facilities.

 Kahalu'u Beach. Off Ali'i Dr., near mile marker 5 (south of White Sands Beach). Gray-sand, palm-fringed beach, protected by a 3,900-foot long breakwater, Pa Oka Menehune—or "menehune breakwater"—and bordered by a coral reef just offshore. This is one of the most popular swimming and snorkeling beaches in the Kona area, which also attracts some surfers and fishermen. The beach has an on-duty lifeguard, picnic tables, pavilions, and showers and restrooms.

 Kamakahonu Beach. Located in Kailua-Kona, off Ali'i Dr., just to the north of Kailua Pier. This is a popular sandy beach, fronting King Kamehameha's Kona Beach Resort. It offers excellent swimming possibilities, especially for children. Facilities here include restrooms and showers.

Keauhou Bay. Adjoining to the south of He'eia Bay; accessed from Kamehameha III Rd.—or Ali'i Dr.—and Manukai St. The beach park is made up of a stretch of rocky shoreline with boulders. There is no sandy beach here, as such, but the bay offers excellent swimming and snorkeling possibilities. Facilities include two sandy volleyball courts, picnic tables, showers and restrooms.

Old Kona Airport Beach Park. At the northern end of Kuakini Hwy. (11), just to the northwest of Kailua-Kona. Popular, 120-acre beach park, nestled along a rocky shoreline, lined with coral and tide pools and backed by a sandy-grassy area. At the north end of the beach is a small, sheltered cove that offers some snorkeling possibilities. The beach park is also quite popular with body-boarders and fishermen. However, swimming in the open ocean here is not advised due to the strong undercurrents. The beach has on-duty lifeguards, picnic tables, showers and restrooms; also pavilions, ball fields, and tennis courts. Park hours: 7am-8pm.

White Sands Beach Park. Located off Ali'i Dr., ¾ mile south of mile marker 3. Popular white-sand beach, variously known as "Magic Sands" and "Disappearing Sands" for the "disappearing" quality of its sand, which actually erodes during the winter months. The beach attracts primarily bodysurfers, as well as some surfers, and is the site of the annual Magic Sands Bodysurfing Championship. Swimming is not advised here, except in calm weather, due to the strong ocean undercurrents. The beach has an on-duty lifeguard, a sandy volleyball court, and showers and restrooms.

South Kona

Ho'okena Beach Park. Situated at Ho'okena, along Kauhako Bay, approximately 19 miles south of Kailua-Kona; reached on Hwy. 11 south, some 18½ miles south of Kailua-Kona—or 2½ miles south of Keokea—to a point roughly midway between mile markers 101 and 102, from where a steep, narrow road dashes off westward another 2½ miles to Kauhako Bay and Ho'okena Beach. The beach features gray sand and pebbles, and is sheltered from the open ocean by a protective coral reef just offshore. It offers good swimming and snorkeling, and also some camping possibilities. Facilities here include showers and restrooms.

Miloli'i Beach Park. Located approximately 30 miles south of Kailua-Kona (or 7 miles south of Kipahoehoe Natural Reserve); reached by way of Hwy. 11 south to mile marker 89, then roughly 4½ miles seaward along a narrow, one-lane road to the village of Miloli'i and the beach park. This is a remote beach area, located directly across from a small market. The beach is bordered by ironwood trees and features lava outcroppings. There are also small, natural pools here, including some sandy-bottomed ones, and sheltered coves that offer good, safe swimming conditions, ideal for children, as well as some snorkeling possibilities. Beach facilities include picnic tables, children's play equipment, and restrooms.

 Napo'opo'o Beach Park. Located roughly 2 miles southwest of Captain Cook (11 miles south of Kailua-Kona); reached by way of Hwy. 160—which goes off Hwy. 11 near Captain Cook—some 4½ miles southwestward from the Hwy. 11 intersection to a T intersection, from where the north fork leads a short distance directly to the beach. The beach is largely pebbly, with several large boulders, situated along Kealakekua Bay. Spinner dolphins are a common sight here. There are also picnic tables and restrooms at the beach park.

North Kona

 Honokohau Beach. Situated roughly 2½ miles north of Kailua-Kona; reached by way of Hwy. 19 north, then off on a small, unmarked road (which goes off Hwy. 19, approximately ½ mile north of mile marker 98) westward a ¼ mile or so to a paved, north-bound road that leads a little way to the beach access road, and so to the beach. Honokohau is a long, curving, sandy beach with a steep slope to the ocean, situated along Honokohau Bay, and part of the Kaloko-Honokohau National Historic Park. The beach is bordered by coral and tide pools, and backed by *kiawe*. It is frequented primarily by fishermen, surfers, and nudists. The beach has restroom facilities.

 Kiholo Bay. Situated 18 miles north of Kailua-Kona; reached by way of Hwy. 19 directly north to mile marker 81, then off on a trail (which actually goes off Hwy. 19 some 250 yards south of mile marker 81) another ¾ mile westward to the bay. There are two black-sand beaches here, located along a small peninsular tract jutting out at the north end of the bay. Both offer excellent swimming and snorkeling possibilities. Also, at the southern end of the bay is a freshwater, spring-fed natural pool, Luahinewai Pond, with good swimming possibilities as well. There are, however, no facilities at the beaches.

 Kona Coast State Park. Located off Hwy. 19, along Mahai'ula Bay, approximately 1¾ miles north of Wawaloli (OTEC) Beach; accessed on a small, dirt road that goes westward off the highway, between mile markers 90 and 91. Beautiful, long, crescent-shaped white-sand beach, lined with palm trees and *kiawe*. Offers good, safe swimming and snorkeling along its northern end. There is also a popular surf break here, off Kawili Point, on the north side of the bay. Facilities here include portable toilets, and a lifeguard. The beach park is open 9am-8pm.

 Kua Bay (Manini'owali Beach). Situated approximately ½ mile to the north of Makalawena Beach; reached on Hwy. 19 and a dirt access road—which goes west off the highway (19), just to the north of mile marker 88—¾ mile or so to the beach. Manini'owali is a crescent-shaped, white-sand beach, nestled between lava outcroppings on the north side of Pu'u Kuili, a 342-foot cinder cone. It offers good, safe swimming, except during high surf, and also some body surfing possibilities. The beach is backed by *a'a* (rough) lava fields and ancient rock walls. There are no facilities at the beach.

Makalawena Beach. 2 miles north of Kona Coast State Park, off Hwy. 19; accessed on a four-wheel-drive access road that goes southwestward off Hwy. 19, from a point approximately midway between mile markers 88 and 89, some 1¾ miles to the beach. The beach is long, curving, and sandy, backed by shallow sand dunes and ironwood trees, featuring a series of coves and inlets that are separated by lava outcroppings. It offers excellent swimming, snorkeling and surfing. Also, roughly midway along the beach, just inland, is the 12-acre 'Opae'ula Pond—a waterbird sanctuary where stilts, coots and ducks can be seen—and just over the sand dunes, in the lava, is a small freshwater pool.

Pine Trees Beach. Off Hwy. 19, 3 miles north of Honokohau Bay (5 miles north of Kailua-Kona); accessed on a mile-long shoreline road south from Wawaloli (OTEC) Beach—located just to the north of Pine Trees Beach—which, in turn, is reached by way of a small access road off Hwy. 19, a ¼ mile south of mile marker 92. This is notably one of the Kona Coast's most popular surfing spots, named for its grove of mangrove trees which are frequently mistaken for pine trees. The beach itself is sandy, situated between lava outcroppings, and bordered by coral. Swimming is not advisable here due to adverse ocean conditions. There are also no beach facilities here. Park hours: 6am-8pm.

Wawaloli (OTEC) Beach Park. Located 1¼ miles south of Keahole Airport (5¾ miles north of Kailua-Kona); reached by way of Hwy. 19 to a small access road that goes west off the highway, a ¼ mile south of mile marker 92, leading another mile or so directly to the beach park. Wawaloli is essentially an undeveloped beach park, frequented primarily by picnickers and fishermen. There is no sandy beach here as such, and swimming, too, is not recommended due to adverse ocean conditions. Park facilities include restrooms and showers. Park hours: 6am-8pm.

South Kohala |

Anaeho'omalu Beach. Situated some 24 miles north of Kailua-Kona, in South Kohala's Waikoloa Beach Resort area; reached by way of Waikoloa Beach Dr.—which goes off Hwy. 19, just to the south of mile marker 75—westward, a 100 yards or so past the Waikoloa petroglyph trailhead, to the first stop sign, then left (southward) another ½ mile to the beach parking lot. The beach is long, sandy, and palm-fringed, lying directly in front of the Royal Waikoloan resort, curving along Anaeho'omalu Bay, sloping gently down to the ocean. It offers excellent swimming, snorkeling and windsurfing possibilities. It also has picnic tables, showers and restroom facilities. The beach park is open to the public daily, 6am-8pm.

Hapuna Beach Park. The entrance to the beach is located 1¼ miles north of the village of Puako (or 7 miles north of the Waikoloa Beach Resort), off Hwy. 19. This is one of the most beautiful white-sand beaches in Hawaii, approximately ½-mile long—lying largely between two lava outcroppings—and averaging nearly 365 days of sunshine a year. The beach park encompasses some 61 acres, and is the site of the annual Rough Water Swim, a one-mile swim, scheduled for the Fourth of July. The beach offers excellent swimming and snorkeling possibilities, especially along its north end, and also bodyboarding and bodysurfing. During high surf, however, swimming and other water activities are not encouraged due to the dangerous undercurrents. Also, board surfing is prohibited here. The beach has on-duty lifeguards, picnic tables, a snack bar, and showers and restrooms.

Kalahuipua'a Beach. Located at the Mauna Lani Resort, roughly 2 miles north of Anaeho'omalu Beach and the Waikoloa Beach Resort; accessed on Mauna Lani Dr. (which goes off Hwy. 19 just to the north of mile marker 74), 1¼ miles west from the highway to the Historical Park parking lot, from where a ¼-mile paved walkway leads through the park directly to the beach. Kalahuipua'a is a beautiful white-sand beach, bordered by a coral reef, fronting Mauna Lani Bay Hotel, at Nanuku Inlet. It offers excellent swimming and snorkeling possibilities. Facilities include showers and restrooms.

Kauna'oa Beach. Situated along Kauna'oa Bay, at the Mauna Kea Beach Resort, directly in front of the Mauna Kea Beach Hotel, a mile or so north of Hapuna Beach; reached by way Hwy. 19 and Mauna Kea Beach Dr.—which goes west off Hwy. 19, approximately a mile south of the intersection of Hwys. 19 and 270. This is one of the most beautiful white-sand beaches in the islands, quarter-mile long, crescent shaped, and lined with palm trees. It offers excellent swimming and snorkeling, and also a safe area for children along its southern end. Additionally, the beach is an ancient nesting site for hawksbill sea turtles. Facilities here include restrooms and showers.

Keiki Beach. Located at the Mauna Lani Bay Hotel; reached by way of Mauna Lani Dr., which goes off Hwy. 19 just north of mile marker 74. Small, sheltered, crescent-shaped sandy beach with shallow water, situated adjacent to Kalahuipua'a Beach, on the south side of Nanuku Inlet. The beach is ideally suited for children, with good, safe swimming and snorkeling. Beach facilities include showers and restrooms.

Spencer Beach Park (Ohai'ula Beach). Located a little way from the Mauna Kea Resort area, off Hwy. 270, ¼ mile northwest of the intersection of Hwys. 19 and 270. Good, sandy beach, shaded by kiawe trees and backed by a grassy area. The beach, also known as Ohai'ula Beach, is quite popular with families, offering safe areas for children. It also has good swimming, snorkeling and, occasionally, bodysurfing possibilities. Beach facilities include picnic tables, barbecue pits, on-duty lifeguard, basketball and volleyball courts, showers and restrooms. Also camping possibilities.

Waialea Beach. Located approximately 6 miles north of the Waikoloa Beach Resort (or 4 miles north of Kalahuipua'a Beach); reached by way of Puako Rd. which goes westward off Hwy. 19, ½ mile or so north of mile marker 70, and an unmarked dirt road that goes north off Puako Rd., a ½ mile from the highway (19), to lead to the beach access road and on to the beach. This small, undeveloped beach, also known as "Beach 69"—for the number on the public utility pole located near the head of the access road leading to the beach—is backed by kiawe trees and private homes. It is a good place for swimming and snorkeling during calm weather. There are no facilities here.

North Kohala |

Kapa'a Beach Park. Located off Hwy. 270, 2¼ miles north of Lapakahi State Park (or 1¼ miles north of Mahukona Beach Park). Small, remote, and largely undeveloped beach park, backed by kiawe trees. The park is frequented primarily by fishermen, but it offers good swimming possibilities in a small rocky cove along its southern end, as well as some snorkeling, scuba diving, and camping. There are also good views from here, of the island of Maui and Mount Haleakala. Beach facilities include a pavilion, picnic tables, showers and restrooms.

Keokea Beach Park. Situated some 4½ miles east of the town of Kapa'au (at the north end of the island), approximately 1½ miles east of the Kamehameha Rock; reached by way of Hwy. 270, 4 miles or so east of Kapa'au, then northeastward another mile on a road that goes off the highway (270) directly to the beach. The 7-acre beach park, with its rocky shoreline, is situated along picturesque Keokea Bay. The park is frequented primarily by picnickers. Facilities here include covered picnic tables, and showers and restrooms. Some camping possibilities.

Mahukona Beach Park. Located just off Hwy. 270, on the south side of the old Mahukona Harbor, a mile north of Lapakahi State Park, and accessed by way of a short, ½-mile paved road that goes off the highway (270). Small, grassy beach park, situated along a rocky shoreline, with crystal clear waters and abundant marine

HAWAII | Beaches

life. Offers excellent snorkeling possibilities; also some swimming, scuba diving, boating, fishing, and camping. As an added bonus, the beach park offers views of East Maui, looking across the Alenuihaha Channel. Facilities here include picnic tables, restrooms and showers.

Hilo

 Hilo Bayfront Park. Situated along Hilo Bay, alongside the Bayfront Highway. Half-mile-long, gray-sand beach, bordered by ironwood trees. The beach is frequented primarily by picnickers, windsurfers, and fishermen; it is also used as a launching point by canoe paddling teams. Beach facilities include showers and restrooms.

 James Kealoha Beach Park. Off Kalanianaole Ave., approximately 4 miles from downtown Hilo (or ¾ mile east of Onekahakaha Beach Park. Well-liked beach park, also known as "4 Miles"—for the distance from the beach to the Hilo Post Office—situated at the head of a small bay, with a shaded, grassy area to the back of it. There are several sheltered coves here, mainly along the eastern part of the bay, offering good swimming and snorkeling possibilities. Also near the east end of the bay, just offshore, is *Peiwe*—or Scout—*Island*, with a handful of ironwood and hala trees. The beach park has showers and restroom facilities.

Keaukaha Beach Park. Situated along Puhi Bay, off Kalanianaole Ave., near the intersection of Baker Ave., approximately a mile east of the intersection of Kalanianaole Ave. and Kamehameha Ave. Keaukaha is a small beach park with several little coves. There is, however, no sandy beach here. There are also no facilities at the park.

 Onekahakaha Beach Park. Located ½ mile east of Keaukaha Beach Park, off Kalanianaole Ave. and a short access road, Onekahakaha Rd. (which goes northward off Kalanianaole Ave.). Popular beach park; features a large ocean pool with a shallow, sandy bottom, protected by a breakwater, ideally suited for children. Beach facilities include pavilions, picnic tables, showers and restrooms; also on-duty lifeguard. Some camping possibilities.

 Richardson's Beach. Located roughly a mile east of James Kealoha Beach Park, at the Richardson Ocean Park Center, off Kalanianaole Ave. Small, black-sand beach, backed by a sea wall and a grassy area. Offers good swimming, snorkeling and bodysurfing possibilities. Beach facilities include an on-duty lifeguard, and showers and restrooms.

Hamakua Coast |

Honoli'l Beach Park. Located 2 miles north of Hilo, off Hwy. 19; accessed from Nahala St. and Kahoa St., approximately ¼ mile off the highway (19). Popular surfing spot. The beach also has at its north end a large pond that is ideal for swimming; however, swimming in the open ocean is not encouraged here due to the strong currents. The beach has showers and restroom facilities.

Kolekole Beach Park. Approximately 11 miles north of Hilo; reached on Hwy. 19 and a short access road that goes off the highway, ¼ mile north of mile marker 14. The beach is situated near the mouth of Kolekole Stream, which is fed by the Akaka Falls. Swimming is not recommended here due to adverse ocean conditions; however, there is a safe, natural pool along Kolekole Stream, just inland from the bridge overhead, which offers some swimming possibilities. Beach facilities here include pavilions, picnic tables, showers and restrooms. Also some camping possibilities.

Laupahoehoe Beach Park. Located some 24 miles north of Hilo; reached more or less directly on Hwy. 19 and a mile-long access road—marked "Laupahoehoe Point"—that goes off the highway, approximately ¼ mile north of mile marker 27. The beach park is actually situated on a small, flat peninsula that juts out from the cliffs formed by a lava flow. The beach is lined with ironwood and palm trees, and is frequented primarily by picnickers and fishermen. There are also good views of the coastline from here, looking southward. Facilities include picnic tables and restrooms. The beach park also offers some camping possibilities.

Waipio Beach. Located in the Waipio Valley, at the top end of the Hamakua Coast, some 48 miles north of Hilo; reached by way of Hwy. 19 north, approximately 38 miles from Hilo, to the intersection of Hwy. 240, then 240 directly northwestward another 9½ miles to the Waipio Valley Lookout, from where a steep, narrow road descends ¾ mile into the valley and leads to the beach. Waipio Beach is a beautiful, and somewhat secluded, black-sand beach, lined with ironwood trees and stretching approximately a mile, with the distinction of being one of Hawaii's longest black-sand beaches. The beach attracts primarily fishermen, as well as some dedicated suffers. Swimming is not advised here due to the strong ocean undercurrents. There are also no beach facilities here.

Puna |

Isaac Hale Beach Park. Situated approximately 30 miles south of Hilo, along the eastern end of Pohoiki Bay, and reached more or less directly on Hwys. 132 and 137, journeying southward; alternatively, if you are at Puna's Lava Tree State Park, follow Pohoiki Rd. some 4½ miles southeast to the beach park. Isaac Hale is a small, 2-acre beach park with a black-sand beach, and one of the most popular spots along the Puna coast. It offers good swimming and snorkeling possibilities during calm weather, and also has a boat ramp, ideal for boating enthusiasts. The beach park is also quite popular with surfers and fishermen. The beach itself is lined with boulders and palm trees, and near the center of it, approximately 75 feet inland from the shore, there is a small, natural pool—which is part of the Pohoiki Warm Springs—some 16 feet long, 8 feet wide and 4 feet deep, filled with freshwater warmed by the Kilauea Volcano. The beach park also has portable toilets.

Kehena Beach. Located 7 miles southwest of Isaac Hale Beach Park (5 miles southwest of the MacKenzie State Park Recreation Area), off Hwy. 137, just west of mile marker 19. Kehena is a black-sand beach, lined with palm and ironwood trees, originally created in 1955 by lava flows from Kilauea. The beach is quite popular with nudists. No facilities.

Kau

 Mahana Beach (Green Sands Beach). Located approximately 65 miles south of Kailua-Kona, just east of South Point; reached by way of Hwy. 11 directly south, some 51 miles, to the intersection of South Point Rd., then South Point Rd. south another 12 miles to South Point, from where a dirt trail leads 3½ miles or so eastward to the beach. This is of course Hawaii's only green-sand beach, nestled in a cove formed by a littoral cone, Pu'u O Mahana, which was created by a lava flow from Mauna Loa as it entered the ocean. The green sand is actually comprised of eroded olivine crystals from the littoral cone. The beach itself offers some swimming possibilities during calm weather. No beach facilities.

 Ninole Cove. Located ½ mile or so southwest of Punalu'u Black Sand Beach. The cove can be reached by following Punalu'u Rd. north a little way to the SeaMountain Golf Course, directly across from where a jeep road leads ¼ mile southwestward to the shoreline at Ninole Cove; alternatively, you can follow the shoreline from Punalu'u Beach to Ninole Cove. There is a small black-sand beach here, nestled in a cove, dotted with boulders along its western end. The beach is frequented primarily by net fishermen. It also offers some swimming possibilities. No beach facilities.

 Punalu'u Black Sand Beach. Located at Punalu'u, roughly 10 miles east of Na'alehu (68 miles southeast of Kailua-Kona), at the end of the short Punalu'u Rd. which goes off Hwy. 11, just past mile marker 54, directly south to the beach. The black-sand beach here is lined with palm trees along its northeastern end, and offers good swimming and snorkeling possibilities, as well as some camping. Park facilities include picnic tables, restrooms and showers.

Whittington Beach Park. Located some 61 miles southeast of Kailua-Kona (approximately 3 miles from Na'alehu), and reached directly on Hwy. 11 and a small access road that goes off the highway, a ½ mile or so past mile marker 62. The beach park comprises a grassy area and lava outcroppings; there is no sandy beach here. Facilities include a picnic area, restrooms and showers. Also some camping possibilities.

Hiking Trails

[Permits are required for overnight backcountry hikes in the Hawaii Volcanoes National Park. Permits can he obtained from the Kilauea Visitor Center at the park, either in the morning of the proposed hike, or after 12pm on the day before the trip. There is a 7-day limit for all backcountry trips in the park.]

South Kona

Captain Cook Monument Trail. Located in the Captain Cook-Napo'opo'o area, with the trailhead located on the ocean side of Napo'opo'o Rd., approximately 200 yards west of the Hwy. 11 intersection. This is a strenuous, 2½-mile trail that descends some 1,400 feet to the shoreline, eventually leading southward along the shoreline to the Captain Cook Monument. There are some swimming and snorkeling possibilities along the coast at the monument.

North Kohala

Pololu Valley Trail. Trailhead located at the end of Hwy. 270, at mile marker 28.93, approximately 8 miles east of Hawi. Strenuous, 4-mile trail, which descends into the picturesque, mile-long Pololu Valley, where there is also a black-sand beach.

Hamakua Coast

Switchback Trail to Waimanu Valley. Located in the Waipio Valley, with the trailhead located on the north side of the valley, roughly 100 yards inland from Waipio Beach. Strenuous, 9-mile switchback trail that emerges from Waipio Valley, climbing some 1,200 feet to the top of a ridge, then traverses no fewer than 14 gulches, before finally descending into the nearby Waimanu Valley (which is similar to Waipio Valley, but smaller).

Hawaii Volcanoes National Park

Mauna Iki (Footprints Trail). Trailhead located off Hwy. 11, ¼ mile east of mile marker 38. 8.8-mile trail, which journeys through a dry, arid area with no shade trees, at an elevation of around 3,000 feet. It passes by, roughly ¾ mile from the trailhead along the highway, some eroded, historic footprints in lava, dating from 1790. The trail finally merges with the Kau Desert Trail and ends at Hilina Pali Road.

Mauna Loa Trail. Grueling, 39-mile round-trip trail to the summit of Mauna Loa, which has an elevation of 13,679 feet. The trail sets out from the end of Mauna Loa Rd.—which goes off Hwy. 11—some 11 miles northwest of the highway (11), at an elevation of 6,662 feet, journeying some 19½ miles to the summit and back. Ideally, the hike, which includes a 7,017-foot climb, should be staged over 4 days—2 days in each direction—with suggested overnight breaks at the Red Hill Cabins which are located approximately 7½ miles from the trailhead, at an elevation of 10,036 feet, and the Mauna Loa Cabins, situated near the summit, at an elevation of 13,250 feet. This hike should only be attempted by those in excellent physical condition; hikers may experience altitude sickness and hypothermia.

Crater Rim Trail. Located in the Kilauea Caldera area. Moderate, 11.6-mile loop trail, which begins and ends at the Kilauea Visitor Center, paralleling Crater Rim Road for the most part, and taking in the same sights as the road. This is an all-day hike.

Halemaumau Trail. Also located in the Kilauea area, this trail goes off the Crater Rim Trail, 0.1 mile north of Volcano House, then descends into the Kilauea Caldera and journeys across the hot, arid caldera floor, eventually leading to the Halemaumau Overlook, some 3.2 miles distant. There are good views of the Halemaumau Crater from the Halemaumau Overlook.

Byron Ledge Trail. A moderately strenuous, 2.7-mile trail, which goes off the Halemaumau Trail, 0.6 mile northeast of the Halemaumau Overlook, and loops back to the visitor center. The trail essentially offers an alternate route for returning, after crossing the Kilauea Caldera on the Halemaumau Trail, to the Kilauea Visitor Center and Volcano House.

Sulfur Bank Trail. The trailhead is located at the Kilauea Visitor Center. The trail offers an easy, 0.3-mile walk to the steaming sulphur hanks.

Sandalwood Trail. Easy, 0.7-mile trail; begins on the west side of Volcano House, and ends at the "Steaming Bluff." Offers good views of the Kilauea Caldera.

Devastation Trail. Trailhead located at the junction of the Crater Rim Road and Chain of Craters Road, approximately 3 miles south of Volcano House and the Kilauea Visitor Center. Moderate, 0.6-mile trail; passes through an "ohia lehua" forest and over a 1959 eruption site. The trail also passes by the Pu'u Puai cinder cone, offering great views of the Kilauea Iki Crater.

Thurston Lava Tube Trail. Located along Crater Rim Road, 1½ miles east of the junction of Crater Rim Road and the Chain of Craters Road. This is an especially popular, 0.3-mile loop trail, which sets out through a lush, fern forest, and passes through a 450-foot-long lava tube—which is nearly 20 feet high in places—formed as a result of the outer part of the lava flow cooling and hardening and the inner portion continuing to flow, eventually draining to create a hollow tube.

Kilauea Iki Trail. Strenuous, 4-mile loop trail, which begins at the upper (north) end of the Thurston Lava Tube parking lot, and continues, counter-clockwise, through the Kilauea Iki Crater, descending some 400 feet to the floor of the crater. This trail should be attempted only during morning and late afternoon hours, due to the excessive heat and lack of availability of water.

Halape Trail. Trailhead located at the Kipuka Nene Campground, off Hilina Pali Rd., approximately 5 miles southwest of the Chain of Craters Rd. 7.2-mile trail, which journeys through dry, arid tracts, before descending some 3,000 feet to the ocean.

Pu'u Loa Petroglyphs Trail. Easy, 1-mile trail, which begin 16 miles south of the Crater Rim Rd., off the Chain of Craters Rd., and leads to a large petroglyph field with over 15,000 ancient petroglyphs etched into *pahoehoe* (smooth lava).

Campgrounds

National Park Campgrounds

[Permits are required lor camping in Hawaii's national park campgrounds, and there is a 7-day limit. There is no camping fee. For camping permits and information on park campgrounds, contact the Volcano House, P.O. Box 53, Hawaii Volcanoes National Park, HI 96785; 808-967-7321/www.volcanohousehotel.com.]

Hawaii Volcanoes National Park

Kipuka Nene Campground. In the Hawaii Volcanoes National Park, off Hilina Pali Rd., 5 miles southeast of the Chain of Craters Rd. Offers overnight campsites, and picnic tables. Also several hiking trails nearby. No camping fee.

Namakani Paio Campground. Located 3 miles west of the Hawaii Volcanoes National Park, on the inland side of Hwy. 11, roughly ¾ mile east of mile marker 32. Popular campground, with large grassy area. Facilities include picnic tables, showers and restrooms. No camping fee.

State Park Campgrounds

[Permits are required for camping at state park campgrounds, and there is a 5-day limit. There is no camping fee. For camping permits and information on state park campgrounds, contact the Department of Land and Natural Resources, Division of State Parks, Box 936, 75 Aupuni St., #204, Hilo, HI 96720; 808-974-6200/*www.state.hi.us*.]

Hapuna Beach Park. Entrance to the beach is located 1¼ miles north of the village of Puako (or 7 miles north of Waikoloa Resort), off Hwy. 19. 61-acre park with campsites. Excellent, sandy beach with swimming, snorkeling, bodyboarding and bodysurfing possibilities during favorable ocean conditions. Lifeguard on duty; also picnic tables, snack bar, showers and restrooms.

Kalopa State Park. Situated approximately 37 miles north of Hilo, on the Hamakua Coast; reached by way of Hwy. 19 north to Kalopa Rd.—which goes off Hwy. I 9, a ½ past mile marker 39—then inland on Kalopa Rd. another ¾ mile to Kalanai Rd., which leads, 2¼ miles farther, to the park. 100-acre park, at an elevation of approximately 2,000 feet. Offers developed campsites and cabins in a lush Hawaiian rainforest. Also good hiking possibilities, with several self-guided nature trails winding through the park. Facilities include picnic areas, showers and restrooms.

MacKenzie State Recreation Area. Located in the Puna district, a little over 2 miles southwest of Isaac Hale Beach Park, off Hwy. 137. 13-acre park, with undeveloped tent campsites, situated in quiet, shaded area with ironwood trees. Picnic tables, pavilion, restrooms. Also some fishing possibilities.

Manuka State Wayside Park. Approximately 40 miles south of Kailua-Kona, in the Kau district; located off Hwy. 11, at mile marker 81. Lovely, 8-acre park with developed campsites. Arboretum on premises, featuring native Hawaiian plants, with 2-mile loop trail leading through the gardens. Park facilities include covered picnic tables, restrooms, and phone.

County Park Campgrounds

[Permits are required for camping at county campgrounds, and there is a 1-week limit during summer and 2-week limit during winter. There is also a fee for camping, of $1.00 per adult per night. For Camping permits and information on county park campgrounds, contact the Department of Parks and Recreation, County of Hawaii, 25 Aupuni St., Hilo, HI 96720; 808-961-8311/*www.hawaii-county.com/parks/parks.htm*.]

South Kona

Ho'okena Beach Park. Situated at Ho'okena, along Kauhako Bay, approximately 19 miles south of Kailua-Kona; reached on Hwy. 11 south—some 18½ miles south of Kailua-Kona, or 2½ miles south of Keokea—to a point roughly midway between mile markers 101 and 102, from where a steep, narrow road dashes off westward, another 2½ miles, to Kauhako Bay and the Ho'okena Beach Park. Campsites overlooking gray-sand and pebble beach. Restrooms, and showers. Also swimming and snorkeling possibilities.

North Kohala

Kapa'a Beach Park. 2¼ miles north of Lapakahi State Park (1¼ miles north of Mahukona Beach Park), off Hwy. 270. Small park with largely undeveloped campsites. Activities here include swimming and fishing. Also views of Maui. Picnic tables, restrooms.

Keokea Beach Park. Situated some 4½ miles east of the town of Kapa'au (at the north end of the island), approximately 1½ miles east of the Kamehameha Rock; reached by way of Hwy. 270, 4 miles or so east of Kapa'au, then northeastward on a road that goes off the highway (270), another mile, directly to the beach park. The 7-acre park offers some campsites, overlooking a rocky shoreline, along Keokea Bay. Park facilities include covered picnic tables, restrooms, and showers.

Mahukona Beach Park. Located just off Hwy. 270, on the south side of the old Mahukona Harbor, a mile north of Lapakahi State Park, and accessed by way of a short, ½-mile paved road that goes off the highway (270). Offers campsites near rocky beach. Good views of East Maui, across Alenuihaha Channel; also excellent snorkeling possibilities. Picnic tables, showers, restrooms.

Spencer Beach Park. Located on the Kohala Coast, a little way from the Mauna Kea Resort area, off Hwy. 270, ¼ mile northwest of the intersection of Hwys. 19 and 270. Campsites in grassy area shaded by kiawe trees. Good, sandy beach, with excellent swimming and snorkeling possibilities. Park facilities include basketball and volleyball courts, picnic tables, barbecue pits, showers and restrooms.

Hilo

James Kealoha Beach Park. Off Kalanianaole Ave., approximately 4 miles from downtown Hilo (or ¾ mile east of Onekahakaha Beach Park). Campsites available in shaded, grassy area. Some swimming and snorkeling. Park facilities include picnic tables, showers, and restrooms.

Onekahakaha Beach Park. Located in the Hilo area, ½ mile east of Keaukaha Beach Park, off Kalanianaole Ave. and a short access road, Onekahakaha Rd. (which goes northward off Kalanianaole Ave.). Popular park, attracting families for weekend camping. The park also has a large, shallow ocean pool with a sandy bottom, protected by a breakwater, ideally suited for children. Also picnic tables, pavilions, showers and restrooms.

North Hilo

Kolekole Beach Park. Approximately 11 miles north of Hilo; reached by way of Hwy. 19 and a short access road that goes off the highway, ¼ mile north of mile marker 14. The park has a county campground. There is also a beach area here, near the mouth of Kolekole Stream, which is fed by the Akaka Falls in the nearby Akaka Falls State Park—3½ miles inland. Park facilities include pavilions, picnic tables, restrooms and showers.

Laupahoehoe Beach Park. Located some 24 miles north of Hilo; reached more or less directly on Hwy. 19 and a mile-long access road—marked "Laupahoehoe Point"—that goes off the highway, approximately ¼ mile north of mile marker 27. The beach park, lined with ironwood and palm trees, has some campsites overlooking the ocean. The park also offers good views of the Hamakua coastline, looking southward. Facilities here include picnic tables and restrooms.

Puna

Isaac Hale Beach Park. Situated approximately 30 miles south of Hilo, along the eastern end of Pohoiki Bay, and reached more or less directly southward on Hwys. 132 and 137; alternatively, if you are at Puna's Lava Tree State Park, follow Pohoiki Rd. some 4½ miles southeast to the beach park. This small, 2-acre park has some undeveloped campsites along a beach area lined with boulders and palm trees. Also, just inland from the shoreline are the Pohoiki Warm Springs, where there is a small, freshwater pool, approximately 16 feet long, 8 feet wide and 4 feet deep, warmed by the

Kilauea volcano. The beach park also offers some swimming and snorkeling possibilities in calm weather, as well as a boat ramp, and portable toilets.

Kau

Punalu'u Black Sand Beach. Located at Punalu'u, roughly 10 miles east of Na'alehu (60 miles southeast of Kailua-Kona), at the end of the short Punalu'u Rd. which goes off Hwy. 11, just past mile marker 54, directly south to the beach. There are campsites situated along a black-sand beach that is lined with palm trees. Good swimming and snorkeling possibilities. Park facilities include picnic tables, showers, and restrooms.

Whittington Beach Park. Located some 61 miles southeast of Kailua-Kona (approximately 3 miles from Na'alehu), and reached directly on Hwy. 11 and a small access road that goes off the highway, a ½ mile or so past mile marker 62. Offers campsites in grassy area with lava outcroppings. Facilities include a picnic area, showers and restrooms.

Tours and Activities

Helicopter Tours

Helicopter tours are quite popular on the Big Island, and a good way to see the island, with tour companies offering flights over Waipio Valley, the North Kohala Coast and the Hawaii Volcanoes National Park. Tours generally originate at the Hilo International Airport, Keahole Airport on the Kona Coast, or any of several smaller heliports around the island. Typically, tour companies utilize one or more of three different types of helicopters—the Aero-Star, a 6-seater, with all six seats by the windows, offering good views to all passengers; the Hughes 500, a 4-seater, which also offers window seating to all passengers; and the Bell Jet Ranger, another 4-seater that has only three window seats, with one passenger being confined to a center seat and, consequently, lesser views. Tours last anywhere from 35 minutes to 2 hours, and cost $135-$530 per person. For reservations and more information, contact any of the following:

Blue Hawaiian Helicopters. Operates from the Hilo Heliport in Hilo and the Waikoloa Heliport in Kohala; (808) 961-5600/(800) 745-2583/www.bluehawaiian.com. Offers three different scenic aerial tours: the Circle of Fire plus Waterfalls, which takes in the

Kilauea Volcano as well as tropical rain forests and some water-falls; the Big Island Spectacular, which includes Kilauea and the Hamakua Coast and North Kohala; and the scenic Kohala Coast Adventure. Cost: Big Island Spectacular, $424-$477 per person; Kohala Coast Adventure, $228-$250 per person; Circle of Fire Tour, $210.00 per person.

Paradise Helicopters. Operates out of Kona as well as Hilo; (808) 969-7392/(888) 349-7888/*www.paradisehelicopters.us*. Offers 45-minute to 3½-hour island tours in either the 4-passenger Hughes 500 or the 6-passenger Bell 407 helicopters. Coastal tours, as well as aerial tours of lava flows over the Hawaii Volcanoes National Park. Cost: Volcano and Waterfall Adventure (from Hilo), $185.00 per person; Doors Off Experience, $175.00; Hawaii Experience Tour, $385.00; Volcano Waterfall Landing (from Kona), $530.00.

Safari Helicopters. Hilo Heliport, Hilo; (808) 969-1259/(800) 326-3356/*www.safariair.com*. Aerial island tours on board air-conditioned A-Star 350 helicopter. Two tours are offered: the Volcano Safari and the Deluxe Waterfall and Volcano Safari. Tour cost: Deluxe Waterfall and Volcano Safari, $209.00 per person; Volcano Safari, $149.00 per person.

Sunshine Helicopters. (808) 871-0722/(800) 469-3000/*www.sunshinehelicopters.com*. Offers aerial tours of the Hawaii Volcanoes National Park, taking in the molten lava flows into the ocean from the active Kilauea volcano, as well as the towering Mauna Loa and Mauna Kea, and the picturesque Hamakua Coast. Cost: Kona-Big Island Volcano Deluxe, $390.00 per person; Kohala-Hamakua Coast Tour, $185.00 per person; Kilauea Volcano Tour, $190.00 per person.

Tropical Helicopters. Hilo International Airport, Hilo; (808) 961-6810/(866) 961-6810/*www.tropicalhelicopters.com*. Offers three different tours in Bell and Hughes helicopters: a 35-minute Volcano Tour which takes in Kilauea and the site of current volcanic activity; a 45-minute Fire and Falls Adventure, which includes Kilauea as well as Hilo's Rainbow Falls; and a 45-minute Ultimate Experience, which is an "open-door" adventure over Kilauea and Hilo. Cost: Volcano Tour, $132.00 per person; Fire and Falls Adventure, $157.00 per person; the Ultimate Experience, $180.00 per person.

Plane and Glider Tours

Big Island Air. Keahole Airport, Kailua-Kona; (808) 329-4868. Offers a 1¾-hour Circle Island Tour, which takes in all the highlights of the island. Cost: $289.00 adults, $199.00 children.

Sightseeing Tours

Mauna Kea Summit Adventures. Kailua-Kona; (808) 322-2366/(888) 322-2366/*www.maunakea.com*.. Guided tours to the summit of Mauna Kea, with pick-ups at both Kona and Kohala; tours include viewing through an astronomical telescope and an instruction in astronomy. Tour cost: $185.00 per person.

Polynesian Adventure Tours. Kailua-Kona; (808) 329-8008/833-3000/(800) 622-3011/*www.polyad.com/bigisland.htm*. Offers two sightseeing tours on the island: the Grand Circle Tour, which includes the coast, rainforests and the Kilauea Caldera; and the Hawaii Volcano Adventure, which explores the Hawaii Volcanoes National Park. Cost: Grand Circle Tour, $68-$75 adults, $50-$60 children; Hawaii Volcanoes Adventure, $59.00 adults, $44.00 children.

Robert's Hawaii Tours. Kailua-Kona; (800) 899-9323/(808) 329-1688/*www.robertshawaii.com*. Narrated tours of the island's attractions, with several different pick-up locations. Two different tours are offered: the Kona Highlights Tour which takes in all sights on the Kona Coast; and the 9-hour Island Tour, which circles the island, including all the Big Island attractions. Tour cost: $60.00 per person for the Kona Highlights Tour; $80.00 per person for the Island Tour.

Waipio Valley Shuttle & Tours. Kukuihaele: (808) 775-7121/*www.waipiovalleytour.com*. Offers 1½- to 2-hour narrated sightseeing tours of the Waipio Valley in a four-wheel drive vehicle, taking in the valley's waterfalls and lush taro patches. Tours originate in the Waipio Valley. Tour cost: $45.00 adults, $20.00 children.

Waipio Valley Wagon Tours. Kukuihalele; (808) 775-9518/*www.waipiovalleywagontours.com*. 1½-hour tours of the Waipio Valley, which include a ride in a mule-drawn wagon. The tours are narrated, highlighting the valley's history and legends, and take in spectacular scenery. Tour cost: $45.00 adults, $22.50 children.

Horseback Riding

Cowboys of Hawaii. Parker Ranch, Waimea; (808) 885-5006/*www.cowboysofhawaii.com*. Offers 2-hour morning and afternoon horseback rides through the Parker Ranch; also 1½- to 2-hour sunset rides taking in vistas of Waimea. Cost: $79.00 per person for any of the rides.

Kings' Trail Rides. Off Hwy. 11, Kealakekua; (808) 323-2388/*www.konacowboy.com*. Offers 4-hour horseback rides on the 21,000-acre Kealakekua Ranch, on the slopes of Mauna Loa, overlooking Kealakekua Bay. Cost: $135-$150 for 4-hour ride (including lunch).

HAWAII | Tours and Activities

Parker Ranch Rides. Kamuela (Waimea); (808) 885-7655/ *www. parkerranch.com*. 1½- to 2-hour ranch rides on the 175,000-acre Parker Ranch in upcountry Waimea. Features open pasture land and panoramic views. Cost: $79.00 per person.

Waipio Na'alapa Trail Rides. Kukuihaele; (808) 775-0419/775-0290/ *www.naalapastables.com*. Guided, 2½-hour rides in the Waipio Valley, with commentary on the valley's history and its people, as well as useful information on identification of indigenous plants and flowers. The trail journeys across streams and past water-falls. Cost: $89.00 per person.

Boat Tours and Snorkeling Excursions

Atlantis Submarines. Kailua-Kona; (800) 548-6262/(808) 329-6626/*www.goatlantis.com*.1-hour excursions aboard an 80-ton, 65-foot-long submarine, descending to depths of 100 feet, explor-ing a 25-acre natural coral reef. Tour cost: $84.00 adults, $42.00 children.

The Body Glove. Kailua Pier, Kailua-Kona; (808) 326-7122/(800) 551-8911/*www.snorkelkona.com*. 3- and 4½-hour morning and afternoon snorkeling cruises aboard a 55-foot trimaran; includes a complimentary continental breakfast or deli-style lunch, and use of all snorkeling equipment. Also whale watches and scuba div-ing. Cost: 3-hour cruise, $66.00 adults, $44.00 children; 4½-hour cruise, $105.00 adults, $65.00 children; whale watches, $66.00 adults, $44.00 children; scuba diving, $57-$77.

Captain Beans' Cruises. Kailua-Kona; (808) 329-2955/(800) 899-9323/*www.robertshawaii.com*. Lively, entertaining sunset dinner cruise, featuring Polynesian music and dance. No children under 21 years. Tour cost: $66.00 adults, $37.50 children.

Captain Zodiac Rafting Expeditions. Honokohau Harbor; (808) 329-3199/*www.captainzodiac.com*. 4-hour morning and after-noon rafting-cum-snorkeling expeditions to a marine preserve at Kealakekua Bay, near the Captain Cook Monument. Lunch, bever-ages, and snorkeling equipment are included. Also 3-hour whale watches. Cost: $93.00 adults, $77.00 children; whale watches, $70.00 adults, $60.00 children.

Fair Wind Cruises. Keauhou Bay; (808) 322-2788/(800) 677-9461/*www.fair-wind.com*. Sailing and snorkeling trips aboard a 50-foot trimaran to a marine conservation area at Kealakekua Bay. Includes a continental breakfast and barbecue lunch. Also whale watches. Tour cost: cruises, $69-$105 adults, $43-$65 children; whale watches, $55.00 per person.

Kamanu Charters. Honokohau Harbor; (808) 329-2021/*www. kamanu.com*. 3-hour sailing excursions on board the catamaran

"Kamanu"; includes snorkeling at Pawai Bay, a tropical lunch, and complimentary beer, wine and juice. Cost: $80.00 adults, $48.00 children.

Red Sail Sports. At the Hilton Waikoloa Village, Waikoloa; (808) 886-2876/(877) 733-7245/*www.redsailhawaii.com*. 4-hour snorkeling excursions on board a 50-foot catamaran; includes continental breakfast, lunch, beverages, and use of snorkeling equipment. Also, 2-hour sunset cruise, with complimentary pupus and beverages. Tour cost: snorkeling excursion, $71-$82 adults, $39-$46 children; sunset cruise, $62.00 adults, $34.00 children.

Sea Paradise. Keauhou Bay, Kailua-Kona; (808) 322-2500/(800) 322-5662/*www.seaparadise.com*. Daily sailing and snorkeling excursions to Kealakekua Bay on board a 46-foot catamaran. Also scuba diving tours and sunset dinner sails. Cost: $65-$140 adults, $40-$59 children.

Sea Quest Rafting & Snorkeling. Kailua-Kona; (808) 329-7238/*www.seaquesthawaii.com*. Offers morning and afternoon snorkeling tours on Kealakekua Bay, taking in sea caves and lava tubes; also whale watches along the Kona Coast. Cost: snorkeling tours, $49-$79 adults and $39-$57 children; whale watches, $53.00 per person.

Whale Watching Adventures with Captain Dan McSweeney. Holualoa; (808) 322-0028/*www.ilovewhales.com*. 3½-hour whale-watching cruises, departing from Honokohau Harbor, daily at 9 a.m. and 1pm; includes a tropical lunch. Tours are conducted by a noted mammal biologist and whale researcher. Tour cost: $69.50 adults, $59.50 children.

Scuba Diving

Scuba diving is a popular recreational sport on the Big Island, with several different companies offering introductory scuba dives as well as tank dives for certified divers. Dives are offered both from the shore and from boats. Rates range from $85-$130 for introductory dives, to $90-$190 for tank dives; transportation and equipment are generally included. For more information or to schedule dives, contact any of the following dive shops:

Big Island Divers. 74-5467 Kaiwi St., Kailua-Kona; (808) 329-6068/(800) 488-6068/*www.bigislanddivers.com*.

Bottom Time Hawaii. 74-5590 Luhia St., Kailua-Kona; (808) 331-1858/(866) 463-4836/*www.bottomtimehawaii.com*.

Dive Makai Charters. Honokohau Harbor, Kailua-Kona; (808) 329-2025/*www.divemakai.com*.

East Hawaii Divers. Pahoa; (808) 965-7840.

Jack's Diving Locker. 75-5819 Ali'i Dr., Kailua-Kona; (808) 329-7585/(800) 345-4807/*www.jacksdivinglocker.com*.

Kohala Divers. Kawaihae Shopping Center, Kawaihae; (808) 882-7774/*www.kohaladivers.com.*

Kona Coast Divers. 75-5614 Palani Rd., Kailua-Kona; (808) 329-8802/(800) 562-3483/*www.konacoastdivers.com.*

Nautilus Dive Center. 382 Kamehameha Ave., Hilo; (808) 935-6939/*www.nautilusdivehilo.com.*

Red Sail Sports. Hilton Waikoloan Village, Waikoloa; (808) 886-2876/ (877) 733-7245/*www.redsailhawaii.com.*

Sandwich Isle Divers. 75-5729 Ali'i Dr., Kailua-Kona; (808) 329-9188/(888) 743-3483/*www.sandwichisledivers.com.*

Sportfishing

Sportfishing is one of the most popular recreational activities on the Big Island, especially along the Kona Coast, with scores of tour operators offering sportfishing charters. In the Kona area, boats usually depart from the Kailua Pier or Honokohau Harbor. Charters are for a full or half day, with prices ranging from $250-$550 for half-day charters to $350-$850 for full-day charters; rates generally include all equipment as well as ice and beverages on the trips. Sportfishing trips are also available to individuals on a share-boat basis, with prices ranging from $85-$100 per person. For more information and reservations, contact any of the following:

Aerial Sport Fishing, Kailua-Kona, (808) 329-5603; *Anxious Fishing Charter,* Kailua-Kona, (808) 326-1229; *Billbuster Charter,* Kailua-Kona, (808) 329-2657; *Blue Hawaii Sportfishing,* Kailua-Kona, (808) 326-2255; *Catchem One Sports Fishing,* Kailua-Kona, (808) 329-2670; *The Charter Locker,* Honokohau Harbor, (808) 326-2553; *Foxy Lady Sport Fishing,* Honokohau Harbor, (808) 960-3009; *Humdinger Sport Fishing,* Kailua-Kona, (808) 325-3449; *Illusions Sportfishing Charters,* Kamuela, (808) 960-7371/883-0180; *Jun Ken Po Sportfishing,* Kailua-Kona, (808) 987-2291; *Kona Activities Center,* Kailua-Kona, (808) 329-3171; *Kona Charter Skippers Assoc.,* Kailua-Kona, (808) 936-4970/329-3600/(800) 762-7546; *Kona Rainbow Sport Fishing,* Kailua-Kona, (808) 325-1775/989-4982; *Lady Dee Sportfishing,* Kailua-Kona, (808) 322-8026/936-1110/(800) 278-7049; *Layla Sport Fishing Charters,* Kailua-Kona, (808) 329-6899; *Lei Aloha Charter Fishing,* Kailua-Kona, (808) 329-3171/938-3503/(800) 367-5288; *Mariah Sportfishing,* Kailua-Kona, (808) 325-1691/936-3993; *Marlin Magic Sport Fishing,* Kailua-Kona, (808) 325-7138/960-1713; *Pamela-Big Game Fishing,* Kailua-Kona, (808) 936-4970/329-3600/(800) 762-7546; *Sea Wife Charters,* Kailua-Kona, (808) 329-1806/(888) 329-1806; *Sea Genie Sport Fishing,* Kailua-Kona, (808) 325-5355/936-4234; *Sea Dancer,* Kailua-Kona, (808) 322-6630/936-4689; or *Wild West Sport Fishing,* Kailua-Kona, (808) 322-4700/327-9494.

Kayaking

Aloha Kayak. (808) 322-2868/(877) 322-1441/*www.alohakayak.com*. Offers 2½- and 4-hour guided tours to sea caves and snorkeling hotspots in the Keauhou Bay area. Also offers one- and two-person kayak rentals. Cost: 2½-hour tour, $50.00 adults, $25.00 children; 4-hour tour, $65.00 adults, $33.00 children. Kayak rentals: $20-$30 for a half day, $25-$40 for a full day.

Parasailing

UFO Parasail. Kailua Pier, Kailua-Kona, (808) 325-5836/(800) 359-4836/*www.ufoparasail.net*. Offers 7- to 10-minute flights, at 400 to 800 feet, on an hour-long boat ride. Cost: $52.00 for a 7-minute flight; $62.00 for a 10-minute flight.

Windsurfing

Ocean Sports. Anaeho'omalu Beach, Waikoloa; (808) 885-5555/ *www.hawaiioceansports.com*. Offers windsurfing lessons and equipment rental. 1¼-hour beginner lessons are $60.00 per person; equipment rental is $30.00 per hour.

Golf Courses

Hapuna Golf Course. 62-100 Kauna'oa Dr., Kohala Coast; (808) 880-3000/*www.hapunabeachhotel.com/HBP/golf*. 18 holes, par 72, 7,114 yards. Green fees: $145.00. Pro shop, driving range, putting green; also restaurant on premises.

Hamakua Country Club. Hwy. 19, Honoka'a; (808) 775-7244. Small, 9-hole oceanview course; par 33, 2,520 yards. Green fees: $15.00. Facilities include a snack bar and restroom.

Hilo Municipal Golf Course. 340 Haihai St., Hilo; (808) 959-7711. 18 holes, par 71, 6,006 yards. Green fees: $30.00 weekdays, $35.00 weekends. Pro shop, putting green, restaurant.

Hualalai Golf Course. At the Four Seasons Resort, 100 Ka'upulehu Dr., Ka'upulehu; (808) 325-8480/325-8000/*www.fourseasons.com/hualalai/vacations/golf.html*. Jack Nicklaus-designed, 7,117-yard, par 72, 18-hole championship course. Green fees: $195.00. Pro shop, driving range, putting green, restaurant.

Kona Country Club. 78-7000 Ali'i Dr., Kailua-Kona; (808)

322-2595/*www.konagolf.com*. Offers two 18-hole championship courses: the par 72, 6,748-yard Ocean Course, and the par 72, 6,634-yard Mountain Course. Green fees: $160.00 ($104.00 during twilight hours) for the Ocean Course; $145.00 ($94.00 twilight hours) for the Mountain Course. Pro shop, driving range, putting green, restaurant.

Mauna Kea Beach Hotel Golf Course. At the Mauna Kea Beach Hotel, One Mauna Kea Beach Dr., Kohala Coast; (808) 882-7222/882-5405/*www.maunakeabeachhotel.com/MKB/golf*. 18-hole, Arnold Palmer-designed championship course; par 72, 6,736 yards. Green fees: $210.00. Pro shop, driving range, putting green; also restaurant.

Mauna Lani Resort Francis H. I'i Brown Golf Course. At the Mauna Lani Resort, 68-1310 Mauna Lani Dr., Kohala Coast; (808) 885-6655/*www.maunalani.com*. Offers two 18-hole courses: the par-72, 6,993-yard North Course; and the par-72, 7,029-yard South Course. Green fees: $205.00 for either of the courses; $90.00 during twilight hours; $35.00 for cart rentals. Facilities include a pro shop, driving range, putting green, and restaurant.

Naniloa Country Club. 120 Banyan Dr., Hilo; (808) 935-3000. 9 hole, par 35, 2,740 yards. Green fees: $30.00 weekdays, $40.00 weekends; $7.00 for cart rentals. Pro shop, driving range, putting green.

SeaMountain at Punalu'u Golf Course. Punalu'u; (808) 928-6222. 18 holes, par 72, 6,500 yards. Green fees: $49.50 (including cart rental) on weekends; $46.50 on weekdays. Pro shop, driving range, putting green; also restaurant.

Volcano Golf and Country Club. At the Hawaii Volcanoes National Park, Hwy. 11, Volcano; (808) 967-7331/*www.volcano-golfshop.com*. 18-hole, par-72, 5,965-yard course, situated at an elevation of 4,000 feet. Green fees: $63.50 (including cart rental); $51.00 during twilight hours. Pro shop, driving range, putting green; restaurant.

Waikoloa Resort Beach Golf Club. At the Waikoloa Beach Resort, 1020 Keana Pl., Waikoloa; (808) 886-6060/(877) 924-5656/*www.waikoloagolf.com*. Dramatic, 18-hole, Robert Trent Jones-designed course; par 70, 6,566 yards. Green fees: $195.00 (including cart rental). Pro shop, putting green, driving range; also restaurant.

Waikoloa Resort King's Golf Club. At the Waikoloa Beach Resort, Kohala Coast; (808) 886-7888/(877) 924-5656/*www.waikoloagolf.com*. 18 holes, par 72, 7,074 yards. Green fees: $195.00 (including cart rental). Pro shop, driving range, putting green.

Waikoloa Village Golf Club. At the Waikoloa Village, Waikoloa Rd. (off Hwy. 19, Kohala Coast; (808) 883-9621/*www.waikoloa.org*. Robert Trent Jones-designed course; 18 holes, par 72, 6,791 yards. Green fees: $75.00 (including cart rental). Pro shop, driving range, putting green; also restaurant on premises.

Tennis

Hilton Waikoloa Village. 425 Waikoloa Beach Dr., Waikoloa; (808) 886-1234/(800) 445-8667/*www.hiltonwaikoloavillage.com*. 6 courts. Court fee: $20.00 per person per hour.

Keauhou Beach Hotel. 78-6740 Ali'i Dr., Keauhou-Kona; (808) 322-3441/(800) 688-7444/*www.outrigger.com*. 6 courts with lights. Court fee: $6.00 per hour, or $10.00 per day.

King Kamehameha's Kona Beach Hotel. 75-5660 Palani Rd., Kailua-Kona; (808) 329-2911/(800) 367-6060/*www.konabeachhotel.com*. Offers 2 courts with lights. Court fee: $10.00 per hour.

Mauna Kea Beach Hotel. 62-100 Mauna Kea Beach Dr., Kohala Coast; (808) 882-7222/(800) 882-6060/(866) 774-6236/*www.princeresortshawaii.com*. 13 courts available for day use. Court fee: $18.00 per person per hour; off-peak hours (11 a.m.-3 p.m.), $9.00 per person per hour.

Royal Kona Tennis Club. At the Royal Kona Resort, 75-5852 Ali'i Dr., Kailua-Kona; (808) 329-3111/(800) 919-8333/774-5662/*www.hawaiihotels.com*. 4 courts, lighted. Court fee: $5.00 per hour, $7.00 per day.

Waiakea Racquet Club. 400 Hualani Dr., Hilo; (808) 961-5499. 2 courts available, for day-use only.

Waikoloa Beach Marriott. 69-275 Waikoloa Beach Dr., Kohala Coast; (808) 886-6789/(800) 922-5533/*www.marriott.com*. 6 day-use courts available. Court fee: $4.00 per hour, or $5.00 all day.

Public County Tennis Courts

There are several public tennis courts on the Big Island, maintained and operated by the Department of Parks & Recreation, 25 Aupuni St., Hilo; (808) 961-8311/935-1842; for availability and more information, call the department's office. Among the public county courts are the following:

In South Hilo: *Ho'olulu Park.* Cnr. Pi'ilani and Kalanikoa Sts., Hilo. Offers 5 outdoor courts and 3 indoor courts with lights. *Lincoln Park.* Cnr. Ponahawai and Kino'ole Sts., Hilo. 4 courts with lights. *Lokahi Park.* Puainako St., Hilo. 2 courts, lights. *Malama Park.* Mimaki St., Hilo. 2 courts, no lights. Mohouli Park. Mohouli St.. Hilo. 2 courts, no lights. *Panaewa Park.* Located across from Prince Kuhio Plaza, Hilo. 2 courts, no lights.

In North Hilo: *Hakalau Park.* Located in Hakalau. 2 courts, no lights. *Papa'aloa Park.* Located in Papa'aloa. 2 courts, with lights.

In North Kohala: *Kamehameha Park.* Located in Kapa'au. 2 courts with lights. In South Kohala: *Waimea Park.* Hwy. 19, Waimea. 2 courts with lights.

In North Kona: *Kailua Park.* Kailua-Kona. 4 courts with lights. *Kailua Playground.* Kailua-Kona. 1 court with lights. Keauhou Park. *Kailua-Kona.* 1 court, no lights. *Old Kona Airport Beach Park.* Located at the north end of Kuakini Hwy., Kailua-Kona. 4 courts with lights. *Kailua Playground.* Located on Kuakini Hwy, ¼-mile south of Hualalai Rd., Kailua-Kona. 1 court with lights. *Harold H. Higashihara Park.* On Kuakini Hwy. (11), ¼-mile south of mile marker 115, Kailua-Kona. I court, no lights.

In Kau: *Na'alehu Park.* Hwy. 11, Na'alehu. 1 court with lights. *Pahala School Grounds.* Kamani St., Pahala. 2 courts, with lights.

Luaus

Friday Night Luau. At Hale Ho'okipa at the Kona Village Resort, Kailua-Kona; (808) 325-5555/(800) 367-5290/*www.konavillage. com.* Authentic Hawaiian luau with an imu ceremony featuring the removal of the kalua pig from the earthen oven. Also Polynesian entertainment, and a guided tour of the village. Luaus are offered on Friday nights only, and begin at 5.00pm. Cost: $88.54 adults, $53.65 children. Reservations recommended.

Hilton's Legends of the Pacific Luau. At the Hilton Waikoloa, Waikoloa Beach Dr., Waikoloa; (808) 885-1234/(800) 445-8667/ *www.hilton.com/hawaii/waikoloa/index.html.* Lavish Hawaiian buffets, with traditional Polynesian foods. Also features Polynesian show, with dance and music of the islands. Luaus offered on Tuesdays and Fridays, starting at 6.00pm. Cost: $78.00 adults, $39.00 children (ages 5-12). Reservations suggested.

Island Breeze Luau. At King Kamehameha's Kona Beach Resort, 75-5660 Palani Rd., Kailua-Kona; (808) 326-4969/*www.island-breezeluau.com.* Traditional luau in beachfront setting. Begins with a royal pageant and torch lighting, and includes an imu ceremony and Polynesian revue. Luaus are offered on Tuesday, Wednesday, Thursday and Sunday nights, beginning at 5.00pm. Cost: $65.00 adults, $29.00 children. Reservations recommended.

Royal Kona Resort. At the Royal Kona Resort, 75-5852 Ali'i Dr., Kailua-Kona; (808) 329-3111/*www.hawaiianhotelsandresorts.com.* Authentic Polynesian buffet with sunset cocktails and Polynesian revue. Also hula performances. Luau dinners on Monday, Wednesday and Friday nights, at 5.00pm. Cost: $72.00 adults, $27.00 children. Reservations recommended.

Mauna Kea Beach Hotel Luau. At the Mauna Kea Beach Hotel, One Mauna Kea Beach Dr., Kohala Coast; (808) 882-7222/(800) 882-6060/*www.maunakeabeachresort.com.* Traditional luau. Polynesian entertainment, featuring hula chant and dance. Luaus on Tuesday nights. Cost: $82.00 adults, $41.00 children (5-12). Reservations suggested.

Island Events

January

Third Weekend. *Volcano to Hilo 31-Mile Ultra Marathon and Relay.* Ultra marathon, from Volcano (at the Hawaii Volcanoes National Park) to Hilo, drawing nearly 100 participants. Features 20-30 ultra runners and around 10-15 relay teams. More information at (808) 969-7400/*www.hilomarathon.org.*

Hulihe'e Palace Concert Series. Held at the Hulihe'e Palace in Kailua-Kona. Monthly concerts of Hawaiian music, song and hula, with each concert dedicated to one of Hawaii's monarchs. Concerts begin at 4pm and are presented to the public free of charge. For more information, call (808) 329-9555 or visit *www.huliheepalace. org.*

Mastercard Championship at Hualalai. Held at the Hualalai Golf Club at Hualalai Resort. Annual, televised event, featuring some of the world's top golfers as they vie for $1.6 million in prize money. For more information, call (800) 417-2770 or visit *www.pgatour. com.*

Fourth Weekend. *Hilton Waikoloa Village USTA Challenger Tennis Tournament.* Week-long tournament, held at the Kohala Tennis Garden at Hilton Waikoloa Village on the Kohala Coast. Features some of the world's best men's and women's professional tennis players, competing in both singles and doubles matches. For more information, call (808) 886-1234 or visit *www.hiltonwaikoloavillage.com.*

February

First Weekend. *Waimea Cherry Blossom Heritage Festival.* At the historic Waimea Church Row Park. Features agricultural as well as arts and crafts demonstrations, and distribution of cherry trees for planting in the Waimea area. Also ethnic food concessions, live music and entertainment, and displays of local fine art, Hawaiian quilts, ikebana and Japanese kimono—including demonstrations on how the kimono are designed—as well as Japanese calligraphy and traditional Japanese tea ceremonies. More information at (808) 961-8706/885-5433/*www.calendar.gohawaii.com.*

Second Weekend. *Hilo Chinese New Year Festival.* Held in historic downtown Hilo. Features dancers and fireworks. Also food concessions and cooking demonstrations, live music and entertainment, and children's Chinese costume contest. For more information, call (808) 933-9772

Fourth Weekend. *Annual Grow Hawaiian Horti/cultural Festival.*

Held at the Amy Greenwell Ethnobotanical Garden in Kona. Features educational talks, discussions and demonstrations centered around native plants and gardening, and Hawaiian art and culture. Also plant sales, children's activities, Hawaiian food concessions, and live entertainment. More information at (808) 323-3318/*www. bishopmuseum.org/calendar/february.html* or *www.calendar. gohawaii.com.*

March

First Weekend. *Big Island Woodturners Exhibit.* Wailoa Center, Hilo. Month-long show. Features a variety of wood-craft, including decorative items such as bowls, furniture, sculpture, and musical instruments. Also wood turning and carving demonstrations. The show is sponsored by the Big Island Woodworkers Guild. For more information, call (808) 933-0416 or visit *www.bigislandwoodturners.com.*

Kona Brewers Festival. Annual festival, held at King Kamehameha's Kona Beach Hotel in Kailua-Kona. Showcases some 30 Hawaiian and mainland breweries serving over 60 different beers. Also features tropical culinary offerings from at least 25 restaurants, as well as live entertainment, including hula and fire dances, bluegrass, Hawaiian and rock music, and a "trash fashion" show. More information at (808) 331-3033/334-1884/*www.konabrewersfestival. com.*

Third Weekend. *Big Island International Marathon.* Held in the Hilo area. Features a scenic course that follows the "Coast of Old Hawaii," winding past waterfalls, over one-lane bridges and along lava beaches. Food and entertainment at the finish. The event includes a traditional 26.2-mile marathon, a 10.8-mile run, and a 3.1-mile run or walk. More information at (808) 969-7400/*www. hilomarathon.com.*

Fourth Weekend. *Annual Kona Chocolate Festival.* Held at the Outrigger Keauhou Beach Resort in Kailua-Kona. Features a night of champagne, wine and live music on the Kona Coast, with some of the island's best chefs, caterers, and candy and ice-cream makers offering gourmet chocolate confections. (808) 937-7596/*www. konachocolatefestival.com.*

April

Third Week. *Merrie Monarch Festival.* Held at the Edith Kanaka'ole Stadium in Hilo. This is one of the most colorful and popular festivals on the island, honoring Hawaii's King David Kalakaua, the "Merrie Monarch." Highlights of the festival include a prestigious hula competition, featuring over 20 halau (or hula dance clubs); event usually sells out ahead of time, drawing nearly 8,000 spectators. Also music and live entertainment, arts and crafts, and a Merrie Monarch Royal Parade through downtown. For a schedule and more information, call (808) 935-9168 or visit *www. merriemonarchfestival.org.*

Hula Heritage Festival. At Kalani Honua Retreat and Conference Center. Features Hawaiian songs, dance, and crafts. (808) 965-7828/(800) 800-6886/*www.kalani.com.*

Fourth Week. *National Park Week.* Held at the visitor center at Pu'ukohola Heiau National Historic Site in Kawaihae, on the Kohala Coast. Features exhibits and displays of weapons used during early-day wars in Hawaii. For more information, call (808) 882-7218.

May

First Weekend. *Lei Day Celebration.* Celebration of Hawaiian leis, with an island-wide lei-making competition, held at the Hilton Waikoloa Village on the Kohala Coast. Features colorful leis, made from flowers, feathers and shells; also crowning of Lei Queen, a royal court procession, hula competition, and other traditional Hawaiian dances and songs. For more information, call (808) 885-1234.

AstroDay 2K6. Held at the Prince Kuhio Plaza in Hilo. Annual event, featuring Mauna Kea Observatory exhibits and demonstrations, as well as students' science projects, StarLab Planetarium shows, IR cameras, scholastic robotic demonstrations, liquid nitrogen demonstrations, telescope viewing, and children's activities. Also Hawaiian cultural displays and Hawaiian slack key music. More information at (808) 932-2328/*www.astroday.net.*

Second Weekend. *Asian and Pacific Islander Heritage Day.* Held at the Pu'ukohola Heiau National Historic Site at Kawaihae on the Kohala Coast. Cultural awareness activities include workshops and demonstrations centered around the crafts of lei-making, lauhala weaving, coconut frond plaiting and woodcarving. Also crafts fair and farmers market. For location of events and more information, call (808) 882-7218 or visit *www.nps.gov/puhe.*

Hamakua Music Festival. Held at the Peoples Theatre in Honoka'a. Four days of jazz concerts, featuring some of the best resident and touring performers. For a schedule of performances or more information, call (808) 775-3378 or visit *www.hamakuamusicfestival.com.*

Big Island Film Festival. Held at Waikoloa, at the Waikoloa Beach Marriott and Hilton Waikoloa Village. Celebration of the independent narrative film and filmmakers. Includes films, music, receptions, parties, symposiums and awards ceremonies. More information at (808) 557-5200/(808) 883-0583 or *www.bigislandfilmfestival.com.*

100K Saddle Road Ultra Marathon and Relay. Annual marathon run, leading along the island's remote Saddle Road, beginning in downtown Hilo and ending at Waimea. Draws more than 100 runners, including 15-20 ultra runners who complete the race. Also features 2- to 5-person relay teams. More information at (808) 328-9395/*www.hurthawaii.blogs.com.*

Orchid Show and Mother's Day Plant Sale. Two-day show, held at Hale Halawae on Ali'i Drive in Kailua-Kona. Features orchid exhibits and displays from Big Island growers. Also plant and art sale. Hosted by the Kona Orchid Society. For more information, call (808) 938-0179.

Third Weekend. *Annual Lauhala Weaving Conference.* Held at the Kona Village Resort in Kona. 40-plus master weavers gather to share their art with newer weavers. Includes a luau, talk-story and ho'olaulea (celebration of Hawaiian music, dance and food). For more information, call (808) 325-5203.

Memorial Day Weekend. *Keauhou-Kona Triathlon.* Half ironman course, and a qualifier for the Ironman Triathlon, including a 1.2-mile swim, 56-mile bike race and 13.1-mile run, beginning and ending at Keauhou Bay on the Kona Coast. There is also an Olympic course available for participants, featuring a 0.9-mile swim, 24.8-mile bike ride and 6.2-mile run. For more information, call (808) 329-0601.

June

First Weekend. *King Kamehameha Celebration in Kailua-Kona.* Annual parade down Ali'i Drive in Kailua-Kona. Features colorful floral floats, marching units, pau riders and decorated vehicles. For more information, call (808) 586-0333.

Second Weekend. *King Kamehameha Statue Draping, Games, Ho'olaule'a.* Held at Kapa'au, North Kohala. Lei-draping, followed by a celebration featuring Hawaiian food, music and dancing. For more information, contact the King Kamehameha Celebration Com-

HAWAII | Events

mission, (808) 586-0333.

King Kamehameha Day Celebration. Celebrations held in the towns of Kapa'au and Hawi in North Kohala. Popular annual event, honoring Kamehameha the Great. Features more than 100 colorful floats, mounted groups, marching bands and pa'u riders. Also Hawaiian food, music and dance. For more information, call (808) 889-0169.

Third Weekend. *Dolphin Days.* Held at the Hilton Waikoloa Village on the Kohala coast. Three-day event, centered around the resort's resident dolphins. Includes a food, wine and music festival, with preparations from Hawaii's top chefs, paired with fine wines and boutique brews, as well as world-class jazz. Also silent art auction, and tennis tournament. More information at (808) 886-1234/ *www.dolphindays.com.*

Annual Kona Classic. Held off the Kailua-Kona coast. Sport-fishing tournament with cash prizes. This is part of the Maui Jim Hawaii Marlin Tournament series. (808) 327-1440/960-0978/*www. konatournaments.com.*

Fourth Weekend. *Establishment Day.* Two-day event, held at the Pu'uhonua O Honaunau National Historical Park on the Kona Coast. Celebration of the establishment of the park as a National Historical Site. Features a royal court, and traditional Hawaiian crafts, including demonstrations of lei making, lauhala weaving, and arts and crafts, Hawaiian games, and tasting of Hawaiian food. For more information, call (808) 328-2288/328-2326/328-9877 or visit *www.nps.gov/puho.*

July

First Weekend. *Parker Ranch Rodeo and Horse Races.* At the Paniolo Park in Waimea. Parker Ranch paniolos (Hawaiian cowboys) participate in horse races and other traditional rodeo events, including team roping, double mugging, team penning, and wild cow milking. For more information, contact the Parker Ranch office, at (808) (808) 885-2303/885-7311/*www.parkerranch.com.*

Big Island Bonsai Show. At the Wailoa Center, Hilo. Fascinating presentation of the Bonsai culture, including Bonsai demonstrations. Sponsored by the Big Island Bonsai Association. For more information, call (808) 933-0416.

Turtle Independence Day. Held on the Fourth of July, at the Mauna Lani Hotel and Resort. The Mauna Lani Resort, jointly with the Sea Life Park on Oahu, raises green sea turtles on its property, then releases into the ocean on this day every year these endangered sea creatures. For more information, call (808) 885-6622.

Second Weekend. *Hawaii Volcanoes National Park's Kilauea Cul-*

tural Festival. Held at the Hawaii Volcanoes National Park, Features demonstrations of Hawaiian crafts, including lei weaving, coconut basket weaving, net throwing, fishing, canoe building, making ti leaves capes and sandals, planting dry land taro, using medicinal plants, beating kapa cloth, carving wood and crafting drums. Also instruction in playing Hawaiian musical instruments, traditional Hawaiian food, and talk story with Hawaiian elders. More information at (808) 985-6011/*www.nps.gov/havo*.

Third Week. *Big Island Slack Key Guitar Festival*. Annual festival featuring many top slack key guitarists, held at the Afook-Chinen Civic Auditorium in Hilo. (808) 961-5711/*www.ehcc.org*.

Big Island Hawaiian Music Festival. Held at the Hilo Performing Arts Center on West Kawili Street in Hilo. Features some the top slack key guitar performers, as well as ukulele steel guitar and falsetto musicians. More information at (808) 961-5711.

Fourth Weekend. *Kilauea Volcano Marathon and Rim Runs*. Held at the Hawaii Volcanoes National Park. More than a 1,000 international runners compete in three different races: the "World's Toughest Measured Marathon," featuring 26.2 miles of back-country trails; a 10-mile run around the summit of the Kilauea Caldera; and a 5-mile race into the Kilauea Caldera. For more information, call (808) 985-8725/*www.volcanoartcenter.org*.

August

First Weekend. *International Festival of the Pacific*. Held in Hilo. The festival, also known as the "Parade of Nations," features a lantern parade with floats, and cultural displays and music from throughout Asia and the Pacific region. For more information, call the Japanese Chamber of Commerce at (808) 934-0177 or visit *www.international-festival.com*.

Second Weekend. *Hawaiian International Billfish Tournament*. At the Kailua Pier in Kailua-Kona. This is one of the oldest and biggest marlin fishing tournament in the world, which began in 1958. Draws over 350 competitors from some 18 countries, and features catches weighing nearly 1,000 pounds each, There is also a parade through the town of Kailua-Kona at the start of the tournament. For more information, call (808) 329-6155.

Pu'ukohola Heiau Annual Cultural Festival. Held in Kawaihae, on the Kohala Coast. Celebration of Hawaiian culture, with demonstrations of Hawaiian arts and crafts, ancient Hawaiian games and dances, and tasting of Hawaiian food. For more information, call (808) 882-7218 or visit *www.nps.gov/puhe*.

September

First Weekend. *Aloha Festival.* Month-long festival, with events staged throughout the island, many of them in Hilo, Kailua-Kona and Waimea. Features a variety of Hawaiian pageantry and dem-onstrations in lei making, poi pounding, coconut husking, mat weaving and Hawaiian-style quilting. Also arts and crafts, food, island fruit tasting and entertainment—including original Hawai-ian music and hula dancers—and a paniolo parade (Waimea) and taro festival (Kona). For a schedule of events and more information, contact the Aloha Festivals office, at (808) 589-1771 or visit *www. alohafestivals.com*.

Queen Lili'uokalani Long Distance Canoe Racing Champion-ships. On the Kona Coast. Long distance, 6-man outrigger canoe races, between Kailua and Honaunau, along an 18-mile course Features separate divisions for single and double hull canoes, for men and women. More than 150 crews from Australia, Tahiti, Canada and the U.S. participate, with over 1,300 paddlers. There is also a parade clown Ali'i Drive in Kailua-Kona. More information on (808) 331-8849.

Second Weekend. *Annual Poke Contest.* Held at Hapuna Beach prince Hotel on the Kohala Coast. This is a key event in the Aloha Festival, celebrating Hawaii's soul food, the "Poke": a marinated Hawaiian preparation of seared, cooked or raw seafood. Samples of creations of both amateur and professional chefs are offered to the public for tasting. More information at (808) 880-3205/*www. PokeContest.com*.

Big Island Farm Fair. Held at the Old Kona Airport State Park. Annual family event, featuring agricultural displays, Hawaii-grown products, games and carnival rides. More information at (808) 324-6011.

Third Weekend. *Hawaii County Fair.* Old-time county fair, sponsored by the Hilo Jaycees, held at the Afook-Chinen Civic Auditorium in Hilo. Attracts over 75,000 people. Features a variety of displays and exhibits, carnival rides, and food concessions. For more information, call (808) 935-5022/961-8223.

October

First Weekend. *Ironman Triathlon World Championships.* Annual event, drawing more than 1,400 participants from some 49 coun-tries. The challenging competition features a 2.4-mile swim, 112-mile bike ride and 26.2-mile marathon. The race begins and finishes at the Kailua Pier in Kailua-Kona. For more information, contact the Ironman Office at (808) 329-0063 or visit *www.ironmanlive.com*.

Second Weekend. *Tahiti Fete of Hilo.* Held at the Afook-Chinen Civic Auditorium in Hilo. Colorful 2-day event of Tahitian dance and music, with dance troupes from Tahiti, Hawaii, mainland U.S., Japan and Mexico competing. Includes hula and Samoan dance performances, as well as food concessions and Polynesian arts and crafts. More information at (808) 935-3002/*www.tahitifete.com.*

Third Weekend. *Hawaii International Film Festival.* 10-day annual festival, featuring films from Asia, the Pacific and the U.S., which highlight the cross-cultural diversity of the Pacific Rim. Screenings are held at theaters throughout the island (as well as on other islands), and there is no fee for viewing. For a schedule and more information, call (808) 528-3456 or visit *www.hiff.org.*

November

First Weekend. *Kona Coffee Cultural Festival.* Two-week celebration of Kona's famous coffee, held in Kailua-Kona. Events include coffee bean picking contests, tours of local coffee mills and farms, and a parade through downtown Kailua-Kona, along Ali'i Drive. Also arts and crafts, food concessions, and a variety of entertainment. For More information at (808) 326-7820/*www.konacoffeefest. com.*

December

First Week. *Mauna Kea Beach Hotel's Annual Invitational Golf Tournament.* Held at the Mauna Kea Golf Course at the Mauna Kea Beach Hotel, Kohala Coast. 120 amateur golfers participate in this championship tournament. For more information, call (808) 882-7222/882-5400.

HAWAIIAN GLOSSARY

The Hawaiian language, in its simplicity, contains only seven consonants—H, K, L, M, N, P, W—and five vowels—A, E, I, O and U. All words—and syllables—end in a vowel, and all syllables begin with a consonant. The vowels, typically, are each pronounced separately—i.e., a'a is pronounced "ah-ah," and e'e is pronounced "ay-ay"; the only exceptions are the diphthong double vowels—ai, pronounced "eye," and *au,* pronounced "ow." The consonants, on the other hand, are never doubled.

Hawaiian consonants are pronounced similar to those in English, with the notable exception of W, which is sometimes pronounced as "V," when it begins the last syllable of the word. Hawaiian vowels are pronounced as follows: A- "uh," as in among; E - "ay," as in day; I - "ee," as in deep; O - "oh," as in no; U - "oo," as in blue.

For travellers to the Hawaiian islands, the following is a glossary of some commonly used words in the Hawaiian language.

a'a — rough, crumbling lava.

ae — yes.

ahi — tuna fish.

ahupua'a — pie-shaped land division, extending from the mountains to the sea.

aikane — friend.

alanui — road, or path.

ali'i — a Hawaiian chief or nobleman.

aloha — love, or affection; traditional Hawaiian greeting, meaning both welcome and farewell.

anu — cold, cool.

a'ole — no.

auwe — alas!

awawa — valley.

hala — the pandanus tree, the leaves of which are used to make baskets and mats.

hale — house.

hale pule — church; house of worship.

hana — work.

hahana — hot, warm.

haole — foreigner; frequently used to refer to a Caucasian.

hapa — half, as in *hapa-haole,* or half Caucasian.

haupia — coconut cream pudding, often served at a *luau.*

heiau — an ancient Hawaiian place of worship; shrine, temple.

holoholo — to go for a walk; also to ride or sail.

honi — a kiss; also, to kiss.

hui — a group, society, or assembly of people.

hukilau — a communal fishing party, in which everyone helps pull in the fishing nets.

hula — traditional Hawaiian dance of storytelling.

imu — underground oven, used for roasting pigs for *luaus.*

ipo — sweetheart, or lover.

ka'ahele — a tour.

ka'ao — legend.

kahuna — priest, minister, sorcerer, prophet.

kai — the sea.

kakahiaka — morning.

kama'aina — native-born, or local.

kanaka — man, usually of Hawaiian descent.

kane — male, husband.

kapu —taboo, forbidden; derived from the Tongan word, *tabu.*

keiki — child; a male child is known as *keikikane,* and a female child, *keikiwahine.*

kiawe — Algaroba tree, with fern-like leaves and sharp, long thorns, usually found in dry areas near the coast. Kiawe wood is used to make charcoal for fuel. The tree was introduced to Hawaii in the 1820s.

koa — native Hawaiian tree, prized for its wood which was used by early Hawaiians to craft canoes, spears and surfboards. Koa wood is now used to make fine furniture.

kokua — help.

kona — leeward side of island; frequently used to describe storms and winds, such as *kona* storm or *kona* wind. Also, south.

ko'olau — windward side of island.

kukui — Candlenut tree, characteristic in its yellow and green foliage, generally found in the valleys. Kukui nuts are also used in *leis.* Kukui is Hawaii's state tree.

kuleana — home site, or homestead; also responsibility, or one's business.

kupuna — grandparent.

lamalama — torch fishing

lanai — porch, veranda, balcony.

lani — the sky, or heaven

laulau — wrapped package; generally used to describe bundles of pork, fish or beef, served with *taro* shoots, wrapped in *ti* or banana leaves, and steamed.

lei — garland, wreath, or necklace of flowers.

lilikoi — passion fruit.

limu — seaweed.

luau — traditional Hawaiian feast.

mahalo — thanks, or thank you.

mahi-mahi — dolphin.

maile — native vine with shiny, fragrant leaves used in leis.

makahiki hou — New Year; *hauoli makahiki hou,* Happy New Year.

make — to die, or dead.

makai — toward the ocean, or seaward.

malihini — stranger, newcomer.

mana — supernatural power.

manu — bird.

mauka — toward the mountain, or inland.

mauna — mountain.

mele — song, chant.

menehune — Hawaii's legendary little people, ingenious and hardworking, who worked only at night, building fishponds, heiaus, irrigation ditches and roads, many of which remain today.

moana — the ocean; open sea.

mo'o — lizard, dragon, serpent.

mu'umu'u — long, loose, traditional Hawaiian dress.

nani — beautiful.

nui — big.

ohana — family.

ono — delicious.

pakalolo — marijuana.

palapala — book; also printing.

pali — cliff; also plural, cliffs.

paniolo — Hawaiian cowboy.

pau — finished, all done.

GLOSSARY | Hawaiian Words

poi — a purplish paste made from pounded and cooked *taro* roots; staple of Hawaiian diet.

puka — hole, opening.

pupu — appetizer, snack, hors d'oeuvre.

pupule — crazy; insane.

tapa — cloth made from beaten bark, often used in Hawaiian clothing.

taro — broad-leafed plant with starch root, used to make poi; staff of life of early Hawaiians, introduced to the islands by the first Polynesians.

ti — broad-leafed plant, brought to Hawaii by early Polynesian immigrants. *Ti* leaves are used for wrapping food as well as offerings to the gods.

waha — mouth; *waha nui, a* big mouth.

wahine — female, woman, wife.

wai — fresh water.

wiki — to hurry; *wikiwiki,* hurry up.

VOLCANIC GLOSSARY

a'a — rough, clinkery lava.

andesite — a lava relatively rich in silicon content, and of lighter color than basalt.

ash — volcanic ejecta characterized by fine, sand-sized particles.

basalt — dark, heavy lava, rich in iron and magnesium, but with a low silicon content; commonly found in Hawaii.

caldera — large, circular volcanic depression.

cinder cone — conical hill, created by the fine ejecta found around a volcanic vent.

crater — bowl-shaped volcanic depression, smaller than a caldera.

ejecta — volcanic rock, ash and other fragments thrown out by a volcanic eruption.

eruption — forceful ejection of volcanic debris onto earth's surface.

fault — fracture in earth's crust, where one or both sides have moved with respect to the other, parallel to the fracture.

fault zone — a geographical area with several parallel faults.

hot spot — a stationary hot area in the earth's mantle in which the zone just below the earth's crust melts, producing magma. The magma rises through weak regions in the surrounding rock, and erupts to form volancoes.

lava — hot, molten rock forced out onto the earth's surface, and the rocks created when the lava solidifies and cools.

magma — hot, molten rock, beneath the earth's surface.

olivine — a greenish mineral, comprised of iron, magnesium, silicon, and oxygen.

pahoehoe — smooth, ropy lava.

pele's hair — fine, hair-like volcanic glass.

pillow lava — a type of lava formed when pahoehoe lava enters water.

pit crater — small crater, formed by a collapse.

pumice — light, glassy, gas-rich volcanic fragments.

pyromagma—fluid basaltic magma, highly gas-charged.

pyroxene — group of dark-colored minerals, composed primarily of silicon, iron, magnesium, aluminium, and oxygen.

rift zone — extremely fractured area, extending downward from the summit of volcano, along which many eruptions occur.

seismic swarm — large number of earthquakes, occuring over a short period of time, beneath a specific geographical area.

shield volcano — broad, low, dome-shaped volcano, built up by flows of very fluid basaltic lava.

vent — an opening where volcanic debris reaches the earth's surface.

INDEX